COMMON GROUND

ALSO BY MELANIE GREENE

Hearts of Honey Wine Series

Common Ground *(Livia & Greg)*

Still Waters *(Amalia & Dante)*

Dunway Siblings Series

Feather in Her Cap *(Jeannie & Brendan)*

Twelve Scorching Days *(Sarita & Scorch)*

Margo of the Bells *(Margo & Karl)*

Away With a Stranger *(Andi & Cole)*

Pier 3 Coffee Series

Mocha for Mateo *(Alicia & Mateo)*

Cappuccino for Callie *(Abraham & Callie)*

Latte for Leyla *(Austin & Leyla)*

Curiosity (Amity & Josh)

Polar Opposites *(Audra & Salt)*

Roll of the Dice Series

Rocket Man *(Serena & Dillon)*

Ready to Roll *(Janice & Miguel)*

Eye of the Tiger *(Natalie & Evan)*

Let the Good Times Roll *(Chloe & Gabriel)*

Roll of a Lifetime *(Rachel & Theo)*

Roll Play *(Kim-ly & Tómas)*

On a Roll *(Gillian & Vic)*

Roll in the Hay *(Anton & Cisco)*

COMMON GROUND

HEARTS OF HONEY WINE

BOOK 1

MELANIE GREENE

First edition: November 2024

Common Ground / by Melanie Greene

Cover Design by Melanie Greene

ISBN: 978-1-941967-51-5

For Emilia, who made me Great

CHAPTER 1

"Y'all, I'm telling you, you've never heard such quiet." Livia Delacroix aimed her camera through the slightly wavy glass front door of Chata Bed and Breakfast. She'd signed away most of her inheritance to buy the small hotel, sure her mom would have approved of Livia making it the business of her dreams.

Almost entirely sure. Sure enough to make up for any smidges of anxiety that she was in over her head, relocating to the town she hadn't even seen since she was thirteen.

So it was okay if her first impressions of Chata were ... lonelier than she'd hoped. Outside, there was nothing but dusk and—well, nothing. Dusky sky, undulating dark line of trees, hills and fields impossible to see.

She kept her narration upbeat as she moved up the stairs. Probably she'd edit it out. Overlay a more sensible audio when she put the video together. Her friend Maggie had advised her to talk through this first gander of her new venture. Her initial reactions could be gold. Livia hid all her doubts, and kept talking. "I know what you're thinking: how do you hear quiet, right? But I bet you know what I mean. It's nothing but crickets and owls out here. Are they crickets, do you suppose? Grasshoppers? Frogs? What chirps at night?"

Maggie would be snorting about now if she heard this footage. Livia grinned, pausing at the first guest room door. "My intuition says they're crickets. So I'm sticking with that. And if it turns out the charming little town of Honey Wine, Texas, is overtaken with marauding locusts, y'all can laugh at me later. Okay. This first room is called Persimmon."

She switched on the overhead light and gasped. Remembered to keep her camera steady and her dismay curtailed.

Livia had expected some surprises, sure. She'd bought the place sight unseen, with only outdated website photos, vague memories of a brief stay with her mom, and a good report from her structural engineer as evidence that she hadn't lost her hard-won good sense.

Not that she'd been slip-shod about the process. Kent Stipple, the former owner, wanted to sell fast without involving realtors; he'd grumbled that there was nothing they could do he couldn't manage himself. Chata B&B had been his wife Sissy's passion, but she'd died over a year earlier, and he was ready to retire. Livia had talked to him about everything Chata—which translated to "cottage" in Czech. How cute was that? A sweet nod to the Bohemians that had settled the Hill County town of Honey Wine back in the mid-1800s.

Before closing, she'd gone over the accounts with a fine-tooth comb and reviewed every report. She knew that she'd find that Chata was as much rough as diamond. But she'd signed the papers, rented a trailer, and now stood in the middle of Persimmon, ready to concede that she might not have been entirely prepared for this undertaking.

She was tempted to call Mags and brainstorm solutions that would let her back out of this venture unscathed. Only the thought of her friend's sardonic comments kept her from outright fleeing.

The building itself had all the rustic charm she'd remembered. Good bones. The common areas were slightly worn, but the kitchen was large, with gracious windows overlooking the ranks of trees. The high end appliances, only a few years old, circled a large central island.

Every time she explained how Chata was everything she'd always dreamed of, Maggie and other friends from their hotel management program found increasingly less polite ways to call her a fool. Sure, Livia had entertained secret doubts, even while working through her never-ending 'before I move' checklist. But she'd ridden up the uneven, unpaved drive to the building, just as twilight settled the surrounding hills into dusky tranquility, and felt peace descend.

All traces of that peace fled when she walked into Persimmon.

"Right. Well. The layout isn't bad. We have a spacious king bed, daybed tucked against the wall, this great brick and tile fireplace. Desk and two—oh."

Her attempts to cheerfully narrate the video skittered south.

"Yeah, so this will not be in the final cut. Do you see how that armchair's missing half its fabric down the side? Do you see how it clashes with the wallpaper?" She laughed shortly. "Not that I'm likely to keep that up. Top of the list of things to replace, honestly. Or top, so far."

She trailed off as she spotted ragged holes in the foam under the frayed fabric of the armchair. Not obviously made by animals, but if critters were the culprit, she wouldn't be surprised. Spinning slowly, she took in the room. It was a good size. The window and doors were sturdy. She couldn't smell mold or mildew. In fact, the B&B's air was pleasant, thanks to the cedar or cypress or whatever other fragrant trees that covered the property.

She could work with it.

She had to. She'd sunk every one of her options into it.

Boosting a smile into her voice, she said, "I love Persimmon. It is unique. One of a kind." Or so she hoped. She still had to investigate Chickasaw, Mulberry, Loquat, and Jujube.

She undercut her entire point by focusing in on the fireplace mantle, where five angels perched. They were all different styles—ceramic, plaster, something that might be cornhusk.

And then she zoomed in on the four mismatched lamps. The angular brass 70s-era one by the porch door. On the desk, a porcelain urn-shaped base with celadon glaze and a gilt-rimmed inset of a pastoral French scene. The one on the left bedside table, with a scrolled plaster of Paris base topped with a bust.

"I think that's Mozart," she told her camera, of the bewigged man with a flouncy shirt and a violin resting against his chest. "Could be Brahms? Not Beethoven, though. I'd recognize him for sure. Shame I can't read music, because whoever's symphony is decoupaged on the shade might give me a hint."

She was going to have to cut so much wobbly camera work when she edited this video. Livia barely had her shaking shoulders under control by the time she'd circled to the other bedside table. And then she lost it again.

In the ill-lit photos on the website, Persimmon had seemed full of wood and charming rag rugs and comfortably upholstered furniture. She couldn't begin to remember what the lamps had looked like. But definitely not like this.

She'd have remembered this.

The final lamp base was boldly painted resin of a cowboy astride his horse, and the dangling light switch was his lasso. She managed a close-up of his seen-too-much, far-reaching gaze, before shutting off the recording and collapsing on the mercifully comfortable bed.

She took a quick photo to text to Maggie, because she needed to share the hilarity. Needed to have at least some sense of not being completely alone as she explored her new home and business. It might get creepy otherwise, all this darkness, and the chirping bugs, and the boards that creaked underfoot.

And if she felt totally alone, she might start wondering what she'd gotten herself into.

Buying Chata sight unseen hadn't seemed that wild a plan. Sure, when she'd made the offer, Mags and the others had mentioned that most people didn't blow their inheritance on some property hundreds of miles from any place they'd ever lived, even with all her research about the town's growing tourism economy. Didn't go from managing the high thread-count luxury of a European-style Dallas hotel to sole proprietorship of a five-room B&B on the outskirts of a small Hill Country town. No matter how quaint it looked on the website. No matter her sepia-tinged memories of that one spring break getaway she and Mom had spent at Chata. Or the remembered comfort of the safe haven Mom had tried to create for the two of them post-divorce, back before they'd locked horns in an unresolved clash, followed by Livia's impetuous flouncing away.

Her mom, the one of comfort and support, would have wanted Livia to pursue her dreams. And if she caught herself rubbing her thumb over the contours of Mom's old ruby ring on her right hand at the thought, that was just a habit. It meant nothing.

She pretended that if she said it enough, she wouldn't be making it up. Pretended that she knew what her mom would have thought about her wild venture. Pretended that Mags didn't know damn good and well that Livia was pretending.

Prior to discovering Chata, Livia would have said things were fine. No, she and Mom hadn't been close since before Livia left for college, but they talked a few times a year. Mom consistently said how much she just wanted Livia to be happy, even if she never seemed to grasp the difference between the unsophisticated, resentful suburban girl Livia had been at seventeen and the well-traveled, competent hotelier she'd become.

So after Mom's death, she'd gone on with life as usual. Well, life as usual, if her usual life hadn't been contaminated by those five long years with Terry, and also, somewhere in the sub-structure, the festering disconnect from her mom. Really, what went on as usual was work. Always work.

And then she'd covered someone's shift and wound up stuck on front desk duty one slow evening, with little to distract her from idle thoughts of the directionless expanse of her future.

And Livia preferred not to think about the directionless expanse of her future.

Between occasional calls from guests, she'd read an industry magazine cover to cover, and ran across Kent's ad. "For Sale: rustic B&B in scenic Honey Wine. Newly updated, regular occupancy, make Chata's past a part of your future." The black-and-white photo showed a wood-frame three-story house with porches wrapping each level, absolutely surrounded by trees and empty sky.

Livia's heart had unaccountably leapt when she'd seen it. It took a good few minutes of staring, hand to her chest, before she reconciled it with that half-buried memory of her and Mom eating pie at a diner, plunging into a deep blue swimming hole along the river, and reading on a porch while hummingbirds darted overhead.

By the time her shift was over, she'd read every review of Chata B&B on three travel sites, half-memorized the layout of Honey Wine from the town's tourism page, and surreptitiously logged in to her bank account so she could stare, again, some more, at the balance that had landed there after probate on her mom's will was cleared.

The next morning, she'd phoned Kent.

Chata was still there. Still for sale. She could afford it.

Within a couple of weeks, they'd worked out a deal. Within a couple of months, the deal had closed.

She'd kept meaning to take some time off, to make the five-hour drive to see it again in person, but giving notice to the hotel had sent the owners into crisis mode. They'd recruited her straight out of college and shepherded her to her current position; it had been the definitive move she'd needed to make to escape Terry's cycles of control. Livia wanted to leave things in experienced hands. Which meant interviewing. And more interviewing. And then hiring, and training, and more training. By the time they'd squared everything away, it was her closing date, so she checked her gut, found she was still inordinately excited about Chata, and signed the papers.

It was almost weirder that she never met Kent than it was that she hadn't seen Chata in fifteen years. They'd used different branches of the same title company. She'd hired a local inspector and surveyor to check the place out, and he'd sent his books to her once they'd signed the sales contract. All in all, Livia was pretty impressed with how honestly the old guy had represented his property. Everything he'd said—that the bathrooms were outdated but functional, and the driveway uneven, but the well water was pure and the kitchen was commercial quality—checked out. For all his hard-to-understand mumble-grumble over the phone lines, and his distrust of realtors that had led him to place the sales ad, Kent had kept the place in good repair and, most importantly, kept heads on beds. Repeat heads on beds, actually—there were folks on the review sites that mentioned they returned to Honey Wine every couple of years, and always stayed at Chata.

It boded well. And what Livia really, deeply, desperately wanted in her life was something that boded well.

She wasn't a fool. Her friends said it was nothing but magical thinking, when she'd been careless enough to tell them that Chata just felt right, but there was more to it than what they termed her "run away to the country and pretend that the simple life's the life for you" philosophy. First off, she wasn't running. She'd always planned on owning her own place someday, from the moment she'd enrolled in the hospitality program. And she'd done damn well in school—damn well at her job, too. All of it in service of her dream—to have business cards reading "Livia DeLacroix, Owner."

And now she could.

If it also meant she could leave behind some bad memories and a handful of the less charming aspects of Dallas, that was nothing but a bonus.

After the shocks of Persimmon, she gave up on attempting to record her initial impressions of Chata, stowing her phone while she explored the rest of the rooms. They were definitely … singular. She'd examine closer in the light of day, but most of what she clocked seemed, as expected, cosmetic. Kent had included all furnishings and decor with the deal, other than the stuff in the top floor owner's suite.

Livia had a few furnishings of her own in the trailer—her comfortable desk chair, the dinette set from her apartment, a storage chest she'd mostly packed because it had been with her so long it was hard to imagine a new life without it. The few of her mom's stained-glass windows that survived after cleaning out her house. But mostly she'd brought clothes, books, electronics, and her stack of pillows and bedding. She carted a few armloads up to the owner's suite before returning to Persimmon, and settling down against the rickety brass headboard to make notes by the light of the atrocious lamps.

It ought to have been enough to exhaust her into sleep, even with the strange surroundings. But her mind leapt in chaotic rhythm, cataloging the night sounds—surely those were crickets—and flashing on odd new worries. Would her wifi be strong in all the guest rooms? What if her guests were used to some unknown favorite breakfast treat of Kent's and resented her famous jalapeño cornbread muffins? What would she find to replace the collection of scary angels on Persimmon's mantle?

After a half-restful night, Livia started early the next morning, unloading the trailer all by her lonesome. So Maggie could just bite her skeptical tongue. Never mind that she left the table and half her boxes stacked in the entryway for the time being. Livia needed to return the trailer and deal with her own transportation needs before she could do much of anything else.

She followed all the twists and turns to the interstate and zipped up to a nearby town where she could finally unhitch. Of course, if she'd realized how difficult the road up to Chata would be on her sedan's suspension, she could have skipped installing a trailer hitch on it and bought something sturdier to begin with. But never mind. She searched for used car dealers while waiting on the rental trailer paperwork, glad she'd kept easy access to her car's title while organizing herself for the big move. It took the expected bit of negotiation, but by the time Livia stopped by a grocery store to stock up, she was in her brand new, pale blue, slightly used pickup. Bonnie, she named it, short for the state flower, bluebonnets, which carpeted the Hill Country every spring.

The salesperson took a picture of her sitting in the truck's cab, which she sent to the Dallas group text before heading back to Chata.

Back home.

Livia was pretty darn proud of herself.

Even if no one else was around to hear her brag about it.

By the middle of her third morning at Chata, Livia was dying for someone to brag to. Not for the sake of the bragging —though her lists were kick-ass levels of thoroughness—but because the crickets and deer and the corpses of dried out millipedes filling one corner of Bonnie's garage were all the company she'd had, and it would have been nice to see a familiar face. Or even an unfamiliar one.

Too bad she'd had Kent block off bookings for several weeks so she could renovate and settle in.

Mags pointed out, during one of the calls Livia was initiating too often, that if Livia could go through the entire process of buying Chata without driving down to see the place, she shouldn't already be begging her friends to visit.

"But you'll love these hills," Livia wheedled. "You should see how purple and azure the sky is as the sun sets over the treetops. And watching the stars come out! It's like nothing you'd ever see in Dallas. You know you'd enjoy that."

"Yep, one day. I have my doubts about your motives just now."

"Some friend."

"Live with it. Now go away. I know you keep calling so I'll get fired for personal calls at work and not have that as an excuse to stay put."

She snickered, as her friend must have intended. "You saw through my diabolical plan?"

"I'm clever that way. Go make a grocery list or something. I sent the crumb cake recipe, by the way. Check your email."

"You're the best."

"Damn straight. Don't forget it."

"Love you, Mags."

"Yeah, yeah. Later." Maggie hung up.

Livia carried her third cup of morning coffee up to her top floor suite. She'd begun moving some of the weirder—but still in decent shape—furniture up to her own space, giving her more latitude to rearrange and redecorate the guest rooms. She was measuring for new blinds when a cloud of dust down the hill caught her attention. It grew closer. By the time Livia moved to the window with the best view, she'd discounted a pile of possibilities. The satellite internet guys weren't due for three more days. The mailman left everything down by the street. Kent had called from Louisiana the previous day to report that he'd gotten a royal flush at the poker tables. Though why he'd thought Livia needed to know that, she wasn't sure. Maybe he wanted to give her an opening in case she needed to yell about the millipedes.

So she wasn't expecting anything to be climbing up her rocky driveway. She checked her cell phone was getting a signal and ducked back into the shadows, hoping to see without being seen. A dusty SUV swung into the parking area, barely missing Bonnie, and the silence once it was off was as loud as had been the noise of it trekking up the hill.

Livia stood back and watched as an athletic, tall, dark, and possibly handsome—under his ball cap it was hard to tell—stranger emerged and turned to stare, balefully, straight up at her top-floor window.

CHAPTER 2

Sometime past dawn, Greg pulled up to his last charging station of the trip. He jogged in the fresh air while his SUV charged up, ready for the road trip to bring him home at last. He'd been driving all night; he'd intended to set out from Mississippi far earlier than midnight—hell, he'd intended to make the drive two months later, company documents in hand, letting Uncle Kent know in advance so he'd be ready to sit down and listen to what Greg had to say.

But that sure as shit wasn't happening now.

"Papers are signed," Uncle Kent had said. Like there wasn't anything he could do about it.

Okay, there wasn't. Legally, fine, he was all tied up. But like hell was he going to sit back, while the plans he'd been making for two years just evaporated around him. So he'd given notice to his boss at the excursion company, gotten out of his lease, and hit the road. Well, gone to The Raft for good-byes, which weren't as brief as he'd intended, then hit the road.

After a few jumping jacks and press-ups, Greg dug a sand-wich out of his cooler and slid back behind the wheel, letting his phone tell him what he already knew: in a few hours, he'd be back in Honey Wine. It had been five, six years since he'd been there on any kind of regular basis. Not that he figured the town would have changed, in its essentials. Not that he figured the folks with their disapproving eyes had cleared out, like he couldn't tell what they still thought of him. Like they were subtle about it.

Still and all, it wasn't the whole town against him. Especially since Uncle Kent moved to be near his his brother—and the casinos—in Lake Charles. Plus, Greg held some kernel of brattiness within him that looked forward to rubbing their noses—the noses that wrinkled at him since his childhood, sure he'd never amount to anything—in his success. He hadn't gone so far as to practice the "that's right, I'm hot shit, never thought you'd see that, did you?" look in the mirror, but he may have imagined an encounter or two.

That was before Kent went and sold the place out from under him. To some stranger, some city gal, some non-relative. Probably she had the kind of slick wiles and bona fides the old man valued over anything Aunt Sissy wanted for the land. She might even've confused and bamboozled him in the bargain.

Not that it justified his uncle forgetting about Greg. Aunt Sissy would never have done it, no matter how slick the city gal was. Aunt Sissy had known Greg had dreams and plans and was on his way to achieving them. She must have told her husband. She would have mentioned it, even the bones of his ideas, enough that Kent would have known not to just up and sell it to some wily city gal without talking to Greg first. Dad and Sissy had smiled over it, once: Greg's plan to reunite the land his Forst grandparents had split between their kids. And with Sissy gone, Greg and his dad were the last Forsts left. He'd once figured that would mean something to Uncle Kent.

But his uncle hadn't sounded the least contrite when he called to announce his new address. "Sold Chata," he'd said, like it was no big deal. Just a thing he did, entirely his own business.

Technically, yes. Never mind Greg's land next door. Never mind his dreams. Never mind what Sissy must have wanted.

Shit. Aunt Sissy would have wanted it, wouldn't she? She hadn't been merely humoring him and Dad?

Greg chucked the PB&J in his trash bag, queasy. It had never occurred to him that Aunt Sissy might have told Uncle Kent specifically not to sell to Greg.

But Kent held the rope swing incident against him, more than a decade on. Apologies hadn't mattered—not to him. Everyone else forgave him, even his mom. As for Aunt Sissy, she was never hard to convince of his basic innocence. Sissy had been soft. Especially with Greg. Seemed to realize he needed it more than most, not that he would have ever outright said so. Maybe that was a result of her being raised alongside his dad, who also never outright said anything. Sissy had the knack of knowing stuff about what people needed—it was downright mystical, this little nothing-sized old Czech lady, able to tell in the merest glance what was up deep inside everyone she met.

Greg had seen her in action over and over, when he was the summer help at the B&B. He'd be cleaning the kitchen and Sissy would glance in to say, "Pitcher of iced tea and some cookies out here, okay?" and he'd bring it out to the porch where Sissy had her guests installed in rocking chairs, relating some folktale or teaching them to distinguish the various trees. And whatever thing she was saying, by the time she'd finished, the guests were smiling fondly, or were energized and ready to tackle new adventures, or had reached across to hold hands.

Greg didn't think he had the same power. But Kent didn't, either, and he'd run the place nearly two years after Sissy died, so it wasn't like that was a good reason to keep Chata from him.

Whatever the man's reasons—he'd stayed stubbornly quiet when Greg asked—it'd spurred Greg to amp up his timeline and head back to Honey Wine straight away. He didn't know what he could do about it, but the first step was to get there, and get a look at the city gal who'd gone and stolen his dream.

Livia stepped cautiously out onto the front porch. Up close, he wasn't that tall. Just something to do with the perspective from the third-floor window, then. He was handsome, indeed, now that she could see his square face and high cheekbones, which had the same horizontal slash as his narrowed eyes and his dark brows. If he looked that good mad, Livia was dead curious what he'd look like laughing. Though maybe it was already a laughing face, and he just had odd expressions. Since he was a total stranger appearing out of nowhere to glare at her, she really couldn't say.

"Can I help you?"

The guy didn't even blink for a moment, then glanced at the surrounding emptiness.

Now that wasn't at all creepy. Maggie would have a field day. *"Hey, some muscle-bound man just drove up to my isolated house in the woods and is staring at me like I ran over his favorite dog and he needs to enact retribution, and I opted to walk out to him without even dialing 911 first. What's up with you?"*

Too many years in the service industry, clearly. "If you're lost, I can get you a map to town," Livia tried, glancing from his Mississippi plates to her phone to check the signal.

"Not lost."

Well, that helped answer none of her few dozen questions. But despite the two-word answer, his voice was friendly enough.

"Well, then. Welcome to Chata B&B. I'm Livia DeLacroix,

and I'm afraid we're not open just at the moment. I'd be happy to give you referrals in the area, if you need a place to stay." Unless this guy was the kind of regular who thought he could just show up and get a room based on his long-standing history with the place, she still didn't have a sense why he was standing there.

He shifted, dropping his shoulders in a way that let Livia relax a fraction. His eyes stayed narrow, though, when he said, "I'm Gregory Forst. I live next door."

He didn't glance left or right, much less point helpfully at a nearby rooftop. Not that Livia could see any rooftops—her place was nicely isolated, though there was a stretch of power lines down the hill a ways. She waited a beat for more, and got nothing. Okay, then. "Are you the local welcome wagon?"

At that he laughed, and Livia had been right. Wowza. Never mind being laughed at for her sarcasm, never mind the strange man/remote woods horror story set-up; this Gregory Forst was yummy. Instant fantasy material. Fabulous. Just what she needed. The boy next door was a stone cold hottie. And mysteriously antagonistic.

And possibly a liar liar pants on fire, given the out-of-state plates, but when she glanced at the bumper of his SUV, he noticed. "I've been working over near Jackson, but I grew up here. My dad and my Aunt Sissy inherited this land way back when. She married Kent, and they started Chata up on their half of the property." He finally pointed, uphill at an angle past the back of the B&B, not that Livia had noticed anything but trees that way. "Dad didn't do more than build a little house there for the three of us. It's mine now."

"Uh-huh." Articulate, Livia. Real conversationalist there. But she'd seen pictures of Kent and Sissy Stipple on the Chata website. Even given that Gregory Forst wasn't as tall as she'd originally thought, he had a lot more size to him than tiny Sissy had. Sissy was pixieish and fair, with big round eyes and gray-blonde hair falling to brush her tiny round chin.

Figuring for gender and generational differences, Livia still failed to see a single trace of her in the delectable specimen before her. "So, Kent never mentioned I'd have his nephew as a neighbor."

Gregory's jaw tightened just a tad. "No, well. He didn't know that I'd be moving home just yet."

"And you grew up in Honey Wine?"

He glanced down the driveway towards town. "That I did."

"You know all the locals?"

He nodded briefly. "I know them."

"They know you?"

"They do. Are you looking for them to vouch for me? I'd show you my ID, but I guess it won't prove much. Try Ellie at the Honey Wine Cafe. I bussed tables for her after school for three years. Or Mason, from the trail riding school. I mucked stalls there on weekends."

"Lots of jobs."

"Everyone was bent on keeping me busy, growing up here. Used to work at Chata, too, summers."

Interesting. The touch of hostility about the town, and the fact that he was repeatedly mentioning his connection to her place. Livia sensed an agenda. Well, may as well tackle the bear if it shows up growling on her porch. "And what brings you back to Honey Wine, sooner than expected, Gregory?"

"Greg." He nodded.

Not an answer, Greg. Livia waited.

And waited.

Fine. She could growl, too. "What brings you to Chata, Greg?"

He glanced away, eyes tight. Shook his head. Eventually said, "Sometimes people come and go to my place via your drive and the bridge just up there. My own drive is a twisty pain. Figured I should let you know, in case. And meet you. Welcome wagon, like you said."

With that, he climbed back into his SUV and, lifting a hand in a brief farewell, drove past her along the wooded drive.

Well, that hadn't been a success.

Greg opened the kitchen door of the stone and timber frame house he'd grown up in, dropping his duffle on the dining table as he automatically walked to his childhood room and slammed the door behind him. Took him a couple of beats to notice there was no bed in the bedroom. Couple more beats to remember that he'd moved everything he'd wanted from there into the master after Dad left, replacing the twin bed Dad had obstinately insisted upon with his queen-sized one, stocking the closet with his own clothes and a couple of boxes of memorabilia. And yet every time he'd returned since Dad took to the road, he'd ended up in his old room, staring befuddled at the desk where his bed once sagged.

His encounter with pretty little city gal Livia DeLawhatever sure hadn't helped him feel any more grounded. Defensive, gripping that cell phone like it was her lifeline, acting as if he was trespassing. He hadn't even gotten out of the parking area and onto the porch. Her porch. No longer Kent's porch. Not Sissy's. Nowhere he'd be bringing guests lemonade anymore, not that lemonade runs had been necessarily part of his plans. But he'd had plans.

Big plans.

His degree in forestry management was never going to make him a million bucks, but growing up on this land, spending hours roaming through the trees, observing the wildlife, learning through interaction how the plants and streams and sun and bugs all worked together—it was his calling. And once his YouTube channel had taken off, letting others in on his passion for the ecology of the land, he'd learned how to stash away revenue to pursue something more. He'd envisioned a way to bring others out to the place, make some tourism money while still protecting the ecosystems.

But it wouldn't work, not the way he imagined it, unless he had Chata, too. He needed Chata's land, with its access road, and high bluffs, and the landing area at the low curve of the creek. His half of his grandparents' land filled his soul, but didn't, on its own, give him the same commercial opportunities.

Cesta Adventures, he was going to call his business. "Journey" in Czech, to go with "cottage" for Chata. Sissy would have liked that. His dad did, for sure—he was always saying things like, "Make life an adventure, but come home at the end."

Greg stepped out onto the front porch. If he stood on the far side of the bay window, just past the obstruction of a couple of the older cypress edging the stream, he could see Chata. Mostly just the side and part of the back, but as he watched, the new owner moved onto the second-story porch. She wasn't doing much. Looking around. Jotting something in a notebook. Kicking each of the porch rails, as if Kent would have let any of them go loose for even half a day. Greg smiled, remembering the fall weekend they'd spent replacing the nails in every slat. "Safe side," was about all his taciturn uncle had said when Greg had asked why they were bothering. It had been one of his first days of paid work, early on in his teens. It hadn't occurred to Greg for years that maybe Uncle Kent had been making work for him to do, not until after so many other friends of his family had employed him to bus tables, curry horses, stack lumber, clear garden beds, and otherwise lock him in place with labor that kept him from the kind of trouble his parents frowned on.

Any rate, as Livia was finding out, the porch was sturdy.

Her pale limbs flashed as she moved. Shorts in the dead of winter was a choice, but Greg had ditched his own sweatshirt once he hit home. Was warming up just standing there, watching pretty Livia trying to find fault with Chata.

"Screw it," he muttered to no one, and headed inside for a shower and a nap. Time to develop tactics, because another of his dad's aphorisms had to do with not letting obstacles to your first plan stop you from coming up with a second plan that was even better.

CHAPTER 3

Livia holed up on the sofa in the downstairs parlor, all her notes stacked beside her. Her laptop had practically scalded her legs by the time she'd compiled it all into the most gorgeous spreadsheet. Color-coded, organized by target dates, cross-referenced by room. She was feeling darn good about herself as she hit 'save' and put a copy in her email drafts folder. She couldn't send it to herself until the internet guys got out to her, but it made her feel a little more secure.

And then she almost threw the computer on the floor when an otherworldly shrieking erupted from the dining room.

"What in the holy hell?" Livia caught the laptop and set it on the sofa before she slid into her shoes—better safe than sorry—and snatched up her cell phone before creeping towards the sound.

Not that her phone could protect her from zombies or the Infamous Wailing Ghost of Honey Wine or whatever creature was making the racket. Not that her self-defense training had included weaponry skills, even if she'd had a bludgeon handy.

Livia snagged a broom she'd left against the entry doorway. The handle wasn't even wood, just molded plastic. But maybe the zombie would be freaked by the neon-green bristles and run off.

There was a swinging door between the kitchen and dining room, super-convenient for carrying in platters of bacon or cran-crumble cake, and also for gently spying on the guests. Of course, it wasn't much protection against zombies, who could just as easily swing it in towards the kitchen and attack the broom-wielding fool cowering next to the fridge.

Right. Livia took a deep breath and, broom first, cracked the door open. Nothing. Well, not nothing – plenty of shrieking, and Livia was about eighty-percent sure that one of the chairs on the far side of the table was wobbling, which meant ghost instead of zombie, and Livia wasn't sure that was any better, even if she believed in either paranormal possibility. She edged further into the room, until she got a glimpse of the critter under the dining table, at which point she high-tailed it out to the porch to regroup.

She was peeking in through the dining room windows—one of which was still, *damn it, Livia,* open from her earlier cleaning foray—when the neighbor showed back up.

"You ... okay?" he asked.

Probably the fact that she was crouching and still had a death-grip on the broom clued him in. "Great. Yeah."

He nodded. "Okay."

Livia straightened and looked at Greg. He'd changed; his hair was wet. The black waves tumbled back from his high forehead, and the last thing she needed to be doing instead of calling the exterminator was imagining what his shampoo smelled like. Probably something outdoorsy. Not that she cared.

"Listen, I came to see if I could take you to lunch. Or dinner, later, if you've already eaten. I don't think ..." But Greg's thoughts would remain as much a mystery as the contents of his shampoo bottle, because the zombie-ghost chose that moment to shriek again. Livia was more pleased than she should have been to see him flinch. At least she wasn't a totally overreacting wuss.

"What on earth?"

"It's in the dining room. Some sort of creature."

"Some sort of unhappy creature," he agreed, moving forward to look through the window that was still closed.

The beach. His shampoo smelled like the beach.

"It's a Maine Coon." Greg eased back, relaxed now, and gave her a half-smile.

Livia peeked in the window again, caught the glint of green eyes, a bushy tail. "Are you saying there's some sort of raccoon in my dining room? Should I call animal control?"

"It's a cat."

She eyed him. Tried to gauge if he was laughing at her. "That thing? Making that noise? It's the size of a—I don't know, a king-size pillow!"

Yep. Laughing at her.

"I'm new to town, bud, but I wasn't born yesterday."

He swiped at his eyes. "Sorry. Honest. I swear, it's a cat. Probably semi-feral. They're big bastards, I'll give you that. Pardon my language. But we get a few of them around here. They usually hang out waiting to steal food where they can, if it's easier than hunting. Uncle Kent used to keep some kibble to throw out for them. Them and the foxes. This one likely smelled food and took the notion to come on in and settle down."

Livia leaned into open window to get a better look. The cat—she could see it was a cat now, but ridiculously big—had a bottle-brush of a tail, sable fading to tawny at the base. And it seemed to be trapped under the table. "Is it likely to be rabid?"

Greg considered. "I don't think so. He's not exhibiting the signs, and coming here for food matches his behavior pattern. I used to warn Uncle Kent to stop feeding them unless he was going to trap and domesticate them, but he didn't think it was a real problem."

"So, animal control? Or I just let it out?"

He shook his head. "No need. I'll get him and run him in to the vet to be neutered and checked out. As long as he's healthy enough he can come live with me."

"You're just going to up and adopt him?"

"Cats are okay." Greg shrugged. "Better than having him out there making more feral cats to populate my land. So. You got a box? A big box? And some rubber gloves?"

And like that, Livia was bringing the guy next door into her home—well, the business part of her home—and rigging him out with the supplies he needed to get the Maine Coon untangled from the mini-blind cords he'd knocked to the floor. Livia had removed the blinds while scrubbing the window frames, and stacked them on the dining table, next to the now-ransacked bowl of jalapeño-cheese muffins she'd baked that morning. Greg used one as bait, and pocketed one, Livia suspected, for himself. She wasn't even mad at his sneakiness. They were fantastic muffins.

Before he and the cat left, he looked from the chaos of the dining room to Livia. "I gotta rescind my offer of lunch now." He hefted the box. "You free for dinner?"

She picked him up at six. There was the little cut-through he'd pointed out from behind her place to his. It was barely wide enough, and certainly not smooth enough, to call a driveway. At least the bridge over the property-defining river was strong.

Bonnie handled it all just fine, and Livia wanted to see this supposed homestead of his. Get onto his land. Be in the driver's seat, in case of, like, kidnapping or whatever.

Maggie would just love this, she thought, as the trees

overhead obscured what little light was left in the day. *Sure, Livia, go deeper into the woods, further from civilization, from cell towers, from your last known location.* But Livia's gut wasn't worried, so she decided to trust it, like she had when she'd found out about Chata to start with. Sure she'd been a little taken aback when Greg had first pulled into her parking lot, but something—maybe the casual way he'd set about dealing with the cat—was setting her at ease with him. Plus his hair smelled like the ocean. How much of a threat could a guy with ocean-smelling hair be, really?

He was on his porch, tilted back in a rocker with his feet on the rail. Not whittling, but otherwise filling a dozen stereotypes of a country boy at ease: jeans, ball cap, plaid shirt, beer bottle. "Hey. You want the ten-cent tour before we head out, or are you ready to roll?"

Deferring to the Maggie in her head—*You went into his house? Excuse me, his remote cabin? Where he probably keeps all his duct tape and Bowie knives? Haven't we learned the dangers of traveling to a second location?*—Livia suggested they go straight to town. Greg and his ocean-smelling hair filled Bonnie's cab right up. Livia tried to figure out if he'd feel so right-beside-her if they were in her ex-car, with its center console and back seat and generally more distinct 'you sit there, I sit here' arrangement.

Directions and a little bit of feral cat chat sustained them until they were at the Honey Wine Cafe, which Livia had opted for both because of the info she'd gotten from the Chamber of Commerce website, and because of Greg Forst's supposed history with the place. Plus, she'd emailed the owner before moving, hoping for advice about bulk suppliers, but hadn't heard back yet.

The cafe was cute as all get out. Cedar shingles on the exterior, plenty of hanging baskets lining the porch overhang, and, once inside, warm wood tables along the midnight blue walls.

A passing server in a blue Honey Wine Cafe T-shirt smiled at Livia and told her they could sit anywhere.

"Thanks, Pam," Greg said, which stopped Pam right in her tracks for a double-take.

"Well if it isn't the bane of Ellie's existence!" She rolled her eyes a little and reached out to rub his arm, which knocked his shoulders down a notch. "When'd you roll into town?"

"Just now. As if I'd wait twenty-four hours before I got my hands on a mug of Ellie's coffee."

"We figured you'd been around a while. Ellie heard from Jackson that you were over at Susanna's this afternoon."

And there he had it. The Honey Wine grapevine.

"Susanna's the vet," Greg explained to Livia. He didn't go into the fact that her clinic was across from the hardware and feed store where Jackson Apel and Bill Moll spent their afternoons pretending to be helpful, or to the long-standing rumors about Jackson's relationship with Ellie Cerny, the owner of the Honey Wine Cafe.

He waited for Livia to scoot into his favorite corner booth before introducing her to Pam. They both ordered coffee and the special, and Greg glanced at the time, making a bet with himself about how few minutes would pass before Ellie herself emerged to give the both of them a once-over. His return was more than enough bait on its own, never mind that it was accompanied by a hook as sharp as, "Livia here bought Chata."

He pegged it. Two minutes exactly before he was compelled to stand up and allow Ellie to engulf him with her skinny-strong arms and rub at his shoulder.

Damn, but she'd aged. Pam had aged, but in that middle-years way where mostly it was lips that rested down-turned instead of upturned, plus a crow's foot or two. Ellie, though. Ellie'd turned old.

Probably if she hadn't been his mom's best friend, he wouldn't have especially noticed. But he'd imprinted on Ellie and Mom goofing together in the cabin while he gnawed at wooden blocks. On Ellie and Mom dragging him on longer and more adventurous treks as he grew. On Ellie and Mom laughing when he stormed off ahead, swearing that he could find the path back to the cafe from the swimming hole without what passed for their help. So even as he'd grown up, even when Ellie and Mom turned into just Ellie, he'd always seen her as the thirty-something she'd been in his strongest memories of her and Mom before Mom got sick.

If Mom was around, she'd have white-streaked hair, too. Loose skin under her chin. Maybe even balance issues that would curtail her explorations of the woods. She'd have an AARP card and dietary restrictions and no matter how she and Ellie taunted, she'd never have been able to out-swim him.

"Oh, stop it." Ellie poked him back into the booth. "I don't need your big sad eyes to tell me I look like a crone. I've got a mirror."

He grabbed ahold of her bird-thin hand and pretended he hadn't been about to warble about his long-dead mother. "You couldn't be a crone if you bought out the clearance section Witches-R-Us. I'm just glad you haven't forgotten how to brew the coffee."

"If the coffee was that good, you wouldn't go a decade without it."

"Hardly a decade."

"I'm senile now. I want to call it a decade, I call it a decade. Stop being a brat and introduce me to your date."

She probably had Jackson spying on this whole conversation via webcam, and would be posting the juiciest clips to the town's social media before he was halfway through his chicken parm.

"Ellie Cerny, Livia Delacruz. Livia's the one Kent sold to."

"DeLacroix," Livia corrected, shaking Ellie's free hand.

"Sorry."

"No problem. You'll learn."

Not if he had much to do with it, he wouldn't. Not once he got papers signed the right way, like they should have been to start with.

"Boy ought to learn his date's name."

"She's not my date, El. I only met her today."

"That's right, you've been seeking out Susanna."

"I'm not 'seeking her out.' We trapped one of Kent's strays and I had to get it checked out."

"You did, did you?"

"Yes, Ellie, I did."

"Bet you noticed she's still single, though."

He would not roll his eyes at the woman who was as close as this sometimes vexatious town got to being a parent figure for him. Greg kissed Ellie's cheek. "Look, Pam has food. Go away so I can talk to Livia."

"Nice to meet you, Livia. That old place ought to do well for you, but if it acts up, Greg here's got all the referrals you'll ever need."

Greg didn't comment. Ellie didn't need to know his plans just yet, and Jackson and the rest of Honey Wine could certainly wait until the deed was done. Kent selling Chata out from under him had hastened his return to Honey Wine, before all the plans he'd set in motion panned out, but he'd long ago decided that a fait accompli was the way to go with this town.

Maybe it meant he had more in common with Kent than he'd thought. Otherwise, he wouldn't be facing Livia Dela-not-cruz across a diner table now.

"So you're the bane of her existence, eh?"

The barest hint of pink flared across Greg's face, but his eyes were still resting on the cafe owner's retreating back. And no question but that Ellie had been glowing with pleasure to see him; even Pam had stopped moving long enough to smile fondly at the reunion hug.

"She and Mom were best friends. If—when—I got up to trouble in town, I couldn't make it back home before Ellie had called Mom to tell her all about it."

"So you reformed and never misbehaved again?"

Greg laughed. "Yeah. That's right."

She'd made him laugh again. Mmm. Livia was happier by the second about her decision to move to Honey Wine, if this is what the local populace did for her tingly bits.

"I suppose I can believe you are who you say you are now."

"You were still doubting me?"

"Hey," she shrugged, "you're the one who keeps showing up on my land, then when I go to your place there's not even proof that you have a key to get inside."

He shook his head. "You are one hardened city gal, Livia DeLacroix. Suspicious as all get out."

Okay, that was judgmental. Maybe a little true, too, but did he have to go and say it? "I'll learn small town ways soon enough."

Greg tensed his jaw a moment, then went back to his pasta. "Maybe it won't end up suiting you."

"Beg pardon?"

"Just," he sighed. "Sorry, that's a strange way to talk about this. Okay, you know how I told you Aunt Sissy and Uncle Kent used to hire me over the summers?"

Livia nodded. Her chicken grew less appealing, thanks to the weird vibe Greg was sending out.

"After Aunt Sissy passed, that was near two years back, I'd just left the forest service for an adventure tour company. Dad was wrung out, between how long my mom was sick, and then his sister dying before she was even seventy. He sold his place to me and took off to live, well, he says he'll be on the road until he's sick of the lifestyle, then come settle back in a retirement community. Anyway, by then I'd started making money on my YouTube channel—it's me on eco adventures, like I'm going to run here. I'll send you the link. And I told Dad and Uncle Kent the plan, how I'd set up something on our land. Zip lines, off-roaders, caving, that stuff. And I planned to buy out Kent, so I run them together, right? Like, B&B guests wouldn't have to zip line, and vice-versa, but I make package deals, and between the two I have a good business. But then Kent screwed up and sold to you, but you're not really a country gal, and maybe what you should do is just sell to me, right? And then I'll go on with my plan, and you can find someplace fancier that suits you, someplace with no feral cats or whatever, and we'll both be set."

Greg was leaning far across the table at her, earnest, voice lowered against eavesdroppers, his near-black eyes fixed on hers like he was being the most sensible and helpful creature in five counties.

Setting down her cutlery, Livia pushed up against the booth's back cushion. If she'd been in a chair, she'd have scraped it into the next table, but the booth held her in unnerving proximity to Gregory Forst's intense nonsense.

"You want me to sell Chata to you?"

He nodded.

"Chata, which I just spent almost every dime of my mom's life insurance buying? And you want me to just sell it to you?"

His smile went down a notch, but he nodded again.

"Kent screwed up by selling it to me? And now it's my job

to fix that by selling my business, my home, my—my dream of my future, to you?"

Finally he sat back some, and Livia could almost breathe.

"Well, that was my idea," he said, breaking eye contact.

"That was your idea."

"Right."

And she'd live next door to this guy for the rest of her life? Not great. "Greg, I don't know what baggage you and your uncle have, but I can tell you absolutely, positively, without the slightest room for error: that is never going to happen."

CHAPTER 4

A couple of days later, as the internet installers wound their dust-trailing way back down her drive, Livia's burning indignation at Greg was more of an intermittent simmer.

Kent had screwed up? Screwed up! Did Gregory Forst have a degree in hospitality from one of the best programs in the United States? He did not.

Did Gregory Forst have years of experience, have actual plaques engraved with his name, testifying to his excellence at the hotel business? Livia didn't think so.

She'd cleaned rooms and hauled bags and put in more than enough time at reception desks over the years, going back to her teens. She knew from the ground up exactly what she'd gotten herself into, but Gregory Forst thought she couldn't hack it? Because he'd helped out an indulgent aunt a couple of summers? Far as she'd gathered, Gregory Forst had been playing in trees for years and had no blasted idea what went into her job. No clue how prepared she was to make Chata B&B the best damn B&B in central Texas.

Kent had not screwed up.

Maybe—*maybe*—her outrage could stand to dissipate more. But Gregory Forst owed her some goodness and grace, because hell if she was going to put up with a neighbor belittling her at every turn.

Livia was streaming Beyoncé, bopping around the house with her neon-green broom, corralling as much of her paint-prep dust as possible, when she slid hip-first through the kitchen's swinging door and saw Gregory Forst's damn Maine Coon again. "Countdown" died on her lips as she stared at the creature perched on her dining table, casually helping itself to the tortilla chips she'd left out to snack on as she wandered through.

At the remnants of her bowl of queso.

"Hey!" she waved the broom in its direction, and it barely even raised an eye to her. "I'm serious! Get your paws off my table."

The broom didn't bother it in the least. It didn't shy away from her approach, and when she reached for the bag of chips, the menacing growl was loud enough to drown out the music. Livia remembered the trouble Greg had had getting the beast into a box, and didn't want it unsheathing its claws in her direction.

She closed the dining room windows; really, what was the point of a pretty day if she couldn't air out the house without inviting in the feral outdoors? And made a note to color-code getting new screens fitted as a top priority. After some experimenting, she blocked the door to the kitchen and, satisfied that the beast would stay put for a while, Livia rinsed the dust off her arms and face. It was time for blasted Gregory Forst to take some accountability.

Greg emerged from one of his favorite caves, pleased to find it dry and primed for exploration by his customers. He jotted ideas in his pocket notebook as he headed home, then flipped back a couple of pages to find where he'd started a new plan for dealing with Livia and the problem of Chata.

Not being a total fool, Greg realized that he'd gone about it all wrong. Despite his hopes, he'd realized going in she wasn't likely to just up and sell to him. All he'd meant to do over dinner was broach the idea of working together to build business for them both, as a way in to her good graces. He'd had a sound plan worked out, practically perfected it before he'd gone and gotten sidetracked by rescuing Mittens. Then sidetracked again, seeing how Ellie had aged.

By the time he and Livia were talking at the cafe, he'd almost forgotten that they weren't allies, that she didn't yet trust him, and wasn't already ready to turn to him and confess that she'd bitten off more than she could chew.

So instead of treating her like the strangers they were, he acted like they'd built the rapport he'd hoped for, in the process managing to antagonize and insult her.

Damn fool thing to do.

He gave her a couple of days to forget his mistakes while he reconnoitered his land. There were several trails that needed more clearing than he could do on his own. He'd have to see if Mason could recommend someone good with a chainsaw, but meanwhile, he'd flagged the trees that had to come down and staked out zip line courses so the insurance agent could visualize them during her upcoming site visit. If it all came together like he imagined, the last line would end not far from the trailhead to the caves; he could use the same parking area to pick up zip liners and drop off cavers, or sell packages that allowed the more inexhaustible customers to do both activities.

If he had access to Chata's land from the get-go, he could put up a couple of longer cables and give customers a five-line course that actually crossed the creek, instead of the three-line course that merely overlooked it and crossed a tributary. The caves were all on his side of the creek, but her side included some bluffs that would make excellent landing stages, if only she would agree.

But probably he had to give that idea up. People would enjoy crossing the tributary, no matter how little water they'd really get to see that way. The vistas were plenty fine. Adjusting his plans didn't mean he had to give up on everything.

This was the price for his utter failure of diplomacy at the Honey Wine Cafe. He'd lay out inferior zip lines, and reroute to take advantage of the bluffs once Livia agreed to work with him. Or once she sold to him, bringing him better parking, deeper trails, and access to a vaster customer base. Sucked to put all that on hold, but that was life.

The important thing was to get back on the track to becoming Livia DeLacroix's ally.

Brushing some of the cave dirt off his jeans, he set off across the rocks that made a low-water bridge between the caves and his cabin.

He was leaning on the porch rails, toeing off his damp boots, when he caught sight of Livia approaching on the trail from Chata. Maybe her showing up meant his white flag would be well received.

"Hey, neighbor. How's it going?"

"Don't you 'neighbor' me, bud. I thought you were the one so set on keeping that beast from roaming the countryside."

Or maybe he could just take the white flag and stuff it up his ass. "You mean Mittens?"

That brought Livia up short. She stood on the path, cocking her head up at him. "You named it Mittens?"

"Him. Yeah, I named him Mittens." Mainly to irritate Susanna, the vet, who'd burst into actual giggles when she'd seen him struggling to contain the beast in her waiting room. She hadn't even tried to hide it, leaving him standing at her reception desk employees clocking what had his erstwhile prom date so tickled. Susanna stood there, pen poised over the cat's newly created chart, and started suggesting names like 'Rocky,' 'Monster,' and 'Chewbacca.' Some inner demon —Greg could hardly name which one, it seemed sometimes he had so many—prompted him to come up with 'Mittens' instead. The beast had white paws, after all. And it was better than 'Mr. Whiskers,' which one more guffaw from Susanna would have made inevitable.

It was always like that with him. The less serious people took him, the more determined he became to make them think his glib side was the core of him.

So he'd faced down bigger skeptics than Livia. He didn't even have to fold his arms across his chest and tighten his lips to convey that yes, he had named the cat Mittens, and he didn't intend to let her laugh at him for it.

"Well, Mittens is helping himself to my afternoon snack, and I'd appreciate it if you would fetch him before he does any permanent damage to my dining room."

"Left your windows open again, did you?"

"So you knew he was out roaming the hills?" she shot back, ready to jump to her own conclusions.

No, dammit, he hadn't known. So much for hoping Livia would gloss over that part. Mittens had been sleeping under his desk when he'd headed down to the caves, and though he'd closed up the house, the beast obviously had some tricks up his mittened sleeves.

"Give me just a minute," he said, tugging his socks off and draping them over the porch rail to dry. "Want to come in while I grab his carrier?"

Livia shrugged. She mounted the porch steps, though, so he held the door for her before taking his cold feet inside.

It took effort, but Livia didn't stop short to stare at the place. Of course, she'd been indoctrinated by Persimmon, not to mention Jujube, Chickasaw, and Loquat, which, sad to say, featured wood paneling painted in fuchsia and lime stripes, as well as peach—or maybe it was meant to be loquat-hued—bedding. So it wasn't the hugest shock she'd ever had, seeing Greg's place. Like Chata, it had a solid and secure feel to its construction, but like Chata, it appeared to have been decorated by a sentimental person with no filter.

It looked like the furniture started out mid-century modern, but then something went wrong. The serape rug didn't exactly contrast with the serape print on the sofa, but it didn't match, either. Two chairs had legs reinforced with duct tape, and Livia didn't know if that meant someone was prone to bashing them about, or if it was just a function of age or inferior wood. Pictures of a younger Greg, mostly captured mid-motion and in the outdoors, smiled out of the mismatched frames overflowing the fireplace mantle. A similar cluster of family pics sat atop the tv, which was a box-style set encased in a cherry wood cabinet with Queen Anne details. The most deliberately decorated part of the house was a gallery of nine black frames above the sofa, each holding a colored pencil drawing. Livia stepped closer; they all featured the kinds of natural landscapes she'd discovered around Honey Wine, and each was signed 'GJF.'

She wondered what the J stood for, if these were, like she suspected, pictures he'd created growing up.

Greg was peeking into a room opposite the dining area, calling for the cat as if Livia had invented leaving a home-invading feline back at Chata. "Mittens?"

Mittens.

Heh.

It was his kitchen door swaying open to reveal glimpses of the back porch that Greg ought to be looking at, if he was searching out his cat. Livia cleared her throat, then pointed her chin at it.

Greg sighed. "Okay, I give. Let me put some dry shoes on and throw his carrier in the car. You want a ride back to your place?" He was already shoving his feet into moccasins and reaching for his car keys.

"Sure." She followed him out the back—no crossbows or giant knives in sight, which pleased her imaginary Maggie—and hopped in beside him. Maybe it was his vehicle's bucket seats and openness, maybe it was the fact that he'd proved to be kind of a jerk, but the proximity didn't bother Livia nearly as much as it had when she'd driven him to their dinner at the Honey Wine Cafe. Having him in Bonnie on the way back hadn't been a picnic, but at least she'd been so busy biting her tongue that she hadn't noticed his seascape scent or the way his jeans curved over his thighs.

The SUV was fine, though. Almost roomy. And the path between their homes was short. And she wasn't planning to forget about the whole jerk thing, just because he'd named that beast cat Mittens and his second toes were freakishly long and the sound system blasted NPR before he jabbed the buttons to turn it off.

Nope. Whatever else happened, Livia was going to remember Gregory Forst telling her that his uncle had screwed up in selling Chata to her.

"So, sorry about him," Greg said, once he'd settled Mittens and a handful of tortilla chips in the carrier. The beast wasn't exactly cooperative, but he was no longer growling, which he figured was a step in the right direction. Training him to live indoors was a little more involved than he'd imagined. But if he screwed it up, Susanna would never let him forget it, so Greg would persevere.

Nothing the people of Honey Wine liked better than never letting him forget stuff, after all.

He looked around the dining room, which didn't seem to be destroyed. Though it appeared different. "Hey, where are the samplers?"

"The what?"

"On the walls? 'Home is where the dinner table is,' and 'A cook's love is saucy!' and all those?" His Aunt Sissy had hung a half dozen cross-stitches between the windows, back when she first opened the B&B.

"You mean—you don't mean those awful faded thread things?"

"Awful?"

"You like them? You're welcome to them. They should be near the top of one of those bags," Livia pointed out three black garbage sacks in the kitchen.

"Geez, city gal, what's the plan? Make this place as sterile and soulless as a chain hotel?" Greg could have bit his foolish tongue off at the base. White flag, Gregory Jacquin Forst. Don't keep antagonizing her.

He eyed Livia cautiously. Her ire was up, for sure. She'd shoved her hair under a green bandana, which let him see every spot where her pretty oval face was flushed.

"No, that's okay. I mean, they're yours now. Do what you want with them." If Kent didn't see fit to stop Sissy's hard work from hitting a landfill, who was Greg to intervene? And he had to admit she was right about them being faded. "I just was noticing all the work you've put in here."

"Well, they're still yours if you want to dig them out. I didn't think to ask if you want any of the junk I'm tossing."

"You're ... tossing a lot, then?"

Livia shook her head. "Honestly? Have you taken a good look at this place lately?"

He shrugged and went back to stroking Mittens through

the wire door. Any minute now and the cat would start purring, he was almost sure of it.

"I mean, I couldn't be happier to be here. I couldn't. Chata's great, but it's not like I just needed to give it a good sweeping and be open for business."

"It's not?"

"No. No way. A lot of the furniture is on literal last legs, and I'm sorry if it hurts your family pride, but the decor … look, it was dated when I stayed here as a kid. I'm not trying to sanitize all the character away, but I had Kent close reservations during the transition for a reason."

Greg swallowed his reply, for once, and took another look around the room. There was something to be said for how clean and bright it looked without the knick-knacks and the heavy brocade cafe curtains. Boring, but bright.

"Okay, I see your point. I wouldn't say it's all that bad, but maybe the place could use some updating. TLC, right?"

"A little more than TLC. I'm painting starting tomorrow, and should be able to start putting rooms back together and taking new pictures for the website in a week or so."

Maybe it was the brightness of the room, but it seemed like a lightbulb moment to Greg. "Do you need any help?"

"Sorry?"

"With the painting, I mean. I'm not great at trim and stuff, but I could help with the basics." This was perfect. Get her relying on him already. One step closer to her asking for his help bailing her out of the place.

"Yeah, no. No thanks, I've got it under control."

Greg looked up from Mittens, who was definitely almost relaxed—one eye was half-closed as he rubbed his chin—and found Livia wasn't even close to looking grateful for his offer. She looked more like she'd prefer he just get out of her way. He wasted a moment wishing his Aunt Sissy was there. She always knew how to generate accord between people. But then, if Aunt Sissy was there, Uncle Kent wouldn't have sold to Livia Delacroix in the first place. And hindsight wasn't going to get him anywhere closer to what he wanted.

Right then. Time to bring out the white flag.

"Hey, Livia?" Maybe it was the bandana holding back her hair, but her eyes flashed bright green at him. It made Greg want to leap back almost more than it made him want to step closer. But noticing her green eyes—or her strong arms, or the disarming bluntness she tried to hide behind her friendly smile—was in no way going to get Chata in his hands.

"Gregory?"

Her tone made him grin. He'd bet anything she wasn't thinking good thoughts about him. Greg planned to change that. "Can we sit and talk a minute? Can we—will you let me apologize and start over at this being neighbors thing? I've got some ideas. I mean about Cesta. That's my place, my business: Cesta Adventures. And I know you're busy getting the painting done and all, but if you can take the time to hear me out? Some of the ideas we can work up together, could be good business for us both."

Before answering, Livia leaned forward to look into Mittens's carrier. The cat's eyes snapped open, and he started growling, low but serious. Greg yanked his fingers out of biting range, just in case.

Livia sighed. "Fine. We can talk. Just take that thing home first and make sure he's not going to show up here again."

He wanted to argue that leaving the cat caged was good enough, afraid that if he left, she wouldn't be receptive to his return. But Mittens was still irritable, and Livia had that glint in her eyes again, the same one she'd used on him when he'd forgotten to go slow at the Honey Wine Cafe. All things considered, it seemed wisest to just do as Livia said.

For now.

CHAPTER 5

Freaking ridiculous. Livia stashed the green broom and her other supplies in the cleaning closet. She was actually considering changing into a clean top and fixing up her hair while Greg returned the cat to its new lair. As if, after a dusty day under a bandana, her hair had any chance of behaving. As if he hadn't already seen her in a bleach-spotted shirt.

As if it mattered.

Reminding herself that Greg was a jerk, and presumptuous, and kinda sanctimonious about the beast cat which he went ahead and let roam the hills despite his mini-lecture about feral animals, Livia settled herself at the table. He could just take her as is.

Well, not *take her* take her.

Although …

No. Not in the cards. Jerk. Presumptuous jerk. Sanctimonious jerk. Next-door neighbor, one of three or four people she sorta knew in her new town, and a jerk. With cheekbones made of heaven and biceps built for sin, but whatever. She'd met sinfully lovely men before.

Don't let a bad boy turn my good girl into a foolish woman.

As her mom's refrain burst into her memory, Livia

covered her mouth to stifle a sob. Mom had said it over, and over, and over again. And then some more. It had become the beginning, middle, and end of every conversation they had, those last few weeks before Livia had moved out. The first, and worst, time she'd learned her decisions could be swayed by good chemistry.

She'd been seventeen. Terry was nineteen, but more importantly, Terry's messy bangs flopped into his eyes, and his restless energy only calmed when he focused in on her. On holding her in his arms, on kissing her senseless, on telling everyone in his syrup-fake voice, "I live for Livia."

And he had an apartment. Well, he shared an apartment with a couple of guys who'd been in school with him. And they made room for her stuff on the bathroom counter, the week after she graduated. She'd spent a morning going through all of Terry's T-shirts, throwing out the shabbiest, and when she'd finished folding the rest, she'd made enough space to unpack two duffles' worth of her own clothes into his dresser.

Mom had flipped, of course. She'd tried all kinds to get her to return home, backing down about Terry in the end. Told Livia she'd move her curfew to one in the morning and stop criticizing, if Livia would just spend the last months before heading to college living at home.

"I've got a new home now," Livia had said. Seventeen years old, looking Mom straight in the eye, defiant tip to her chin, sure she knew everything right about how to live her life. Rejecting everything Mom had built for the two of them after Dad walked out.

Once, when Livia was thirteen or fourteen, and it was her and Mom against the world, Mom had joked about how she'd started out in a house of four people—her parents and brother—then tried out three people when she got pregnant and married Dad, but it turned out her favorite was to have just two people in the house.

The thing that still stabbed Livia in the gut was the look on Mom's face, the evening of her eighteenth birthday, when Mom must have given up on Livia answering any of her calls and instead just showed up at Terry's place. And Livia had said, "I'm giving you the chance to try a household of one. Isn't that what you've been working towards all these years?"

Every facet of Mom's face had broken, but she'd forced a smile and said, "I've tried it now. Turns out I was right all along; it's better to have two."

"Maybe you just need to try harder."

She'd kept the snide look on her face as she'd said it. The one she'd practiced in Terry's fly-specked bathroom mirror, just to make him laugh as they waited for the water to warm up for a post-sex shower. And even in the face of that face, her mom had tried smiling again as she handed over a gift bag. She'd wished Livia a happy birthday, and leaned forward like she was going in for a hug, before Livia muttered, "Thanks," and backed off, shutting the door.

Terry helped her talk the department store clerk into exchanging the fancy new purse, even though Mom hadn't included a receipt. In return, she'd given him half her store credit. Well, more than half, if she factored in that she bought him a T-shirt from her portion. He'd complained he was running low.

"I live for Livia." She could gag now, remembering him saying those treacly, vicious, controlling words.

"Livia."

Greg stood, annoyed at feeling intrusive as he looked at Chata's once-familiar dining room, and the closed-off face of the woman transforming it.

"Livia," he said again, a little more gently. Not an hour before, she'd been a warrior, standing by his porch and blasting him for not keeping Mittens indoors. He couldn't think of anything he'd particularly done to cause her to be slumped and deflated now.

Had she realized she was in over her head with the work it would take to get the Chata she envisioned?

With a shoulder-jerking sigh, Livia rose. "Greg. Hey. Come in."

"What's wrong?"

"Wrong?"

"Nothing's wrong?" Jesus. Vaudeville had nothing on them.

She smiled a little. "Sorry, no. Nothing. Just lost in thought."

Yeah, and Ellie was just mildly curious about what he was doing back in town. But if she didn't want to share, it was no skin off Greg's nose. So long as it didn't stop her from listening to his proposal. He got back that buzzing-under-the-skin feeling that suffused him when he thought about Cesta.

If he could get Livia to buy in to just the initial phases … One step at a time. Lay it all out for her, show her how it benefitted them both. He would make it work for Cesta, and wouldn't hurt Chata any. And most important, his plan lined him up to make Chata, in the end, his. As it should be.

So Greg smiled the smile Susanna had once called "insufferably sexy." Livia noticed. At least, she seemed to pull her focus from wherever it had gone and place it on him. And she noticed the folder he was carrying.

"What've you got there?"

"Couple of things. Mind if I sit?" She was nodding as he pulled out his favorite chair—next to the head of the table, so he faced the window with his back to the kitchen. It was the spot most likely to get served first when Aunt Sissy was entering with arms full of dishes. Maybe it was a tactical error, sitting there. Too easy to fall into a sense memory of big family meals, or one-on-one times with Sissy when Dad and Ellie were lost in grief and he was sure no one else in the world understood him. Winter nights, if someone was home at his cabin, the lights were sometimes visible to someone sitting in his favorite chair.

But nostalgia or not, Greg was also sitting in the place he was most comfortable in Chata, and that gave him a boost. He shot Livia another grin as she placed herself at the head of the table.

"We're starting over, right?"

"Over?"

"Okay, sure, not completely over. But you're forgiving and forgetting my getting pushy the other day, and you're forgiving my cat—I know you can't forget him, he's too memorable—and you're up for listening to my plan for Cesta, right?"

Livia smoothed a hand over her hair, only to stop when her fingers hit the bandana. "Remind me again what Cesta means?"

"Journey, pathway, tour. In Czech, of course. So you have cottage and I have trail, basically. And I think that works really well, as side-by-side businesses. It was how I always envisioned it, before Kent—well, we won't jump on that land mine again. I'm sorry, by the way. I mean, for claiming he acted out of turn, and not just for telling you to sell to me. Which I'm also sorry for."

For the briefest of moments, Livia wondered if she'd misremembered Greg's comment at the cafe. Nope. She didn't see the point in being churlish, though, so she let his interpretation of his 'Kent made a mistake' comment stand. Well, she raised an eyebrow at him, but otherwise let it stand.

"And what exactly would Cesta be doing? What kind of journey?"

"Trails. Lots of trails for every level. Caving, hiking, zip lines, ATVs. Electric ATVs," he added before she could grimace at the thought of a half-dozen lawn mower engines waking her guests up every morning. "They're seriously quiet, I'll show you soon. The whole place would have—will have, I mean—practically zero carbon footprint."

Greg opened the folder resting on her farmhouse-style dining table. After jotting "only leave your own footprints?" on the inside cover, he seemed to notice the papers Livia had been trying to decipher and rotated it towards her.

"Is that the boundary map?"

"Yep. It's both our places. Actually, it's the original plat. This is how it looked when my dad and Aunt Sissy inherited from their parents."

He tapped the surveyor's rendering, which named the little creek between their lands as Forst Creek. It was the hypotenuse of the rough triangle that made up her land.

She shook off the remnants of the spaced-out reverie Greg had interrupted. "Is there a reason Sissy ended up with less land than your dad?"

"Sure," he said, and went on to explain that Chata sat on the original house site. Sissy took the land with better main road access and drainage. Greg's dad was working more acreage, but it was undeveloped, with no utilities and nowhere easy to clear for building. While Sissy and Kent expanded the existing building to create Chata, Greg's dad Peter coaxed the land into giving him enough level space to park a trailer house.

"My mom refused to live in it, though," Greg continued. "So Dad had to get the cabin built when he conned her into marrying him."

"Conned her?"

Ha. She'd made him blush. As if those strong cheekbones needed anything else to make him more attractive. Which,

Livia reminded herself, was not something to be thinking about. Ever.

"He, Dad that is, always says it that way. I guess I'm so used to everyone in Honey Wine having heard it. I forget it sounds strange."

She smiled. "What does your mom say about it?"

And now Greg's smile was fading, and he started shuffling through the folder. "I don't really remember."

Of course. His mom and Ellie at the Honey Wine Cafe had been friends. She'd picked up from their conversation that his mom must have passed. "Sorry."

Greg glanced briefly at her, shook his head. "No, it's okay. I don't mean to be maudlin. Mom's gone. It's been a while—I was in high school—but once in a while … Well, I hear a question like that, and realize I don't know the answer. It hits a little."

Livia closed her eyes against the realization that, a decade or more from now, she might still be hit by questions about her own mom. Maggie had accused her of not taking enough time to mourn before offering for Chata. She hadn't laughed her off. She'd known the pain was nowhere near buried. But she was going to have to face the reality that changing every other detail of her life wasn't some magical method of putting the loss of her mom into a securely locked box in her brain. Or in her heart.

Definitely time to change the subject.

CHAPTER 6

Livia tapped Greg's part of the map. "So, where are your trails going? You mentioned caves? Do I have caves? Wait a sec. Are there bats?"

Chuckling, Greg pulled out a sketch, this one of his part of the land. "Yep. Mostly Mexican free-tailed bats, but that population has migrated south now. There's a colony of vesper bats, too, up in the rocky area behind this hill. And a few Eastern pipistrelles hibernate in the caves." As he pointed out the geography of his land, his posture relaxed. Tracing the line of Forst Creek closest to the road, he showed her where the bulk of the caves were, and gestured to the trail that led to them, as well as some hiking paths that emerged at the summit of his highest land. The ATV trail followed a similar route, but circled around another hill and descended through a rougher area.

Livia hadn't ever been on an ATV. Or a zip line. Or within spitting distance of a cave, to her knowledge. Though it looked like her driveway was practically on top of the bats, so what did she know?

Regardless, she found herself charmed by his enthusiasm. Greg was clearly passionate about the land, and his vision for it. And though she didn't want to go off trailblazing herself, she could also see some potential for her guests. He was right to suggest that running specials together could be a strong revenue stream.

As long as he knew what he was doing. Though she had to admit, from her completely ignorant perspective, he had a handle on every question she thought to ask. Except for whether she had bats on her own property—no caves, so that was good, but apparently some kinds of bats didn't live in caves. "The poisonous snakes are more likely to give you a problem, anyway," Greg said, not without a cocky smile.

She had much to learn about life in the country.

Instead of freaking her out, though, the thought of settling in deeper to life in Honey Wine kind of tickled her. She could practically see Maggie's eyes rolling, but the idea of zip lining over the land and finding out if electric-powered ATVs were as silent as Greg claimed sounded … fun.

For years, Livia's life had been all about the kind of beauty that came with elegant furniture and high-quality linens, very urban and very urbane. Now she was thinking about bats and wooded hills and whether she could set up a picnic area by the bluffs she hadn't fully realized were a part of her land. They were up by the tip of her triangle, overlooking the creek. And once Cesta was in business, they'd overlook the zip lines and hiking trails, too. She could encourage adventurous guests to head out for a day of excitement while their more sedate companions enjoyed a stroll to the bluffs with a picnic basket, where they could lounge in the shade and catch glimpses of the action across the creek.

"So, what do you think?"

Livia held up a finger to let him know she'd be right with him and moved to the kitchen, where her laptop sat beside the crock-pot of chili she'd started that morning.

"You want to stay for dinner?" she asked, starting up her Chata organization spreadsheet.

There was that conceited grin of his again. Livia kept on a

neutral, pleasant face, but made a mental note about not giving Gregory Forst even an inch without careful consideration. He was all too ready to charge forward a mile, insisting his way would be a sure-fire success. But her ingrained hospitality had led her to speak before thinking it through.

"If dinner is whatever's making that smell in the kitchen, yeah, I'd love to."

"My top-secret chili recipe. But no jalapeño-cheese muffins today, I'm afraid. You and Mittens depleted my stock."

"Those were really good muffins."

"It's really good chili, too. Should be ready any time, but I want to go through the rest of this first. Let me make a couple of notes." Livia opened a new tab to enter ideas about Relaxing / Adventures. Or maybe she could call it Zip / Zen? Revving Up and Settling Down? She typed them all in separate cells, ready to be played with when she had more time for brainstorming.

"Note away." Greg kept the smug out of his voice. He'd already begun to sell the concept of Cesta to people—potential clients, other marketing outlets, the chamber of commerce hardheads. His dad.

Some of those had been real receptive: the business lawyer his cousin hooked him up with who'd been streamlining the paperwork; his high school buddies; Dad. Others—especially the chamber—didn't seem convinced, leaving Greg unsure of his sales pitch.

So it was a good sign that Livia, with her vaunted knowledge of tourism and hospitality, was impressed. The sparks in her eyes as they talked, and the way she threw out that invitation to dinner? Also good. One step closer to Greg being the one to help her out if she couldn't hack it.

One of Greg's sneakier demons threw out the idea that if

he and Livia had a fling, he could end it once she got attached, making life awkward for her and making her more willing to sell up and leave Honey Wine for good. But before he got too carried away imagining her without the dirt-smeared shirt that was clinging to her curves, a more sensible demon butted in and reminded him that an angry, heart-broken Livia wasn't likely to pick him as her savior.

Damn shame, that. Her curves were delightful.

He really needed to stop staring at her as she concentrated on whatever she was typing. Eventually, she was going to look up and catch him at it. Greg pushed away from the table, noting again how different the view from the long windows looked without Aunt Sissy's curtains and samplers. It maybe wasn't bad, this new way. Strange, for sure, but maybe not bad.

Curious about what else she'd done, he wandered past the unchanged half-bath to the reception room. Other than the desk, which held new computer equipment and was missing Kent's bowl of butterscotch candies, it was about as he remembered it. The curtains and blinds were gone here, too, as well as in the parlor. And with that much extra light pouring into the parlor, he could see the sofa and armchairs he'd sat in for much of his life were, indeed, as threadbare as she'd said.

Huh.

Greg walked across the back porch from the parlor to the kitchen, where he stopped for a couple of glasses of ice water and a closer-up savoring of the chili's aroma before nudging open the swinging door into the dining room.

Arms folded across her chest, Livia stared at him. The eye sparkles were gone, as was that pretend-happy face of hers.

"Something wrong?"

"Wrong?"

Oh, not this again. He handed her a glass. "Brought you some water."

"How very hospitable of you."

Ah. Right. "Sorry. I should have asked. I just wanted to see what you'd done with the public rooms."

"And the kitchen?"

Greg scratched at the back of his neck. "Yeah. Well. I'm probably too comfortable here. I'm sure it'll feel alien once you're done with it."

Livia's one eyebrow arched, which was a neat trick.

"I don't mean alien in a bad way. Just not like the place I know." He tried the killer smile on her. "A place I'd like, of course. But one where I'd ask the owner before helping myself to a drink."

She couldn't help returning his smile. Jerk. Charming, presumptuous jerk. Not that she'd been the best of hosts, ignoring him so she could get down her ideas. Then she'd had a question about the view from the bluffs, which had died on her lips when she realized he wasn't beside her anymore. She'd heard him open the back porch door and had to face the reality that Greg wasn't just the business owner next door. He might have ideas that could serve them both, but under it all, he still thought proprietorially about Chata.

And Chata was hers.

After all, if she was going to have to live with the memories of Terry, and the fact that she and Mom never found their way through to an uncomplicated adult relationship, she was going to do it while she worked her butt off to prove to the spirit of her mother that she was living the kind of dream that the two of them had always talked about. Back when they talked. It was the only way, Livia knew, that she could handle the weight of being her mom's only beneficiary. Life insurance, as an assurance that Livia would lead a good life.

And if this charming, smug, sexy, presumptuous neighbor of hers had his way, this life would be his.

Well, too bad, Gregory Forst. Possession as nine-tenths of the law and all that, and this life—and Chata—were Livia's possessions.

That being established, and Livia would be careful to reinforce how established she was as they continued, he wasn't wrong about the potential for the two businesses to help each other out. She just had to keep him in line, and one thing Livia had learned the hard way was how to establish and maintain her boundaries.

"Please, have a seat," she invited, putting the hospitality face back on. Would be nice to be armored with tidy clothes and fixed up hair, but she could operate without all that fuss. She'd seen him barefoot earlier, after all. Not to mention his ass crawling under her dining table trying to lure the beast cat into his well-protected arms.

Don't think about the jerk's ass, Livia. No matter how it looked all snug in his jeans as he crooned at Mittens. That ass was settled into her dining room chair—*her* chair, not his, no matter how at home he looked in it—and she was going to be all business from here on out.

"What's your timetable?"

"If everything goes well with permits and inspections, I should open by April. But I've been trying to accelerate a lot since moving back. If it looks good in a week or so, I'm aiming to grab spring break revenue in March."

Livia nodded. She planned to reopen the first weekend in February, herself, and be at full capacity in time for Valentine's Day. To that end, she'd been concentrating on the dining room and the two second-floor bedrooms—Mulberry and Persimmon. And if the plumbing problems weren't too bad, Loquat could be ready by the end of the month, too.

"Do you know a good plumber around here?"

Greg shook his head.

"Ah well. I'll search around. I need to start getting bids. And pillows, and bed frames. Which … never mind, that's nothing to do with you. I wanted to ask about the view from the bluffs. Would guests be able to see the zip lines and people on the trails?"

"Well, yeah, probably. Is that a problem?"

"No, no. I was just thinking if I had an adrenaline junkie who's traveling with a couch potato, they could both sort of participate. If you change the definition of participate to mean sit and watch other people do stuff, that is."

For once, his grin seemed spontaneous. "That's great. We could build a lookout stand. There are some trees up there, make it like a treehouse sort of thing."

"With big fat cushions and binoculars and a stock of paperbacks and magazines, yeah," Livia added, watching his finger trace the area on the joint property map. Telling herself not to think it was cute how his square nails were pearlescent pink against the tan of his hands.

"Treehouse luxury. That's perfect, and it'll still work for when—"

Oh, how apt that his hand was currently crossing the boundary between their lands. "When what?"

So now she knew what Greg looked like when he wanted to run away. "Nothing. Never mind."

"You had other plans for around the bluffs?"

"Doesn't matter."

She crossed her arms. "Are they plans you can't execute since I own Chata?"

"Livia, look." He blew out a breath. "Until a couple weeks ago, sure, I thought I'd be the one refurbishing this place. Of course, I thought about zip line platforms and rock climbing up there, things that made sense if I had the bluffs. I don't, and you do, and I've already re-routed the lines. Mapped trails that don't cross the creek."

She looked maybe like she believed him. And just to be totally clear, he added, "The water is all on my side. And I've got hiking trails that end at the creek here. Then the hikers can take a lazy raft ride downstream to end up at the trail-head. It's a great half-day trip."

Livia rolled her eyes. "I know the water's yours. I'm not the one encroaching here. I'm trying to envision how these two things—Chata and Cesta—work together. And for the record, a raft ride sounds like an outstanding way to end a half-day hike. If my guests are going, they're going to start out very full from breakfast, though, so maybe have their treks leave later in the morning, and I can offer brown-bag lunches to picnic on before they raft? Or just a trail bag with granola and water or whatever hikers eat, and meet them with wine and cheese once they're done rafting?"

Greg suppressed a whoop of triumph. She'd bought in. While the momentum was with him, he launched into other ideas about packages he could offer Chata guests. He showed her research he'd done on ad placement for adventure sites he'd gotten familiar with through his online presence, and talked about cross-pollinating their marketing. He proved he hadn't just read some 'Trailblazing for Dummies' book before solidifying his plans.

He had good plans.

Not a month after he'd moved from the Forest Service to the adventure company, Aunt Sissy had shocked them all by dying. It was at her funeral that Dad announced his intention to leave the land. Being in Honey Wine without his wife and sister depressed him, and he wanted to rove the country. "New places, new memories," he'd said, like that was the end of a long explanation and not a four-word conversation closer.

Greg's offer to move home immediately wasn't enough to

curb his dad's wanderlust. He had his private doubts about how long Dad would want to live on the road, but the Forst land was in Greg's hands, and would always be a refuge for Dad when he returned.

After they transferred ownership and sorted out the house, Greg returned to his new job. He'd already gotten the sense that it was the kind of business he wanted to create for himself. In the rest of his time there, he researched what he could import from his Mississippi experiences to Texas, banked revenue from his channel, focused on building a following that associated him with sustainable outdoor exploration, and started the long process of making Cesta a legal entity.

Good plans. Plans he thought Honey Wine would respect.

It hurt, when Kent threw the wrench of selling Chata months earlier than he'd projected, without telling anyone. Without giving Greg a chance to put in his own offer.

His uncle, no matter their history, or maybe because of it, didn't believe in Greg.

That was fine. Greg knew—just knew, down to his gut—that this tentative partnership with Livia Delacroix was a solid step towards showing everyone what it looked like for him to realize his dreams.

CHAPTER 7

Greg showed up again before nine the next morning.

He was beginning to have as bad a habit of wandering to her place as his cat did, and both of them kept zeroing in on her cooking. She'd finally offered him a to-go portion of chili the night before, just to get him to stop talking about how great it was and how much he needed to learn to cook better himself and so forth. It turned out he was right; feed the feral beasts once, and they won't stop showing up on your porch whenever the mood struck them.

"I'm up here," she called when she heard him enter. At least he'd knocked on the door first this time.

"Where here?"

"Mulberry." Livia shoved aside the pile of linens she needed to lug down to the wash and stretched her back. Greg's eyes widened when he got a look at how much furniture she'd shoved into the hallway. Much of it needed throwing out, so she might have been better off wrestling it to one of the porches. That way, she wouldn't have to maneuver it all on the stairs. Then again, getting the bulky stuff over the balcony rail would be a trick she didn't think she could perform.

Fortunately, the stairs were a straight ramp into the reception room. When she started messing with getting anything to or from the third floor, she was going to have to remember some physics or geometry or whatnot to navigate the turn on the stairs. Made her impressed with how Kent had managed to clear out the owner's suite on the top floor.

"I thought you were painting today."

"Well. I am. But once I started laying down drop cloths, I kept tripping over this stuff. And half of it's going anyway, so it may as well not be in my way."

"You're trashing all of this?"

"No, not all. Those two chairs stay. And the mattresses; Kent had good mattresses. I didn't want them near the paint, though, and I have to replace the bed frames, so I went ahead and moved them out."

"Both beds?"

"All of them—the day beds and kings in both rooms. Well, I might be able to tighten up the day bed frame for Persimmon; I was about to look at that."

Greg whistled, spinning to take in all the clutter of the wide hallway. He wasn't bristling like he'd been over the cross stitches, though, which she took as a positive recalibration of his attitude.

"I'll give you a hand hauling it down, if you like."

Well, that was neighborly. Livia wondered if there was a catch. But she'd fed him dinner. It could be quid pro quo.

"Thanks. I was just about to back Bonnie, she's my truck, up to the door. We can load the junk items up and I'll drop them at the dump site, when I go shopping."

He grabbed the other end of the infamous armchair with the torn lining. She'd almost be sorry to see it go, after the warm and fuzzy welcome it gave her on her first night.

Hah.

But speaking of warm and fuzzy … it was too early in the morning for her to be ogling Gregory Forst's biceps. He hefted the chair, maneuvering so he caught the bulk of the weight as he backed down the stairs ahead of her. She shouldn't be staring. Never mind how his T-shirt sleeve strained across his muscles. Or how glossy his curls looked as he passed under the stairwell light. And it wasn't that the armchair was heavy, but she'd definitely grunted an inelegant amount when she'd steered it out of Persimmon's door. Greg just let the thing propel him down the stairs like it was less trouble than a folding chair.

"Livia?"

Crap. He'd caught her staring. "Yep?"

He seemed to bite back whatever he was inclined to say, which was good, given that he'd probably have more trouble with the chair if she shoved it at him and let go. Sure, he was steps from the ground floor, but it would still hurt. "Where were you going to shop?"

"Shop?"

"For furniture."

"Right." This was why it was too early to ogle. Her brain was too easily distracted from actual conversation with things like the view across the tops of Gregory Forst's shoulders. She shrugged as well as she could while they set down the raggedy armchair. "There are a couple of outlets off I-35. I'm just going to start at one place and keep going until I have everything I need."

"Go to Cypress instead."

"Where's Cypress?"

"Not where. Who. My cousin, Cypress. He's got a kind of antiques place, lots of furniture, just on the other side of Honey Wine."

"Your cousin?"

"Yep."

"And his name is Cypress? Like the tree?"

As if he could read her every thought, Greg nodded. "Exactly like the tree. Folks usually call him Cy, but where's the fun in that? And no, I'm not getting a kickback from him."

Livia looked from the holes in the upholstery, to the bags full of weird knick-knacks stacked on the porch behind Greg, and back at the guy whose cabin was just a variation on Chata's too-worn-down-to-be-eclectic decorating scheme.

"His stuff is great. Well-made." She must have still looked skeptical, because he added, "You're almost to his gate by the time you get to the dump. People travel a lot further than that for Artemis Antiques."

Well, Artemis she had heard of. Not just from the Chamber of Commerce web page; it had been mentioned favorably in a few of the travel articles about Honey Wine. Still, his cousin. Livia suspected more up Greg's sleeve.

Besides his burly biceps, she meant.

"I appreciate your mentioning it, but I have a certain look I'm going for, so …"

"Three-quarters of a mile. That's all you'd have to go after the dump. He actually complains about that, you know. One too many locals making jokes about him picking stuff up there for free and turning around and selling it for hundreds of bucks."

As she suspected. "So his 'antiques' are as rust-covered and ripped up as what I'm taking out, anyway?"

"No! No, look. I admit, I'm one of those locals who says it, and he's threatened to wallop me for it plenty of times, but Cy's got pretty beds and all. I'll come along and make sure he treats you right, gives you a good deal and steers you away from anything with critters living inside."

Livia shuddered and backed away from the armchair. "I knew something had gouged out that foam."

Greg laughed. "I'm kidding. And if you swear never to tell Kent or my dad, I'll let you in on a secret."

He really needed not to laugh before she had her second coffee. It was devastating to her ability to form words. But he went on without prompting. "I don't know about the other stuff you're trashing, but you can blame me for this chair. I always slept in Persimmon when I stayed over here, if I could, because from that daybed I could look straight out at my place."

"How come I don't see your cabin from here? Have the trees grown too much?"

"No. Well, maybe. But even then I couldn't see it by day, just at night. If the light was on." He stood there, blocking her front doorway, running his right hand hypnotically back and forth over the headrest of the armchair.

Suddenly, he shrugged and started back up the stairs. "I stayed here a lot in school, when Mom was sick. It was easier on her that way, but they promised if anything happened, they'd put on the porch light so I'd know. If I ever woke up and saw it, I could get Sissy or Kent to see me home. Sometimes I'd drag that chair over by the window for the best view, and I'd kind of pick at the fabric while I dozed."

He just tossed all that over his shoulder. Like it was no big deal. Picked up Mulberry's creaky head and foot boards and started down with them.

Livia hugged her arms to herself a moment before hefting a desk chair with a badly mended leg. Maybe he'd been guileless, or maybe she'd been manipulated, but it seemed she and Greg would be visiting Artemis Antiques.

But first, more coffee.

Once she had Greg riding shotgun on the way to the dump, she asked, "What is with your family and the tree names, anyway?"

"Who else has a tree name?"

"The Chata rooms."

"That's just rustic charm or something. Besides, Cy's from my mom's side of the family."

"Don't you mean branch?"

"Branch?"

"Branch of the family? Because of Cypress?"

"Wow. That's terrible."

She took a hand off the steering to swat at him, but all the hills and curves in this part of the state sure did their best to force her to drive responsibly. "It's not. It's funny. You should have taken me up on that coffee, then you'd know."

"I've had three cups already, but thanks again."

For a bit, they just rode in silence. The winter morning chill, such as it was, had vacated. The sun was working on removing the frost from the grass. Driving mostly west sent long shadows curving out ahead of Bonnie, while Livia and Greg cocooned in the cab.

Shame he was taking up too much space for her cocoon to metamorphose just yet.

"So, listen." Greg shot a quick glance at the road to see why Livia had swerved. It was clear and straight. Interesting. First she scopes him out, then just the sound of his voice makes her jump.

"Yeah?" Her voice was almost steady. His 'get her naked' demon was waggling its eyebrows. Damn demons weren't supposed to be making fun of him.

Banishing it, Greg focused on the plan again. "I was thinking over everything. The cross-promotions and the tree-house and your painting and everything."

"Okay. Sure, me too."

"And you've got a lot to do, physically, in the next several weeks. But I can't do much more than clearing trails before I get my permits, so I've got some time."

"Are you offering to be my hired hand?"

He'd show her what he could do with his hand. Hands. Now the fucking demon was outright laughing at him. "Uh, no. I mean, I'm happy to move furniture some just to be neighborly, but I was thinking more along the lines of a partnership."

"Partnership?" Livia's knuckles whitened around the steering wheel.

"Of sorts. Not a full partnership. I just mean I could give you a hand during the refurbishing phase, plus be in charge of the work on the bluffs—to your specifications, nothing you don't want. But I know the land pretty well, and we were talking about it being secluded, a retreat, but with the views and all. I can cut an easy trail that winds through a couple of glades. I stopped up there this morning after I'd hiked the Upstream Path, and I've got a couple of concepts that I think you'll like."

Livia's fingers were relaxed, her face open, when she looked at him. "What time do you wake up, anyway?"

"Five-thirty."

Her laugh was a completely adorable high breath of "heh," and now the fucking demon was recruiting a couple of other demons to his cause. Greg banished them all. "I don't sleep much. And since I was a kid, I started my day in the woods, if I could manage it. My folks put one of those old-fashioned dinner bells outside the kitchen door. Maybe you saw it? They found it when a neighbor's ranch was being sold for home tracts. It used to call hands in for meals. They'd ring it to get me home in time for breakfast on school days."

"And to think I only ever had an alarm clock."

"Well, city gal, now you're here, you can make up for all the things you've been missing out on." Where the hell had that come from? Greg opted against contemplating the impulse that'd led him to think, much less suggest, Livia being around for the long term was a favorable outcome.

"I'll consider that, thanks. So you want to build my tree-house, is what you're saying?"

Well, yeah. For starters. "I've had some experience with that sort of thing. And I was thinking you could pop a solar cell up there. It'd store enough energy to run lights and a fan, for as much use as it gets. Couple of outlets, too, if you want to play music or whatnot."

"I'm afraid to ask if you've already sketched all this out."

"Nope." Not technically. Not all of it.

"Look, it's a grand idea, don't get me wrong. I've put 'magic treehouse' near the top of my dream list for Chata, but I told you already I sank most of my inheritance into the place. I can't dip into my cushion for the dream stuff, not until I've got money coming in."

"Your dream list?"

"Sure. The things I don't have to do to get running, but ultimately want. Like a treehouse, and new ceiling fans in a few spots, proper furniture for my suite, a hot tub."

"Hot tub?" It was a regular demon party up in Greg's skull. They were making bets about what color bikini Livia would wear in the hot tub, but he was absolutely ignoring them. Besides, he could guarantee them it would be black. He just had a feeling his city gal was all about a classic black bikini.

Not *his* city gal. The city gal.

"Well, sure. It'd be great to have it for Valentine's Day, but it's hardly essential. I've tagged it as something to look at again, maybe before next winter sets in. If I'm doing well. Anyway, all that's just dreams right now. Hence the name of the list. I may well find, once I'm with my guests, that other things are more important. Either way, I've got to keep that money set aside, not drop it on solar cells and lumber right now."

"Slow up. You'll want to take a left just past this curve."

"Thanks."

"Yeah." His bikini-clad vision of Livia was dissolving in the rising mist from the imaginary hot tub as it hit him, again, that she was thinking very long term about Chata and Honey Wine. What's more, she'd been thinking about aspects of Chata that hadn't been in his own plans. The refurbished look, her menus that went beyond basic breakfasts, tech to improve customer interactions. She grew long-term ideas for Chata the way he did for Cesta; the experience she brought to it put his 'continue how Kent and Sissy did things' formula to shame.

"You get it, Greg, right?" Her voice cut through all his deflating hopes.

"Yeah, course." But he'd formed a new plan. "That's what I meant by partnership, actually. I have cash. You know I'd been saving to buy Chata from Uncle Kent."

Livia's eyes narrowed, and not because the sun was coming in at her.

"It didn't happen, fine. I'm not suggesting we rewrite history."

"What exactly are you suggesting?"

Deep breath. This was it. She would agree, or she wouldn't. No, she would, end of story. "What I'm suggesting is, I have cash on hand and I still have ad revenue on my channel. Even with slowing down content while I transition my career. So, yeah, I'm putting plenty into Cesta, but I got great terms on the ATVs, and I came here with more than I needed just for getting it up and running. I can fund the treehouse—sorry, the magic treehouse—and maybe even some of your other dream list things. And like I said, give a hand with the heavy lifting."

Well, she hadn't pulled over and kicked him out of the truck. That was good. "And you'd do all this in exchange for, what? A steady supply of muffins?"

He laughed. "I might. Your muffins rock. Even Mittens agrees."

"Hardy har."

"No, seriously. I mean, they're delicious, but it's a true partnership agreement I have in mind. Written up contract and everything. Here's what it is: we work up our cross-promotion stuff, and when you do the advertisement you were going to do anyway, you include it. You've got more expertise than me on that side of things, so you tell me—advise me—what I need to do for marketing, sales management, all those things. That's your physical contribution to the partnership. But also, I'll be outlaying the money for the treehouse and so on. We sign papers on that as a loan, low interest, long term. Five years, something like that."

"But?"

"But?"

"Don't play me, Greg. There's obviously more on your mind."

A little eerie that she could read him so well when she wasn't taking her eyes off the road, but he supposed he wasn't a subtle negotiator. Lord knew his attempts to talk his way out of trouble over the decades had rarely gone well. Hopefully, he wasn't talking himself into trouble with this plan.

"Okay, sure. One last thing. Like I said, I do the building and some painting or whatnot, put in hours on your property, and you put in hours on the marketing in exchange. We'll come up with some ratio that works there to be even. One batch of muffins gets you an hour of furniture hauling, that sort of thing."

It was getting so that Livia's abrupt laugh had the power to tug his lips into a grin. Dammit.

"That's the dump there, on the right—turn past those green flags. Okay, the labor side of things we work out that way, but for the cash outlay, like I said, I'll give you a loan. But until it's paid back, if you do decide to sell …" Greg's leg jiggled in the foot well as Livia backed the truck up to the unloading bays. Time to dive in and see what would happen next. "If you decide to sell Chata while the loan is outstanding, I get right of first refusal, pricing based on your deal with Kent plus your costs, and any loan balance goes towards the down payment."

CHAPTER 8

At the designated disposal area, Livia hauled the gearstick into Park more forcefully than strictly necessary. Greg was rubbing his palms on his cargo pants; this sign of nerves was the only thing that stopped her from kicking him out of her truck and letting him find his own way back to their side of town.

Well, that and the fact that he was her neighbor.

Also, until he brought back up his notion that she was doomed to fail at her business, his plan was intriguing.

It boiled down to that same gut feeling again, the one that settled in her when she'd first seen Kent's ad for Chata in the back of a magazine. The rightness. The knowledge that this would just plain work for her: for her goals, for her happiness in her career, for her desire to use her inheritance in a way that kept her connected to Mom. She liked Greg just fine, but she really liked her magic treehouse idea. And she liked low-interest loans that would allow her to install some of the elegant but eclectic touches she conjured up for Chata.

Mags would say any number of things about her impulsiveness and her odd decision-making criteria, but Livia stared Greg down for a couple more minutes, to ensure he knew she wasn't to be taken for a fool. "Six-year term, three percent interest, first payment due sixty days after the treehouse gets an occupancy permit."

"A permit for a treehouse?"

"Electricity, stairs, a balcony? This one is going to need a permit."

"You have a budget in mind?"

"How much do you have to spare?"

Greg leaned back against Bonnie's door, relaxing into that full-of-himself pomposity that Livia was sensing was a crutch of some kind. "Fifteen grand, more or less. Tree house will maybe be three to five for materials, depends on if we find any salvage here, a couple more for the solar cell, if you don't need the wattage to run more than a few lights and maybe a space heater in winter."

"And a fan for most of the rest of the year."

"But a ceiling fan, right?"

She nodded, the good gut feelings spreading.

"So five hundred watts should do it. I'll need to hire labor; a grand for that, another one or two for all the things you haven't thought of, like light fixtures and furniture, plus finishes. Should leave you with at least twenty-five hundred to play with, unless this magic treehouse is a lot more elaborate than you were talking last night."

"No hot tub, then."

"No hot tub," he confirmed. And the smug faded from his face, replaced by something hot. Livia refused to interpret his look in any way that conjured an image of Gregory Forst in her putative hot tub.

"Well, it can't be helped. Do we have a deal?"

Greg lifted a hand in salute to the lion-faced guy in a safety vest and hardhat who was approaching her side of the truck.

"Greg?"

"Five-year term. Three and a half percent, but you keep

the sixty days thing. Oh, and I asked my pal Lee about plumbers. He gave me a list of locals for you to check out."

As counteroffers went, it wasn't bad. Still: "Three and a quarter. And the right of refusal goes both ways. If you sell Cesta, I get the option to buy, but both of us base the purchase price on recent fair market value."

He flinched, which did her soul good. See how he liked being told he was doomed to fail. After a pause, he nodded. "Deal."

They were shaking on it when Mr. Orange Vest knocked on her window.

Not that he cared how soft her hands were. His were rough, naturally. He'd not contemplated the texture of his hands before. Ever. People who spend three decades scrambling up woodsy hills or spelunking limestone caves don't tend to notice calluses or the occasional scab. But apparently that didn't preclude him noticing that her hands were soft. Shapely, like her limbs, and smooth, like her skin.

Didn't matter.

He lifted a friendly hand to the dump manager. "Hey, Jackson."

"Greg. Long time." Jackson's smirk showed beneath the creases in his face, and Greg knew that Ellie had wasted no time in filling her maybe-gentleman-friend in on every move he and Livia had made at the Honey Wine Cafe.

At least Jackson toned down his smirk when he turned to Livia. "You must be the new owner of Kent's place."

"I am." No reason in the world for Greg to feel possessive about Livia's hand when she introduced herself to Jackson. Just because she'd just shaken his hand didn't mean she couldn't go and put those cool fingers wherever she wanted to put them.

And there went the hot tub thoughts again. Greg hopped out of the truck and began unloading bed frames while Livia filled out Jackson's paperwork and paid the dump fees. Once they'd joined him, he talked Jackson into admitting that there was a fair pile of milled cedar he could claim, as well as two decent window frames. And when Livia explained that the wood was for her treehouse project, Jackson got all animated and helpful, the old cuss. He pointed them to some timbers that would work as support posts, then dragged Livia off to some secret shed where he kept, as everyone knew but pretended they didn't, the real top-shelf dumped items. She came back wearing a triumphant smile and bearing a hammock and a stained glass lamp shade.

"It's only got one cracked pane, look," she said, re-wrapping it in the old sweatshirt Jackson had dug out for the purpose.

"Nice," he said, just to have something to say. Livia making conquests of the Honey Wine old guard wasn't in keeping with his hopes she'd realize it wasn't the place for her. Not when they'd just agreed on his revised step one for moving her along.

And then Jackson showed up dragging a trestle sewing machine table. "Don't let on where it came from," he said, trying to load it into the truck bed himself.

"Jackson!" Livia bounced on the balls of her feet. "I'll never say a word, but you are an angel."

As if Jackson wouldn't be relaying this entire conversation to Bill as soon as they settled into their habitual chairs over at the feed store after lunch. Rotten old gossip.

"It's missing a drawer," Greg said.

"I don't care, it's gorgeous. It'll be perfect for the guest book in the reception room."

"I thought you were getting rid of all Kent's furniture 'cause it was broken or whatever. Why take broken stuff to replace it?"

"No, but this is gorgeous."

Greg stopped tying down the cedar and looked at Livia, who only had eyes for the ironwork that made up the sewing table's legs.

"It's a little rusty."

"Ah, just hit it with some steel wool and black spray paint. It'll be pretty as the day it was new," Jackson butted in. And then he grunted pointedly, to clarify that he was an innocent, feeble old man who was only doing a good turn for the new resident in town, while Greg was the unreformed reprobate who wouldn't even lift a hand to spare an old friend some suffering. Or so Livia seemed to interpret the grunt, from the brows she lowered in Greg's direction.

He vaulted out of the truck and hefted the table into the back without a lick of help from Jackson. It might have been a perverse move, but he wanted to be sure Jackson knew Greg was on to him. And maybe he wanted Livia's admiring eyes on him.

But mostly he just wanted to finish with what was seeming like a day of fool's moves: hauling her furniture to start with, offering up a long list of contractors and local contacts, escorting her through town like the Chamber of Commerce appointed him as her personal Honey Wine Ambassador. So throughly neighborly of him, and not at all guaranteed to get him what he most needed to succeed.

"I can't thank you enough," Livia said again as she backed Bonnie up to Chata. She hadn't even thought about it when she'd purchased her truck, but it was the perfect height to just unlatch the gate and unload items directly onto the front porch. Another brief touch of serendipity about her life in Honey Wine.

She almost hated to admit it, out of some weird stubborn

pride, but Cypress had been another piece of providence. He'd welcomed them to Artemis Antiques with genuine pleasure at seeing his cousin again, which seemed to do a lot to cure the case of the grumpies Greg had picked up at the dump.

And his showroom. Oh, his showroom, with magic tunnels leading from tables to chairs to odd one-of-a-kind cabinetry, with detours to bedsteads and bookcases and every weird and wonderful thing Livia had never imagined.

Plus, "seeing as you're Greg's neighbor," he'd offered free delivery the next day. She'd actually had to talk him into waiting two days so she could finish up the painting before installing the new furniture.

"Really, Greg, even the dump was a treat." Livia gave Bonnie's door a satisfying slam and swung onto the porch so she could unload the sewing machine table. "I didn't know what to expect. I mean, I grew up in a suburb. I don't think I ever knew anyone who went to the county dump. I was a little nervous. Can you believe that? But Jackson was such a sweetie, and I mean, even without him, the whole thing was fascinating, don't you think? All the stuff people bring out there, and, I don't know, the entire process? I'm probably revealing all my ignorance, but they have forms for what size vehicle you're unloading; I think that's so cool. And it all makes sense. I like that there's ways to reclaim stuff. Plus, after all the emails I sent out before moving here, practically none of them at all useful for what I needed? I thought I'd spend days driving all over the state looking for furniture, and it turns out all I needed was a Honey Wine insider to help me out. All those rusty wheels are spinning smoothly now. Oh, do you want me to unload the treehouse stuff here, or what?"

Greg was standing by the back tire, hands shoved into his pants pockets.

Livia bit the inside of her cheek when she realized that

she'd spent the entire drive home boring him with a series of monologues they could probably title "Unsophisticated Urbanite Delighted by Small-Town Life." Mortifying.

"Right. Sorry. I'm talking a lot. It's just nice to discover—well, you know what I think. I'll hush. Except to say that I've got plenty of chili leftover, if you want a bit of late lunch." She smiled. "And I made more corn muffins this morning. You can have as many as you want, and I won't even factor them into our bargain."

Well, he didn't laugh, but he did ingest another dose of the chill pills he'd discovered at Cy's. "Sounds great, yeah. And if you trust me with your truck, I'll drive up the path some and unload the wood there. I can tarp it in the morning in case the weather changes before we get it up."

The little road from her parking lot across the bridge to his cabin had a slight, un-groomed path veering off to the left just before the river. Livia hadn't imagined driving on it, but Greg didn't lack confidence.

"It's not going to blow my shocks? Or my tires?"

"Your shocks aren't going to be noticeably affected, no."

"Hey. They're not that bad."

Now he did laugh a little. "Okay, sure. It'll be fine. Keys?"

She tossed them to him, then tucked the stained glass lamp shade under her arm and went to microwave their lunch.

After eating, they modified a free loan contract she downloaded, and agreed that the hours they'd exchange would be an off-books deal. At least until, or unless, one of them got too deeply in debt to the other.

"Also, let me look up the discount code I used for the license on my booking software. They have a tourism booking product that looks nice. I don't know what you're using, but mine integrates really well with my site and has a smooth UI. And I think the discount would apply there, too."

"UI?" The genuine confusion in his tone didn't match any

of that bragging he'd done about having a profitable YouTube channel. How had he found success—she'd looked up his subscriber numbers; watched maybe quite a few of his videos —without more digital savvy. At least she now knew his need for her marketing and business help was beyond genuine.

"User interface. And you can customize the booking engine with the look of your site."

He shifted in his chair. "I wasn't going to do any of that."

"Any ... online bookings?"

He nodded.

"How are you getting customers in if they can't book online? This is standard stuff, Greg."

He shrugged. "I'll have an email form. And the phone. I'll keep track in the book. It's like how Aunt Sissy used to do the hotel, and that worked just fine."

She snorted. "Maybe once, but that software your uncle had was in use for a decade or more. You think they weren't integrating with the big booking sites and collecting customer data all this time?"

Greg scraped his hand through the thicket of his hair, which just confirmed that no matter what he did, it always looked the same. Livia wondered what she would have to do to muss it up.

"I've got a computer, Livia. I'm going to buy accounting software and everything. I just don't have the whole online booking thing. I don't think I'll need it."

"And what about me?"

"What about you?"

Lord grant her the patience of a preschool teacher on class picture day. She took a breath. "Well, just picture it, Greg. I'm serving my spicy sausage casserole to my guests, and talking about what they'll be doing in Honey Wine. Someone says what a nice day it is and how they'd like a trek. I grab my tablet and show them your website, click through and see that there are two time slots available, and then their partner pipes up that if they take the early one, she'll have time to browse Cy's shop before they meet up again. All the while, my other guests are listening in and looking at your site, and I get a couple who want to go caving, and another for the ATVs. Since everything is right there in front of us, I can book them in and it won't be a mess of 'wait, Greg, do you have a 10:30 slot?' and 'oh, hang on, no, they want the afternoon, and he needs the extra-large helmet because his head is the size of a watermelon, is it available?' and all that back and forth that makes people say 'never mind, this is too complicated, let's just go to the swimming hole,' and you lose business, and I look inefficient, and both our online reviews suffer."

Greg's arms crossed his broad chest like if his body was enough of a distraction, she wouldn't notice the flush across his cheekbones. "You have a really active imagination," he grumbled.

She shoved the computer away and just stared at him. The sanctimonious jerk. "What I have, Gregory, is years of experience booking activities for guests. They want convenience, everything online. They want to see a website to judge if they'll like a place. They want to feel like they're personally discovering you even though all of your packages and prices are right there for the entire virtual world to find. They want all kinds of things, but most of all, they want instant gratification. For that, you need a great website, and you need to take online bookings."

"And for all that, I need your software?"

"For that, you need something like it, yeah."

"And if I get this thing, you'll build it out for me as part of our deal?"

She narrow-eyed him. "Look, this agreement is about my business skills in exchange for your labor. I know on the face of it, building a treehouse and building a website are both, just that: builds. But the treehouse is something you can complete and walk away. A website never stops needing tinkering, whenever you do anything like add services or update your seasonal offerings. I'll help you figure out whatever booking software you choose—and if you choose the one that's built by my provider that will be easiest—but this is one of those teach a guy to fish moments."

He did a crappy job of concealing his irritation with her. Fair, since she was doing a crappy job of concealing her impatience with him.

"I know what I'm talking about, Greg. Get used to the idea, because you can't establish Cesta without doing all the things I'm telling you."

"Fine." Greg stood, pocketing another muffin. "Since you've got all the business skills, make me a copy of the contract. Oh, and a word of advice from the humble laborer? Before you let that sewing table Jackson found you sit on your wooden porch much longer, or bring it into the house, you'd best to treat it for termites."

Smug. Arrogant. He didn't care how he came across. He was right. Maybe she was right, too, but not so much so that she had to treat him like an idiot. He showed her, though. He showed her the plans for the treehouse, and didn't even react when she went on about how the dump-procured hammock could hang beautifully under the platform. He showed her the bill for the permits he pulled for the thing's construction, which he'd filed down at the municipal building when he was filing his own permits. He showed her everything she'd gotten wrong about the promo materials for Cesta she'd written up. By the time she was done painting and he was done roughing out the treehouse's frame and helping arrange all of her pretty new furniture, Greg had definitely shown Livia a thing or two.

And never mind that she'd done the same for him in

return. Her website designer had taken their info and updated the Chata logo, then created a Cesta logo that echoed, but didn't duplicate it. The H of Chata had a cottage-looking peaked roof that encompassed the rest of the letters, while the S of Cesta was a winding trail that wove over and under the rest of the word. Individually, they looked cool, and together, they almost interlocked, the Cesta-pathway starting at the foot of the Chata-house and leading off into parts unknown.

Greg's buddies Lee and Jorge had put in a couple of hours finishing up the treehouse before helping him clear the ATV trails by loading up chainsaws and running his new machines all up and down the place with little regard for his guide flags. But at least the thing was done, and Livia had thrown a much-appreciated spontaneous hug his way when she'd first stepped onto the seating deck he'd build below the treehouse platform. He led her past the hammock and Adirondack chairs, up the steps to the treehouse itself. It turned out nice—the platform rose into low walls with a timber and canvas roof shading the wicker stools and a chaise lounge he'd coated with several layers of fabric guard.

She touched every surface and gazed out of each window. "It's perfect. Just what I imagined."

"You switch on the power here." Greg hit the rotator switch that sent juice from the solar cell to the building, then flipped on the ceiling fan and the space heater he'd hidden behind a lattice under the window. "It switches off after an hour, so even if people leave lights on, it won't drain the cells."

"Clever."

"I can be clever."

"Never said you couldn't. I'm just admiring this particular piece of cleverness."

Okay, maybe she hadn't, in so many words, insulted him. And maybe her ideas turned out to be ones that made Cesta better, too. He was already profiting from this partnership, even without it becoming the avenue through which he eventually took over Chata. They both were. So whatever snarky things some of the better demons of his nature tried to point out about his long-term plans, he wasn't going to let them make him feel bad.

CHAPTER 9

It was almost the end of January, and Livia was feeling good. Sexy good. She'd dyed her hair that morning, and it was falling straight and silky down around her shoulders. Plus, it had that fake-botanic home dye kit smell that wafted her way every time she ran her hand through to feel the well-conditioned fullness. If it wouldn't actually destroy her hair in the long run, she'd dye it every week just for the texture and scent. One day she would find a shampoo that replicated it, but in the meantime, she was all set for her photos and for whatever else the day would throw her way.

In a few days, the updated Chata site would go live. She'd kept Kent's storefront running while building her own, and had a few upcoming bookings lined up through. With the new site, though, she would update the booking aggregators, issue a press release, and send out junket invites. It all would drive significant traffic her way—their way—throughout spring and into summer.

She was feeling good about her neighbor, too. This bargain they'd struck wasn't working out badly at all, at least for the first part. He was annoyingly resistant to some of her plans, but tended to capitulate in the end. And he'd proved to be more than capable of the heavy lifting tasks he'd undertaken.

The path to the treehouse was going to be gorgeous once the spring growth started, and the treehouse itself was a thing of beauty. Just space enough for a couple to idle in freedom or a few people to share a cozy afternoon. The combination of the reclaimed cedar and new pine was eclectic and homey, and the construction style echoed Chata's rustic charm.

So it was a real sun's in the heavens kind of day, as she opened the front door to a tall, tall drink of water, backlit by the brightening day.

"Ms. DeLacroix? Dante Morales."

"Dante, great, come on in. Call me Livia." She held the door wide to make it easier for the plumber to lift his toolbox and his other, bigger toolbox over the threshold. Strong arms. He moved like molasses, slow but without hesitation.

"You said it's your faucets?"

"Three of the guest sinks are—well, you'll see. Wonky. And one is just ugly, so I figured while I had you here, may as well replace it."

The vendor list Greg had forwarded from his friend had an asterisk next to Dante's name, so she'd taken a chance and called him first. And she was in luck, because he'd been a half-day away from finishing up a job, with nothing booked immediately after it.

"The powder room and kitchen are fine, so it's all upstairs. Want a hand with any of that?"

Dante just shook his head, then ever-so-deliberately began mounting the stairs. Normally Livia would have led the way, but the toolboxes blocked her ability to slide past him on the landing. The man had long legs. Two steps behind him meant she was eyeing his butt all the way to the second floor, and wondering what had ever happened to plumbers's ass cracks. Because if this particular plumber let his jeans ride that low, she didn't suspect she'd object. That'd teach her to think in stereotypes.

And now she was feeling just a little too good about the

plumber. Why were all the guys she met in this town so cute? Hopefully he was competent; Livia wouldn't love being forced to send him away. She explained about the sideways faucet in Mulberry and the dripping cold-water handle in Loquat. He was opening the box on the new fixture for Persimmon when she caught her reflection running a hand through her hair. *Back away from the plumber, Livia.*

"So you got everything you need, then?"

It was less a smile than an event. His lips curved. They parted, more fully on the right than on the left. A crooked incisor, perfectly imperfect, and the barest hint of a dimple in his chin. Then his molasses voice. "When I need something, I will definitely let you know."

Livia forced her hands to stillness. Retreated. Strong, silent, and scrumptious. She was going to have to tell Maggie about him, in detail.

He'd just rounded the stairwell onto the second floor when Greg saw Livia emerge from Persimmon. She was damn pretty, all dressed up for the photographer he'd recommended to come in and get fresh shots of all her updated rooms. Not that he'd minded how she looked in her grungy painting clothes, or any other way, for that matter. He just hadn't seen her hair all flowy and down out of the bandana or braids for a while. Pretty hair. That was all. Livia had pretty hair.

"Hey."

She gasped. "Oh, hey! Sorry, I didn't hear you come in. What's up?"

"The photographer called. She wants me up on the bluffs overlooking the trails, so I'm checking that's okay with you."

"Right. Sure. I suggested it. I thought if we were both in a couple of shots, they might come in handy. And since you made the treehouse, and it overlooks your place, that kind of made sense." She trailed fingers through her hair. If she played with it whenever she wore it down, he was going to start hoping for her to have loose locks more often.

Then someone in Persimmon said her name.

Just like when she'd first seen him round the stairs, Livia jumped a little.

"Someone here?" He'd come on foot, entered through the kitchen door. Hadn't noticed any vehicles.

"Yeah, um, he's …" She walked into Persimmon, Greg on her heels. "Dante. I'm so sorry. Your surname has flown right out of my head."

And then, of all people, Dante Morales walked out of the bathroom. At least, it seemed to be Dante. The man ambled like Dante. He had a crooked tooth like Dante. He had a bush of black hair like Dante.

"Morales," he said. "Maybe if we'd started across the hall, you would know." And he slow-talked like Dante. So Greg could only figure that, along with growing another half a foot in height, little half-speed tag-along Dante Morales had lost all of that baby fat that had stuck around throughout their pubescence. He shook the man's hand.

"It means mulberry. Morales does. Like the room," Greg said, given that Livia wasn't twigging to the joke, and had taken searching Dante's face for, he presumed, an answer. Or maybe just because she liked looking into his face. What did he know? He didn't know, for example, why Dante was in Chata at all. Or why the two of them would be bouncing around between Mulberry and Persimmon. Or why the idea of Livia bouncing around with Dante was kind of pissing him off, even though he'd already told himself too many times that noticing how Livia heated him up was a bad idea for so many reasons. Reasons good enough to hold him back, those times he'd sensed their sizzling chemistry heating up.

Irritating, then, that he was irritated further by Livia

laughing about Morales without looking at him. He was the one who'd explained the joke. Or pun. Or whatever it was. It wasn't funny. Didn't stop Livia from laughing that high "heh" that he liked so much.

"You want to come on in here?" Dante slow-asked her, and before Greg was done picturing the geometry of two adult bodies in the Persimmon bathroom, they were through the door. And she was speaking all happy-voiced under the sound of the water. Greg's mind moved without his permission to the geometry of two adult bodies in Persimmon's clawfoot bathtub.

His mind was still on spatial relations and had to play catch-up when he got to the bathroom door and found the two of them standing over the sink watching the water. It was flowing. Out of the tap. Like water tends to do.

Ah. Greg got it. The wrench on the floor, and the discarded parts on the counter and, oh yeah, the toolbox he was about to stub his toe on. It all added up to an obvious conclusion. Or, obvious to anyone not distracted by Livia's hair.

Which left him unable to ignore, for once, how much he wanted Livia DeLacroix. He'd spent all this time playing like he was mad at her, but all along he'd been pulling out all the stops to impress her. He was worse than a second-grader toting a frog to school and leaving it on the cute girl's desk. Doing all that work just to get a reaction out of her, and then getting brutish because she was paying more attention to another guy.

He'd gone and fallen prey to all kinds of ingrained nonsense, like he never developed past received notions of gender dynamics. Another minute or two and he'd have pulled her pigtails. If she'd been wearing pigtails, instead of that flowy down her back style.

"Your hair's nice." When Livia and Dante both stopped talking plumbing and looked at him, Greg slouched against the doorframe, arms folded casually across his chest in a way that he could pretend wasn't calculated to get her looking at his biceps like she sometimes did. "For the photos, I mean. You look nice."

"Thanks, Greg."

He nodded. "Sure. The rooms, too. Look nice." They really did. She'd combined Kent's stuff with the new things from Cy, and kind of arranged it all in a way that made Persimmon look both familiar and fresh.

Dante had that crooked tooth pointing his way, and Greg belatedly remembered that even when he was the tag-along, Morales could deflate a guy's ego with two or three slow-spoken words. It was time to get out while the getting was good.

"So I'll head out to the bluff, check if any rain got in the treehouse. Meet you up there when you're ready. Good seeing you, Dante."

And as if to pile on, Dante said, "I'll be talking Livia into a tankless water heater. Let's catch up one of these times I'm up here."

At least she was checking out Greg's biceps again. It was the only encouragement he would allow himself to take as he headed off to face his desire and his jealousy and the complexity of his worry that Livia was never going to need a hero to swoop in and save her.

The demon who was never at a lack for words came up with a few ideas about a different role he could play in Livia's life, but Greg was, for once, way ahead of him.

CHAPTER 10

When Livia arrived, the photographer, Patti Clay, was laughing at something Greg had said or done or implied by the insouciance with which he leaned against Livia's treehouse, feet planted wide, and fine backside resting on the railing. It wasn't the first time Livia had noticed the way his hair gleamed in the sun, or the way his body relaxed when he was outside, or the way his face magnetically drew eyes to him. So if Patti Clay noticed all that, too, and it helped her get great photographs for their businesses, good. That's why she'd hired the woman, after all.

Still, it would have suited Livia fine if she hadn't felt like she was interrupting when she climbed the steps to the magic treehouse.

"Y'all ready for me?"

"Come on over, Patti was saying this is a good angle for shots of the two of us," Greg said, leaning forward as Livia approached.

"And I had an idea for inside," Patti said, positioning Livia so that she and Greg were shoulder-to-shoulder, then nudging them even closer. Livia was at least eighty percent listening as Patti explained how she would stage-set them as a relaxed couple enjoying the treehouse, pillows and books and wine glasses with the window on the view behind them. The rest of her attention was distinctly focused on the firm wall of Gregory Forst's chest, the fact that his chiseled jaw was right there at her eye line, his ocean-breeze air mingling with her new-hair-color smell. On her dreamy, scandalous thoughts about their limbs mingling as readily as their scents.

Okay, maybe only seventy percent of Livia was paying attention to the photographer. But that was because Greg shifted, bringing his hand around to rest on her back. Patti had suggested it, Livia was pretty sure. But she was also pretty sure that resting her head against his shoulder wasn't appropriate in this context. It was getting difficult to separate her instincts from her instructions.

She was virtually positive that Patti Clay had said nothing about Greg's thumb tracing up and down her spine. And yet, there it went. Such soft strokes. Just the pad of his thumb, and Livia was fighting not to close her eyes and allow her body to sink into Greg's side.

Really, now that she suspected the presumptuous jerk part of him was mostly a facade, Gregory Forst had stopped being a maddening, devastatingly attractive man. And they worked together well. Being cooperative neighbors and business owners was inspiring good ideas in them both. In short, Gregory Forst had become an appealing, devastatingly attractive man. And his thumb was telling Livia that she appealed to him, too.

She turned her moan into an interrogatory, so Patti repeated her question about the interior shots. It was the easiest thing in the world to let her arrange them lounging in the overstuffed wicker furniture Cy had delivered, their hands stretching across the window between them for evocative shots of their interlaced fingers. And either Patti had moved into professional mode or she'd picked up a vibe between them, because no hint of the flirt remained in Patti's interactions with Greg. Not that Livia was looking for it.

Still, when Patti said she would return to Chata on her own to start on the interior shots, Livia didn't offer to accompany her. She did warn Patti that Dante was working in the bathrooms. "Just let him know if you need him out of the way. He said he could clean up his work in a jiffy whenever you want."

Greg snorted at that, but he also made no move to rise from the chair beside her.

After all the painting and scrubbing around Chata, Livia's hands weren't as smooth as before. Though when Greg had become the archivist of Livia's skin texture, he wasn't altogether sure. What he was sure of was that he'd touched her more in the previous hour than in all the days since they'd met. All hail Patti Clay, with her artful way of pressing Livia into his arms.

A couple of fat squirrels raced across the porch. Once their skittering had faded, the treehouse was nothing but the silence of their two chests breathing. Greg's body, alive in every place Livia had been, overrode any sensible things he might have said.

"I like your hair like that."

She laughed that laugh of hers. "You said."

"I did?" Crap.

"In Persimmon. But thanks. Again."

Right, Persimmon. Where Dante was slow-moving in that newly tall, trim frame of his. He cleared his throat and stepped closer to Livia. Close enough to smell her hair and for his skin to warm in anticipation of being on her skin. "Sure. I mean, for the photos it looks good. It seemed like she got some good stuff."

She blurted, "I should check she's got all she needs at Chata."

"I should have her come shoot out at Cesta, supplement all my videos," he said, at almost the same time. But they were closer to each other. And no closer to the door.

Her eyes weren't so green in this wood sanctuary he'd built for her. He was examining them, trying to name the shade—it was whatever the name was for pin oak leaves in the fall, just before they turn—when it occurred to him he'd thought of it as her sanctuary. For her.

As if she would never need him as a swooping-in hero to take over at all.

Something tightened in Greg's face, and Livia stepped away before she could throw herself at him. Before she could find out if it was a good or a bad thought he'd had. Or a really bad, good thought.

"Oh. I meant to ask you," she said, and really, she did mean to ask him. Just not necessarily while they were listening to the wind rustle the tree leaves while the air between them grew stiller and heavier. She started for the door. "You mentioned about that outdoor sculptor, Amalia? I checked her stuff out. It's so vibrant, I love it. We got to talking, and I dropped your name, with great success, I think. She agreed to work up a bid on street signage with my new logo. For you, too, if you want it. You'll need a sign anyway, and the Chata one is so faded I almost missed the turn my first time here. I checked with the permit department. We can go at least one and a half times larger than what's there now. So Amalia got me her quote, and it's not bad at all."

He shuffled a few healthy paces behind her as they headed out. "I was just going to paint a four by eight sheet of outdoor ply and mount it."

"Right, I know, but I want you to look at this bid. It's a good price, and if you go down there, she's got some pieces that'd give you the general idea. You'll see what I mean. It would make an impressive statement."

They were several steps down the path before he spoke again, and there was something of the jerk back in his voice. "If that's how you want to spend your loan, fine. That wood sign has stood for a long time, and I was planning on repainting yours when I did mine. It wouldn't be the first time. Kent had me touching it up as one of my first jobs around here."

And there he went again. Livia may have let her subconscious run a little wild after weeks of watching Greg engaged in the physical labor that did nothing to hide his body, or the strength that gave it such a universal appeal. But he still have that annoying tendency to be sanctimonious about Chata. She didn't need to hear quite so many of his stories about Aunt Sissy and how the entire world loved her, and how she loved Greg, and how Chata was full of Forst family history, no matter how many cross-stitches and angel dolls Livia cleared out.

Even if he some of his stories were like the one about how the chair in Persimmon had developed holes. There was a difference, Livia had noticed, in those occasional anecdotes. A genuine peek at Greg's heart.

But then, he came up with the possessive stories. Like the previous evening, when Livia mentioned that Kari Kabot, who had long worked housekeeping for Chata, was back from the month-long trip she and her husband had taken. Greg hadn't seemed able to resist a tale about the afternoons he'd spent minding Kari's daughters while she worked, spinning a simple babysitting gig into a nostalgic reverie about an arrowhead collection that just happened to reside in the curio cabinet of Chata's parlor. Very 'I know this place and the people within it like the back of my manly hand.'

Except if he was so attached, why'd he spend all his adult life working in Mississippi or wherever? Sure, he'd been saving up to start Cesta Adventures, but did he have to do it so far from this land he claimed to love?

Before she could ask, his smile had softened, and his eyes had creased, and he'd confessed that when he was fourteen and Kari's girls twelve and seven, he'd taken them out to a swimming hole near the bluffs, where a rope hanging from a high cypress branch allowed them to catapult out from the bank and drop into the cool deep water. Nicole was big enough to swing on her own, but he'd waited in the water after his turn with some half-formed idea about 'catching' her, just to tell Jorge and Lee he'd hugged a girl. He hadn't suspected Nicole had a similar agenda of her own, and they were tentatively touching their lips together when Lynne's screams of outrage that neither would get out of the water to help her reach the rope swing drew Uncle Kent out to the creek. "Mom and Dad lectured me for two weeks, and took my swim trunks away. They banned me from the water all summer."

"And did you stay out?"

He'd laughed and looked around covertly, like there was anyone within miles to overhear them. "I went skinny dipping every chance I got. It wasn't even that great after the first law-breaking thrill, but I had to, or Jorge woulda called me obedient."

So instead of wiping the smug smile off Greg's face with an announcement that Kari was happy to come to work for Livia, she'd passed along some of the news about Lynne and Nicole, and Nicole's baby boy, that Kari had shared during their informal interview.

"Kari and Mason are grandparents?"

"For a year now, it seems."

"Huh." And then Greg's smile wasn't soft or smug, but a little sad. "Kent never told me."

It was times like that, when Greg's vulnerability poked through his shell of self-confidence, that Livia couldn't fully parse. Was he ever going to relax his proprietary air and act like the business associates they were? Or even embrace the friendship—the something more—that might grow between them? She couldn't grasp where his head was at, and wasn't sure if he knew from one moment to the next, either.

"All I'm doing is suggesting you look at Amalia's bid. There's no commitment. She'll give me the same price, even if it's one instead of two." A few long strides didn't burn off the irritation he seemed so intent on provoking in her. "You don't have to be constantly throwing history in my face, you know. I love Chata's history, I do, but it's mine now. Mine. And a new sign isn't the last of the changes I'll be making around here."

Fortunately, they'd reached the point where the path split to head to his cabin. Greg paused, and Livia didn't. When she glanced back, because of course she glanced back, he'd finally turned and started towards his own land. Leaving her to move forward alone.

CHAPTER 11

"What the—? What exactly do you mean?" Greg stood at the scratched-up black laminated counter of the building and planning department of Honey Wine's municipal offices, trying not to glare at Mr. Connor. Trust his high school vice-principal to have an equally rigid husband working in city government. Mr. Connor tapped the top of Greg's folder of carefully organized paperwork.

"There are those on City Council with, ah, reservations, as it were, about your proposed use of the land."

"It's my land."

"Yes, but the Chamber of Commerce has a Heritage Initiative. You may have read about it in the *Honey Wine Times*?"

Greg did not roll his eyes. Practically the only good grade he'd ever received in his high school government class was for a paper he'd written proposing a similar initiative. His teacher had him send it to the Chamber of Commerce where, apparently, they'd sat on it for over a decade until he was the one looking for a sign-off.

Mr. Connor took his silence as a yes. "So you know City Council has been, ah, working closely with them to ensure the preservation of undeveloped lands and natural features.

When anyone proposes to modify the land like this, interfering with cave formations, disturbing Native artifacts, City Council will insist on a public hearing before granting a variance. If they approve, I should say."

"It's my land, though." Did the man not understand that point?

"As private land, of course, you are free to modify however your building permits, ah, permit. But you've already incorporated as," he glanced back at the folder, "Cesta Adventures. So it's a public issue, as it were."

Like bloody hell. "The caves are dry, so I'm not disturbing their growth. And years back, Mom had some archeologists with the university do a full survey and they didn't turn up anything more than the arrowheads we already know about. None of this seemed to matter when I first filed."

"Ah, but now you are resubmitting, and that means new eyes on this."

Greg did not curse, no matter the temptation. It had been a damn fool move to file his original business paperwork with the conjoined land map. Counting chickens that had no interest in roosting nearby, now he was submitting the modified Cesta paperwork and running into problems. "Mr. Connor, I haven't modified the land at all. I've only cleared pre-existing trails. Ones I've been on with your son, for that matter, if you want to ask him where his own arrowhead collection came from to start with.

"Yes, but that was before it was a public issue."

Nice how Mr. Connor sidestepped anything to do with Paul. He and Greg hadn't been the best of friends back in high school, but Honey Wine was small, and sometimes an entire crew of guys would end up places together. If he remembered correctly, it was Paul who'd almost gotten stuck in one of the caves, leading to Greg's strict cave buddy rules. It had been a bit of a killjoy, and wasn't great for his reputation, but since Greg's reputation at the time wasn't something he was eager to revive, maybe it was best to leave Paul Connor's antics in the past.

"Okay, spell this out for me. What do I need to do to get the variance?" Chata was zoned for commercial use, Cesta was not; it should have been a cookie-cutter form based on what Greg had researched from other new area businesses. Apparently, those guys flew under the Chamber of Commerce radar or something.

"Well, there is a timeline, as it were, for you to follow. It's detailed in this brochure. Your next step will be to attend the Chamber of Commerce meeting and present your arguments. Your proposal, I should say."

"You can't fight City Hall, eh?" Greg added the brochure to his paperwork.

"I beg your pardon?"

Mr. Connor was either hard of hearing, or deliberately baiting Greg. Maybe Paul had told his parents one too many details about his issues sliding past the soda straw formations in the dry caves.

"Nothing. The next meeting is when, exactly?"

To the man's credit, he passed over every informational brochure he thought might apply to Greg's rezoning request. He even added one on sign permits when Greg's thoughts about Chata's commercial zone led him to thoughts about Livia's slick hair and the tensions of the day before.

And her suggestions about Amalia's art. It was definitely better to think about the signs, and how know-it-all Livia was about them, and her little diatribe. Accusing him of throwing history in her face. As if. Being neighborly, that was all it was, if he told her some things about the well water, or where Sissy always kept the spare batteries and light bulbs, or a story about a couple of repeat customers.

If she wanted to fly like a bat with screwy sonar, who was he to stop her? He should focus on his own business, since his help and friendship were such a burden to her. Gregory Jacquin Forst could take a hint.

He would just stay well out of Livia's flowy-down-her-back hair.

She met Amalia Reyes at the feed and hardware store so they could discuss mounting options for her new sign. When she'd first seen the sheet-metal sculptures dotting Amalia's studio yard, she'd had a moment of disbelief that the petite woman could create such large works of art, but one firm handshake was all the proof Livia needed. And the art spoke for itself.

The way Amalia spoke of her creations, sketching in the air with fluid grace and surety, made her seem larger than life. Livia was caught up in deciding between a monument and a pole mount when Greg wandered in, looking distracted.

"Hey, you okay?"

He blinked from her to Amalia and back. "Oh. Hi."

Whether he was unhappy to see her after their words the day before, or something else was going on, she couldn't tell. But it wasn't in her nature to forget all the positives of how he'd helped welcome her into Honey Wine, or all the up sides to their work together so far. Though she should maybe let him wander off again, she opted for friendly concern. "Greg?"

"Sorry, yeah. Hey, Amalia, good to see you." He did break into a smile when the artist shook his hand. "Thanks for putting together the quote on my sign. I'll get back to you soon, okay?"

"No problem." She pulled out her sketches of the pole mount, and gave him a rundown. For his part, Greg dug through his pack and handed Livia the flyer from the

Chamber of Commerce about sign permits. Which she already had, but she took it as a gesture of peace.

Bill bustled up from the register, more animated than he'd been when it was just the two women browsing. "Got those eyebolts you need for your zippy-do-dah stands, kid."

Maybe because she was watching him for more signs of discord between them, Livia caught the brief moment of sadness that flashed across Greg's face.

"Zip line stands," he said, and seemed to brace himself for more.

"Yep, those. Course, it might be you don't need them anymore if Connor has his way, so I'm going to have to remind you of my special order policy. No cancelations." Bill seemed entirely pleased to be in on some joke Livia wasn't privy to.

"What's happened with Mr. Connor?"

"It was three minutes ago." Greg shook his head. "The gossip mill in this town is something else."

Bill nodded like that was a great fact. "Our Gregory is having some issues with his operating paperwork. Seems he had another of his big ideas and isn't going to be able to follow through."

"That's not right." He turned to face her, and it wasn't so much the truth in his expression, as the pain underneath it that spurred her to his defense.

"I'm excited about the zip lines," she told Bill. "I'm letting my customers know all about the fun they'll be able to have right next door at Cesta Adventures. Greg's been helping me get to know all the local businesses, like yours, so I can build a list of recommendations that will keep tourist dollars in our economy."

Bill harrumphed.

Amalia said, "That reminds me, I had an idea to bring a few sculptures to place at both Cesta and Chata. If y'all are into it. I'll set you up with a commission on anything that sells. It seems like a good way to get my work seen by more people, and might spur some to take the drive over to see my studio, instead of only spending their time on Main and in the creeks."

Predictably, Bill's gaze went across the road to his nephew's art gallery. It left Livia even more curious why she hadn't seen Amalia's art there. Bill huffed again and headed back to the register, typing at his phone as he went.

"I'm very into your idea," Livia told Amalia. "Also into the double-pole mount. Want me to come out to yours to draw all that up in a day or so?"

"Ditto," Greg added. "To the sign and to the art. Except it's looking like I have to hold off on contracts just yet. Got to get through the next council meeting first off."

He explained that he still needed a variance to approve Cesta for a commercial use permit, and that he'd be arguing for it at the next Chamber meeting. It all sounded like a bit of a personal vendetta, the way he described it. But every one of her own encounters with Honey Wine's bureaucracy had been friendly and efficient. Between that and Bill's attitude, it wasn't hard to believe that Greg was running up against some of the town's preconceived notions about him.

"I'll be there to support you," Livia promised.

"We both will."

This time, when Greg looked from Livia to Amalia and back, his eyes were clear and his nod was purposeful. Before he went to collect his hardware, he brushed the back of his hand up her arm, gave her bicep a quick squeeze, and bestowed that smile that was all too effective at sending her thoughts spiraling away from anything to do with her business.

CHAPTER 12

It was a bitter rain, a cold rain, a dismal and gross and splattery rain. Livia was grateful it had held off until after Patti Clay had captured the gentle winter light slanting in over her freshly painted rooms. But for two solid days, it had messed up her plans to refinish the dining chairs out on the porch.

She was grumpily regarding her sandpapers and stains when Greg's rap on the kitchen door startled her.

"I didn't hear you drive up. You didn't walk in this weather, did you?" His boots weren't particularly muddy. His hair was dry, but more than once Livia had watched him shove his much-abused ball cap into the back pocket of his jeans, so until she got a look at his backside, dry hair meant nothing.

Except perhaps that she was looking for an excuse to check out his butt.

Again.

She gestured him to come on in and pulled out a coffee mug.

"Nope. Drove an ATV."

"Those things really are quiet. Oh, there's sweet rolls in the oven if you want to grab one."

Greg's dark brows hitched upwards briefly.

"Two, then. But no more. Kari's coming down in a bit to work on inventory and supplies, and I promised her baked goods."

"Fine." Or probably that's what he was saying, around his mouthful of cinnamon-scented pastry. Only when Livia had mentioned Kari had Greg stopped prying at the largest roll, which was packed tight with its neighbors, and taken the most accessible as his second. He'd never held back from taking the largest when it was just the two of them, so Livia figured he must really like the housekeeper.

"So what's up?" she asked, not letting herself think too much about if she minded him liking Kari more than he liked her.

"Mm. What are you up to today?"

"Not a ton. Patti said she'd be by this evening so we can finalize the site photos, but until then, this rain has stopped me from getting much more done." She'd known it wasn't wise to stay inside working on the website and press releases and placing online orders when the unpredictable January weather was pleasant. But she'd done it. And she may as well apply her hard-earned philosophy of not regretting the past to the very recent past, as well as more distant days.

Besides, her color-coded, cross-referenced spreadsheet had significantly more completed than uncompleted items, thanks to her hours on the laptop. Back in her early teens, right after her dad had left, her mom's ruminating about past regrets had irritated Livia, but she'd always appreciated the importance of Mom's checklists. Sometimes those checklists were the primary way they could tell that they were getting from one day to the next. Even after the ground had stopped shifting under their feet, they both were constantly at the yellow legal pad they'd hung on the fridge, flipping to the bottom page where the grocery list lived, rifling through the front pages to cross off school projects turned in and bills paid and volunteer shifts worked and library materials returned.

Even Mags would have to admit that this aspect of her new life was honoring her mom's memory.

And there she went again, justifying her decision to buy Chata, to take on this unknown life. No regrets. Moving forward. Not fiddling with her ring. "Why? What are you doing today?"

"Came to see if you'll cave with me."

"If I'll what now?"

"Cave."

He'd gone into his casual pose, leaning back, arms crossed as if his chest was the most comfy place in the world to rest. Head tilted so all those horizontal lines in his face took on an appealing slant. The fact that it was deceptive as hell didn't stop Livia from enjoying it. "You want me to go into a cave?"

"Yup."

"With you?"

"Yup."

"In the cold and the rain?"

"It's a dry cave. And sixty-eight degrees year round."

"It's dry and sixty-eight degrees in my house, and no bats."

He grinned, breaking the planes of his face. Didn't stop him from being devastating. Alas. "Aw, come on, Livia. They're hibernating now. And I need a cave buddy."

"What's a cave buddy?"

"Can't go wild caving alone. It's not safe. And I have to get some video for the hearing, show the nosy parkers what the customers will be doing."

"In your unsafe caves."

"The caves are safe." Greg set his mug down a little more loudly than necessary, but his voice was light. "People aren't always careful. I'm careful, but I'm not perfect. They're wild caves, I've got equipment to carry, and besides, if I went down without a buddy, my mom's ghost would cross my threshold and spend long nights tossing small, sharp pebbles at my legs every time I drifted off to sleep."

"Um. Wow? I guess?"

He laughed. So now Livia vibrated when he laughed. She was definitely not going to contemplate this fresh development. "Yeah, my mom's spirit is pretty intent on keeping me in line."

"Clearly."

"So you'll come with me then?"

"If I don't, what will your mom do to me?"

"You're better off not knowing. Besides, think of how authentically you'll be able to rec Cesta to your customers this way. Didn't you just get done promising Bill you'd go zip lining with me?"

Also not up for scrutiny: how his teasing made her want to giggle. Livia glanced again at the relentless drizzle outside. Sighed, cause he had a point. "And if I go with you, exactly how much danger will I be in?"

"None at all."

She gave him a look.

He pulled out his cap and smacked it on his thigh, like that proved something. "I swear. I've been climbing in and out of these caves since I was eight. At least. They're nothing you can't handle, so long as you have a cave buddy."

Giggling, tingling. *Way to stay professional, Livia.* It would help if Greg wasn't using his nice-guy voice on her. He hadn't lectured her about anything, hadn't acted as if caving was beyond her understanding. He was kind of boyishly excited about it all, cajoling her into leaving a note for Kari, putting on her sturdiest shoes and her grungiest jeans, and mounting behind him on his electric-powered ATV, as if it was the seat of honor at the Annual Spelunker's Banquet.

By the time they'd bounced and skidded their way over the bridge to his side and down the trails to the caves, Livia was having trouble not laughing aloud. She was wet! Wet and cold and mud-spattered and vibrating. It was completely ridiculous. And completely fun.

On her own, she'd never have spotted the cave entrance. There was a creek-side trail, barely wide enough for one, for a good five minutes—five good minutes of walking behind Greg, who'd put the cap on his head so his jeans-clad butt was nice and visible below the pack he carried. And there were trees, of course, and rocks, and up and down terrain, and the rain, and low plants, underbrush, weeds, whatever it all was. Presumably all the taxonomy was stored in the brain of Mr. Forest Ranger Greg Forst—and she only stopped herself asking if his surname was why he'd gotten that job, because just thinking the question conjured images of park visitors getting flirty with him over the same topic. She'd seen the thirsty comments on his channel; she knew some in-person remarks would be similarly suggestive.

It wasn't that Livia minded she had what she finally was accepting as lust for the guy next door. It wasn't even that she thought it would screw up this silent partnership thing they had signed up for. It was just that he'd made it perfectly clear, in a million ways, that he wanted her out so he could run Chata himself.

Note to self, Livia: don't go off into the woods with the muscle-bound guy, into a cave no less, with rain washing away any tracks, without at least leaving a note for the housekeeper, on the off chance she's not in cahoots with Greg to start with. Maggie would have an absolute field day, once she got done slapping Livia upside the head. No amount of mentioning how she had good gut feelings about Greg would silence Mags on this point.

"You get a signal out here?"

He half-turned. "Got a call you need to make?"

"No. Nope, just curious." She shot a selfie with the trail behind her and sent it to Maggie.

"If you're nervous, don't be. We're going to be fine. And if something happens to me, and you can't reach anyone, head that way about three, four minutes uphill, and you'll hit the road."

Great. So he wasn't planning on bashing her head in and stashing her in a cave, but he was planning on getting his own head bashed in somehow and sending her for help. Never mind how much she'd enjoyed the ride, this caving thing was unbelievably foolhardy. People did this for fun? He was going to make money this way?

"Ready?" Greg was unpacking his bag, which held a couple of helmets, some gloves, headlamps, a rope.

"Rope?"

He had the little kid grin on again. "In case you want to walk the plank."

"The plank?"

How did he always flummox her into monosyllables? How did his laugh do those things to her nerve endings? "It's only a drop of four feet, but a little tricky to get to. Jorge and Lee and me went through a pirate phase, back when four feet was a bit of a fall, so we made whoever was the captured captain go off it first."

The last thing she needed was to picture the sparkly eyed tyke from those photos on his mantlepiece shouting 'avast me hearties!' and pretending to sword fight. "You know, the more I know you, the more I'm surprised your mom's ghost doesn't throw pebbles at you every night."

"You and me both, honey." He checked her headlamp was working, then flicked on his own. "Let's go."

Livia glanced downstream, but the path didn't pick up again. "Go where?"

Greg held back a waist-high bush of some kind. The barest hint of a depression in the rocks behind it was apparently all the opening he needed to take her on this journey. "In."

Jorge's day job started at eight, and Lee was on the road. Greg had spent a little time debating other Honey Wine locals he could bring with him—his cousin's shop didn't open until mid-morning, and Susanna had asked him about the land when he'd brought Mittens in for his checkup. Paul Connor was around, too, and that would've been pointed, but funny.

Really, though, he had considered none of them so much as come up with reasons to reject them all, in favor of Livia. He'd even thought of a reason she should be his cave buddy. A business reason. It made sense she could tell her guests what it would be like and send more customers his way.

Also, he kinda wanted to see her again, and the rain had stopped him from having any maintenance-type tasks to help her out with. It hadn't stopped Dante, he'd noted, when he'd just happened to be looking towards her place from his den. The plumber had put in plenty of hours around Chata these past few wet days.

Not that it mattered. It was just as well. Better for him, in truth, for when he took over. Even Kent had admitted the hot water heater was under capacity, when he'd called Greg up to remind him property taxes were due at the end of the month.

As if it was Kent's problem. As if Greg hadn't been paying his property taxes since Dad transferred the land to him. He wasn't incompetent, despite what Uncle Kent seemed to think. He didn't need Kent calling at all, when the last talk they'd had consisted of Greg asking why Kent hadn't given him the chance to buy Chata, and his uncle saying he thought it was one of those things Greg wasn't going to follow through on. Like a history of high school truancy meant his adult desires were all imaginary.

"Shit."

"What? What's wrong? Is there a bat?"

God, she was cute. "No, there's no bat. I just left the camera in the bag. Hang on a sec, I'll be right back."

"You're not leaving me down here."

He couldn't help laughing. "Livia. We're not twenty feet from the entrance. It's not even dark yet."

"This isn't dark?"

Oh, this was going to be fun. "No, honey. This is not dark. It's the Twilight Zone."

"You're telling me."

"Seriously, turn off the lamp. You'll see." Still shaking his head, smiling, he ducked under the opening to rummage through the pack. He'd forgotten the canteen, too. And the snakebite kit.

He hadn't mentioned the rattlers to Livia, which he tried to justify because she'd grown up in Texas and ought to know about them. Also, it was hibernation time, and he'd never found them anywhere but in their burrow, which was so far away, it was practically not on his land anymore.

He would really have to install a first aid post near the cave entrance, though. Just to make his insurance agent happy. "Shit," he muttered again. He couldn't take her in without telling her.

"What?"

She'd moved to the entrance and was peering out, headlamp still lit, and tilted up enough to blind him temporarily. "Don't be mad."

Livia backed up a couple of wary steps before answering. "Don't be mad about what?"

"Just remember, I've been in and out of this cave every season for years."

"So you say."

"Never even sprained my ankle."

"Uh-huh."

"Not even a spider bite."

"Okay, I'm leaving."

"And we've got sturdy shoes on."

"Gregory Forst, you'd better say whatever it is right now, or so help me, I am sending my ghost mom to find your ghost mom and the two of them will bash your sleeping head in."

"You're a little violent, aren't you? Now I'm sorry I even brought up the snakes."

Livia moved so fast she bonked her helmet on the overhang. Greg caught her as she stumbled back, steading her shoulders against his chest. "Hey, it's okay. They winter upstream. I swear."

"You make it sound like a vacation. A snake-filled vacation." She twisted away and scanned the ground. The beam of her light jumped rapidly around every cranny and nook.

"Sure, well, they probably like it. They use the same burrow every year. It's kind of cool, actually—I can take you there, if you like. Not to get too close, but there's a spot Mom and Ellie used to take me. You can see where they go, if you know what you're looking for."

The light hit his eyes again. "Yeah, I don't think so."

Greg stepped forward. Just to make her tilt her head up enough to keep his retinas clear of the LED bulbs. As he adjusted both their headlamps, he sensed Livia relaxing, and the triumph and relief he felt was disconcerting.

"What do you say?" he asked, letting his hand squeeze her shoulder again, briefly, and skim down her arm. "Ready to explore?"

Her sigh was deep and thorough. But she smiled a tiny bit. "Sure. Lead on."

She'd been expecting stalagmites and stalactites. And bats. He'd said no bats, but her BS detector told her there would, indeed, be bats. Maybe sleeping as promised, but there. She'd Googled it, and decided not to freak out about the bats. Of course, she'd neglected to Google freaking rattlesnakes, but maybe, if she conceded he'd been right about the bats, she could believe him about the snakes, too. He did have a degree in this stuff. And he'd grown up in Honey Wine.

"How many times have you been snake-bit?"

"Never."

"How about your friends? Family?"

"Nope." He was ducking low. "Watch yourself here. This is the start of real darkness."

"Oh, goody."

He laughed. It still tingled. Not as much, but a little. If her nerves weren't still skittery from thinking about snakes—and from his hands on her shoulders—she probably wouldn't be tingling at all. So there.

But then the chills got real. "Greg." She stilled, pressing her gloved palm to his back and focusing all of her attention on the chamber they'd entered. He stopped, too, and switched on the lantern he'd clipped to his belt. It only threw back the blackness a few feet, so it was her headlamp that ran over the limestone crags and soda straws. Everywhere she looked was another other-worldly formation, and suddenly she was grinning ear to ear, and Greg had matched his movements to hers so his light helped illuminate the shapes.

"Told ya," he said, but not as smugly as he might've. He'd slid back a few inches, and was shoulder to shoulder with her, so when he slipped an arm behind her back to guide where she was looking, they were kind of arm in arm. Livia leaned into him a little, but mostly she was busy taking it all in. The chamber wasn't vast, but it was cool and silent and so different from the wet, green world just a few feet away.

They rounded a wall, Greg now walking behind her with his bared hand low and warm on her neck. "Check out the popcorn." And when he explained about calcite build-up and told her where to look to spot the nearly hidden passage they would take to get to his pirate's plank, she didn't hear a hint of know-it-all in his voice.

"You ready?"

She was ready.

"Okay, we're going down the chimney."

And Livia wouldn't have believed it an hour before, but there she was, foot dangling in the air, back braced against rock, while Greg above her explained how to wend her way down to the room below. He was videotaping her descent, and it made her blush to think she was sounding squeaky with nerves when she couldn't locate the toehold he assured her was there. But given the light conditions, her embarrassment wouldn't likely show on screen.

"Greg?"

"Yeah?" His voice was soothing.

"This is … this is spectacular." Livia looked around, forgetting about the video and his voice and anything Maggie would have to say about anything. She was totally alone, underground. Well, not totally alone. His voice drifted down to her. The lantern's rays were limning the edges of the chimney from which she'd just emerged. But it was Livia and the limestone, shapes and shadows and silence.

She loved it.

Before she'd finished soaking it all in, Greg went and ruined everything with his clompy boots loosing grit on the cave floor, and the suddenly ferocious beam of his lantern, and the bulk of his torso filling up the empty spaces that she had been relishing.

He crowded her. He was loud and bright and in her way and the really, terribly, awful thing about it was, Livia loved that, too.

"Water?" Greg passed over his spare canteen before unclipping the camera again. "Stand here," he said, positioning her so her light caught his favorite helictite while he filmed the room. "It's really only big enough for three or four people in here, but there's a nicely decorated cavity just over there, so my guides can rotate people in and out if they have slightly larger groups."

She looked where he was pointing, of course, so his camera followed her. He was going to have to think out next time where he sent her attention.

"Where to after that?"

"After that, you walk the plank, matey."

She shook her head. "I just dropped down that chimney. That's pretty brave of me. You can't expect me to jump off a cliff, too."

"All the other kids jumped off the cliff."

"Ha ha."

"You can use the rope," he said, which reminded him to unwind it from his waist before they moved down the passage. Once they left their current spot, he wouldn't be able to lift both elbows simultaneously. He draped it over a shoulder and moved the carabiners on his belt so everything hung in front or back.

Livia's eyes were catching all the light, despite being shadowed by the helmet. She was having fun. He was pretty sure she was having fun. She hadn't tossed off any of her judgmental comments or up and left when he'd told her about the diamondbacks. He was sure she'd wanted to for a minute there. But she'd stayed, and caved.

In her helmet and gloves, eyes gleaming like an undiscovered species of arthropod, Livia was some sort of poster model for Cesta. This was what he'd wanted all along. To bring people onto his land, to show them the hidden treasures—not just the wonders of speleothem, but the feeling of going underground, or of sailing above the treetops, or walking the trails like animals and humans had been doing for thousands of years. And until just that moment, Greg had been harboring a small doubt that it was going to work.

Livia's excitement and pleasure were tangible. Greg stepped closer, soaking it up. "Want to try something?"

And she was with him on this adventure, so she nodded. While the light was still bouncing up and down, he reached up and clicked off her headlamp. Then he snapped the lantern back onto his belt and switched it off.

"Ready?"

She got it. She put her hand on his arm, nodding again. "Ready."

Greg turned off his lamp. "Close your eyes for a minute."

She squeezed his bicep, briefly, and he located her arm in the darkness.

"Okay, open." He hadn't meant to whisper, not really, but it was so quiet. He'd gone dark down here with the guys, but none of them had Livia's stillness. One of them would shift and another would talk and another would make fart noises. Or scream, or whistle eerily, or Darth Vader breathe. In the dark with his friends was adventure and noise and more adventure.

In the dark with Livia … It wasn't just that she was still, or that her presence made him still.

It was more than silence. It was a vibrant, interstitial energy. Even through her thick gloves, Livia's hand—hands, now—on his arms reinforced the silent bond between them. He felt her breathing, and his own slowed to match, and those spaces between them grew smaller.

For one nanosecond, Greg had the urge to break their bond. To fill the air with a bird call or to reach for the canteen.

Not to turn on the lights, though. He was content, in this space, to decide that the dark was his ally. To feel that their breathing was attuned to something cosmic and powerful in the life around them. To know that the air bouncing between their bodies was warmer than the currents that flowed through the rest of the limestone room.

Their feet were sturdily shod, but that didn't mean Greg

knew which of them stepped to close the distance, that little distance between them. He slid his hands around, cupping her neck, stroking her spine. The rough fingers of her gloves brushed his nape, and Greg remembered to account for clunky safety helmets as his lips sought Livia's.

There was stillness in their kiss, and silence, in equal measure with the motion and noise. Her lips, and likely his, still held a metallic tang from the canteen, but also the sweetness of cinnamon and sugar. And they were soft, and ready, and eager. So hungry and eager.

He couldn't get to her hair, braided and tucked under the damn helmet, but he could stroke her silk skin, and pressed forward, pulled closer, cursed the presence of the first aid pack. Snake bite kit as literal cock blocker between their two bodies. He ignored it, ignored that frustration because his hands on her skin, his lips on her lips, her body moving with his.

And he kissed her, ran kisses across her cheek and jaw, and she was humming her pleasure and in the cave and with his pounding blood it was all he could hear until he tried to kiss her neck and his headlamp scraped her ear. With a cry, she jerked back away from his damn careless self. After the clunk of her helmet hitting the calcite curtain behind her, the spellbinding darkness became too silent again, a confused and rebuking silence.

Greg fumbled for the switch, flooding their enlarged pupils with light. "Livia. Shit. Are you okay?"

CHAPTER 13

Was she okay?

Was she okay? She was tingly and trembly and half-blind and dear lord, but she was aroused. And he wanted to know if she was okay? He kissed like a demon in this underground cavern, darkness and fingers and lips and bodies touching and no light and no sounds but their breathing and their humming and there was fire between them and he wanted to know if she was okay?

Livia blinked and tried to find her center; tried to find it in herself, and failing that, in the shadowed lines of Greg's face. She was off balance. How could he stand there, touching her, in the shattered darkness, and still be solid, when she was so off-balance?

Plus, her head hurt.

Tentatively, Livia reached up, tucking a finger under the helmet, and winced.

"Oh, shit. Are you bleeding? Let me see."

"No, it's fine." She tried to shake her head but realized that was a bad idea. The helmet's back strap felt tight, but the throb at the the back of her head calmed when she stilled.

"It's obviously not fine."

"It's just sore. No blood."

"I'm so sorry. Here, let me take this off." He was already fumbling at the buckle, and Livia inadvertently sucked air in between her teeth when his actions rubbed the helmet against the sore spot.

"Greg, stop. Just. Hang on." Livia let out a long breath. "I have to wear it until we get out of here, right? So I'd rather leave it on now instead of having to put it back on later, okay?"

He nodded, the headlamp flicking into her eyes again. She switched her own light on and could finally see his features clearly. His soft lips pressed into a straight, tight line. His worried, tender eyes. She couldn't stop herself from touching his cheek, even though the damn gloves were in her way.

"It'll be fine. It's just a bruise, I swear."

"I'm so sorry, honey."

She smiled. "I know. It's not your fault."

Of course, then he traced her ear with his fingertip, which made her flinch, and reminded her that her ear hurt. And that the pain actually was his fault.

"Shit. Sorry."

And then they were laughing—light and low, but laughing, and the air between them was right again. Like it had been before. What a surprise, what a rare thing, that rightness. Livia's gut feelings had been doing some nice things for her in the months since her mom's death.

Well, there was a strange thought. A yank her to a stop in her tracks thought. But there it sat, sudden and demanding in front of her.

Maybe she'd been paying more attention to her gut feelings since losing the anchor of her mom's background presence. Did that mean her mom had inhibited her gut instincts? If so, was that a bad or a good thing?

In some ways, she'd stopped adhering to the life plan she'd created in those immediate post-Terry days, back when

Maggie pressed her into taking the Dallas job. Not just because of how Livia had parlayed her teen job working at a local hotel into a degree in hospitality, which led to the job offer, but because Terry refused to move to Dallas. Rooming with Maggie there, and finding new social circles within their new jobs, broke her out of the isolation Terry had always encouraged. During college, she'd only communicated with Mom via the inscrutable semaphore of tuition bills sent and paid. After graduation, she hoped, but didn't know how to state, that her break from him, her focus on making herself a success, were her apologies to Mom for leaving so abruptly. For not moving back home. All those carefully safe boyfriends and well-mapped career moves in Dallas were designed to fit on an imaginary Mom Would Approve list, no matter what else Livia thought about them.

Deep in a cave, with a growing ache on her skull, was a strange place for Livia to realize that Max and Todd and Jones and that guy with the mountain bike were all manifestations of the man that Livia thought her mom would want her to date. And the failure of those dating experiments has reinforced her deep-seated fear that she would never be successful and self-sufficient enough to proudly go back to Mom and show that she was worthy of the ways Mom had always supported her, no matter how difficult Livia made it.

Even once they'd learned to navigate monthly phone calls and weekend visits twice a year, she never managed an honest conversation about the ways they'd broken apart.

Meanwhile, the source of her physical pain was standing there, checking to see if her pupils were excessively dilated, as if he could tell anything in their current circumstances. What on earth would her mom make of Greg?

"I'm okay."

"You keep saying that, and then you keep wincing."

"Well. I mean, I'm hurt. But I'll get over it. I don't think I'm up for your pirate ship, though."

His laugh was more exhalation than chuckle, and when he squeezed her shoulder again, Livia was back in that dark, hands on each other place. So not all her nerve endings were needed for focusing on her skull. That was a good sign. Livia shucked her gloves so she could properly explore the tender spot.

"No, I think we'll make our way back up, when you're ready."

She nodded, which: ow. She ought to know better. "I think a few more minutes."

"Shit. I mean, sorry." Greg turned around the cavern, his headlamp picking out the amazing rock formations. An entire section where the stalagmites and stalactites had met in the middle, like the clamped teeth of some predator. The flowstone—her new vocab word—like icing melting down the sides of her cinnamon rolls, on a far larger scale. A million hues of brown and gold and grey and white. It wasn't hard to see why he loved the cave.

"Do you want to film anything else before we go up? I can wait here, if you'll be safe on your own."

"Yeah, because I've so clearly shown that taking people down here is a good idea."

"Well, I'd maybe suggest leaving the kissing off the official agenda."

Having the lamps on sure emphasized when he swung his head in her direction. Searchlights, beacons, interrogations. "Hey."

"Sorry! Sorry." Greg turned off the LEDs lasering into her eyeballs.

She took the couple of steps to be within arm's reach again. "How about this? We go film the next chamber. No, listen, I can walk. I can hold a light. These are not the tasks that are going to kill me here. Anything you can get without me having to, I don't know, crawl or fall or duck too much. Deal?"

"You're sure?"

"That's why we're here, right? You need it for the meeting?"

Maybe he couldn't see her face too clearly, but she could see his, and his eyes widened for a moment before he set his lips into that firm line again. "Right. Yeah."

Ha. If he'd had the space to do so, he'd absolutely be leaning against the wall, arms crossed over his chest. She could practically feel his body fighting for a way to assume his casual pose in the confines of the cavern.

"Unless that wasn't why you invited me to go spelunking with you?"

"Nope. That's why. Jorge had to get to work early, so he couldn't help me out."

"So I was the only logical choice."

He shifted the rope from his shoulder to his hand. "And I thought it would be good for you to see the caves, so you could tell your guests about them."

"Makes sense." She was smiling. Surely he heard the smile in her voice, even if he couldn't see it? Even if he was looking at the end of the rope instead of at her?

He shrugged. "Just killing two birds with one stone."

"And here I thought you were luring me down here to bash my head in. Now you've got birds to kill, too?"

Greg almost dropped the rope. "To do what?"

"Bash my head in."

What the hell was she saying? "You thought—you seriously thought I was going to hurt you? I mean, on purpose?"

Because he had hurt her, hadn't he? And as if he didn't feel shitty enough about that, about himself and his carelessness, it turns out she was expecting it of him all along? There was nowhere to back up to. No way to give her more space, or himself, either.

He was trying to step back anyway, but Livia reached out a hand. She wasn't shoving him or anything; she just rested her hand lightly on his waist. Her fingers flexed, briefly, the tiniest of squeezes, but it relaxed him.

"Of course not seriously. I'm not really a risk-taker, Greg, never mind all I've done in the past few months. I wouldn't have come here if I, you know, felt like you were dangerous. If I didn't want to."

"Yeah?"

"Yeah. I mean, I trust you. Of course."

The constriction across his chest was gone now. And never mind the slight twinge to his conscious when she said she trusted him. He wanted her to trust him. She *could* trust him. "Thanks."

"Thanks for taking me down here. It's been great. I mean, mostly." And she squeezed his side again, so he figured that translated to the kissing as being one of the great parts. Which it had been. More than great. Livia's kisses were all light and warmth and enthusiasm. Greg wouldn't have minded at all a repeat performance, except for the fact that, like a fucking jerk, he'd gone and given her a couple of head injuries.

He really needed to get her to the surface and checked out more throughly. "Give me a second. I'll pack up."

"What about the filming?"

"Don't worry about it. I'll get Lee when he's back in town."

"Will you have enough time, though? I want your presentation to go well."

"Livia, really. Don't worry about it. I just want to take you up."

She nodded slightly, and didn't wince, which was an improvement. Or she was trying really hard to hide the pain. Greg's grip on the rope tightened, and he moved to make enough room to secure it around his waist again. Except instead of letting him slide over, Livia put her arms where the rope was supposed to go. "Can you take off your helmet a minute?"

"We need to get you out of here."

"I know. But just for a minute."

She was leaning her torso into his, now, the equipment at his belt not doing a lot to keep her chest from meeting his. After a beat, he hooked one arm behind Livia and, dropping the rope, reached up to unclasp his helmet strap.

"Okay?"

In answer, she drew her hands up and around until her palms rested on his cheeks, her fingers lightly raking into his hair. They both sighed a little, their chests rising in unison in a way that felt as intimate as their earlier kisses had. At least, to Greg it did.

He dropped the helmet down on top of the rope. "I don't want to hurt you."

"You won't."

"Just push me away if I do." His hand was incapable of settling anywhere on her body. Her neck, her spine, the wing of her shoulder blade. The other hand was securely locked around her waist, anchoring her to him.

Livia drew his head down, confident and sure, not at all like someone worried about being bashed again. Deliberately or accidentally. She trusted him. And that was all he could think of as his lips met hers. That trust, so willingly given, so essential at this moment between them.

And, as inevitable as the collision of their mouths, his trust freely given in return. Not only a faith that his passion equalled, and enhanced, hers, but on top of, and under, and around that, the security they'd built working together all these winter weeks.

Her kiss wasn't tentative. It was soft, sweet, purposeful. Carnal, but not ravenous. Her tongue met his without hesitation, but helmet or no, Greg wasn't going to try kissing his way down her neck as he so very much wanted to do. Livia's body was so alive against his, so sexy and touchable and such a turn-on.

He had to stop, or his head would be the one bashed and in pain.

"What?" She was smiling against him.

"What what?"

"You were grinning. What's funny?"

"Nothing."

Livia pulled back a little, but kept her sweet hands on his face. "Nothing?"

"If you must know," he said, leaning in for another kiss before side-stepping away to get his equipment together, "you are making me think crude things about our situation."

"Oh?"

"I'm not telling."

"You're not, are you?"

"Nope." He got his helmet fastened and checked the carabiners on the camera and first aid kid.

"So I'll just have to guess?"

Jesus. "It's childish. Never mind."

"Like how you'd like to go spelunking in my cave?"

He sputtered an inelegant laugh. "God, no!"

"You wouldn't like to go spelunking?"

"Livia."

"Was it about the dangers of snakes in a crevice?"

"I'm ready. Let's head this way."

"Something about the rope, maybe? Your plans for tying me up?"

Keeping his voice level was a challenge. "Watch your head here. It's low."

"Getting wet as you slide your way through a tight passage?"

"Listen, you." Greg turned as they cleared their threshold

into the area under the chimney. He caught sight of her smirk and had to clear his throat. "I know you've just suffered a head injury and all, but I'm about to boost you up and I will be standing here staring at your gorgeous ass as you wriggle your way to the next level. I'm supposed to be concentrating on helping you find all the footholds and getting you safely to the surface. And you're not helping. In the least. So if you get stuck and spend the next thirty minutes with my hands on your thighs and butt because I'm too rattled to figure out how to stop touching you and start helping you, it's going to be entirely your own fault. Are we clear?"

Livia leaned in and kissed him. "You are going to make the most amazing guide. I'm kind of looking forward to this next part now."

He groaned. "Livia."

"Spelunking is my new favorite sport."

"I think you must be concussed. We need to get you to the medical center." He dropped to one knee. "Here, step up on my leg and I'll get you out of here."

But instead of putting her foot on his thigh, Livia stepped up close to him and paused. She smelled of cave rock and sweat and also something fresh, and even though she was wearing the gloves again, when she lay her hands on his shoulders, he felt the electricity between them. It would be rude to nuzzle her breasts. And inappropriate. Even though they were right there in front of him as he knelt in front of her. Without quite knowing when it happened, Greg found his hands were under her sweater's hem, stroking her ribcage.

Livia leaned down, which was fortunate, because otherwise Greg would be struggling to remove her sweater and T-shirt without taking off her helmet, which would have been impossible.

And rude.

And inappropriate.

"I'll tell you what, Greg. You get me out of here safely and maybe I'll let you watch me wriggle my gorgeous ass again sometime. Without all the safety gear involved."

Before he was done touching her, Livia had given him another quick kiss and stepped up on his leg, using the boost to launch herself high out of his grasp, on her way out of the cave.

CHAPTER 14

O*hmygodhe'slookingatmybutt.* Livia scrambled for the next foothold before Greg's hands could guide her. It sure did a lot to stop the blood pounding in her head, what with it swirling around all her nether regions instead. She focused on moving up, equally terrified that he would boost her, and that he wouldn't. He'd called it gorgeous. That was … nice. She giggled, glad he couldn't hear her.

"What'd you say?"

Damn. "Nothing. Doing fine." And she was. Going up was easier, because she could see her goal. The holds were easy to grasp, and she knew it was just a couple of feet until her head and shoulders would be clear of the chimney. Never mind the hot guy watching her from below.

Just as she got her arm over the ledge, the headlamp caught movement. Something skittered, not super close or anything, but at eye level. Livia squeaked, and jerked back, and bonked her helmet again, and groaned.

"Livia? Livia! What's wrong?"

She couldn't disappear, and she couldn't run away, so the best option seemed to be to close her eyes and rest her forehead on her forearm. At least everything was still that way.

"Livia! What's wrong? Answer me." He was crowding her from below, one powerful arm wrapped around her calves, the other hand groping up her legs.

"I'm fine. It's okay, I'm fine. Give me a second." A second to pretend that she wasn't a total novice, scared of cave bugs and reckless with her skull. Another second to let the strength and warmth of his biceps permeate through her jeans. A third second to imagine this much physical intimacy without the constraints of jeans and cave walls.

Right then. She braced herself, took a deep breath, and pressed her way out of the chimney.

Shit shit shit shit *shit*. That thud reverberating down the chute had just about stopped his heart. He was taking her to the hospital, no question. Or at least the drop-in clinic in Honey Wine. He wasn't more than a minute behind her emerging from the chimney, and checking her for injury a minute later.

She was fine. She kept saying she was fine, but he checked and it looked like she was fine. She'd hit her head again. A bug. Scared her. Made her hit her head. But she was fine.

"Just let me look."

"It's *fine*, Greg, I swear. I'm more embarrassed than hurt." But she wasn't exactly steady on her feet.

"Take the helmet off. You don't have to put it back on. We're clear of all the tricky parts."

"Leave it. Let's just go."

"Livia, come on. Take it off."

"You taking yours off?"

"No, but I've got to keep the light on."

"And you think me walking through here without a headlamp is a good idea?"

"I'll go first."

"And I won't be able to see where the floor dips or whatever."

"Then you can go first."

"Greg."

He blew out a frustrated sigh. "This is taking too long. We need to get you out."

"So stop arguing with me and lead the way."

"Take the lantern."

"I don't need the lantern."

"Just take the lantern. I don't want you to slip."

"Fine. Give it here."

Beautiful, stubborn woman. He handed it over, checked her chin strap, checked her shoes were still tied and her head-lamp was angled towards the footpath, and hesitated just a moment before carefully navigating his way in for a kiss.

He was fretting worse than Ellie. But by ignoring his every instinct, Greg managed to press on, weaving through the chambers to bring them back to the entrance. The rain had let up a little, which was great, but the path back to his cabin was as muddy and wet and rocky as ever, so by the time he pulled the ATV into the parking shed, his jaw was locked tight against the need to apologize for a hundred jolts and bumps.

"Come in."

"I'm going to head home."

"No. Come in."

"Greg, look," she started, but he cut her off.

"Sorry. Please. Please come in. I really want to check you out."

"So you said."

At that he laughed. He hadn't been insinuating anything, hadn't even been thinking along those lines. Greg wanted her in his bed, that was true, but to lie down and rest and recover from the disaster of their morning. "You're the one making plans for me to abseil your phreatic zone."

"I think I'm better off if you don't translate that." Her smile was a vise around his heart.

"Probably. Come on. I don't want you to be alone after that much jostling."

"Kari should be there still."

"Oh, Kari's useless in an emergency. Ask her sometime what happened the time Lynne was stung by a yellow jacket when they were out on the trail. She'd never get you to the clinic in time."

"In time for what?"

"I don't know, Livia. You won't come inside, so I can check you out and find out what damage I did." Time to clench his jaw again, because yelling at the gal with the head injury wasn't helpful or necessary.

She got the message, though, and finally let him guide her up the porch steps. He dumped the equipment bag to deal with later, which would be more than enough to bring on the afterlife wrath of his mom, supposing he really believed in that. But the living, breathing Livia was the only one he was concerned with, and despite her protests she looked whiter than usual, and wasn't moving as lightly as she had earlier in the morning.

"Lay down. I'm getting you meds and an ice pack."

"I'm fine."

"Yeah, you're fine. I know. I've memorized that line now, so you can just stop saying it. How's that for a plan? Move it, Mittens," he said.

"Who are you calling Mittens?"

He knew all the joking was a good sign. She couldn't be in that much pain if she could tease. But he shoved the cat aside and threw back the blanket for her anyway, kind of glad that the constant shedding of the cat had trained him to make his bed in the mornings.

So now she was laying in Gregory Forst's bed. He had dudish plaid flannel sheets, which did not at all match the floral blanket that covered them, but which were soft and warmed the feet she hadn't realized were cold until she'd toed off her shoes on his porch. Also, they had that whole ocean-scent thing he'd had going on, even underground.

He also had the thinnest, lumpiest pillow she'd ever encountered. But part of the problem might have to do with the bumps on her head. Livia scooted over enough to position her skull so that none of her bruises were in direct contact with any surface.

"Here," Greg said from the doorway behind Livia. "No, stay there."

His weight dipped the bed, and his fingers were only marginally warmer than the ice he'd wrapped in a dishcloth poultice. She hissed, just briefly, at the cold, but Greg was already stroking her shoulder and upper arm with his other hand. And those goosebumps had nothing to do with the little goose egg on her skull.

Livia reached a hand up to cover his as it brushed her nape. "Hey."

"Hey?"

"You're being very sweet."

His laugh felt rare and rich. A treasure.

And then, without one ounce of casual grace, but still holding the ice pack in place, Greg clambered over her. His solid warm body mangling the barrier of the sheets between them. His curls were finally mussed as they spread on the lumpy pillow beside her. His eyes cave-dark as they searched Livia's face.

"I'm not sweet." And was that ever the truth. The woman was practically curled in on herself in pain, and all he could do about it was stare at her ass, round and inviting under his covers. As if it was there for him to spoon while he reached around to cup her breasts. While he bit into her shoulder and thrust.

He pressed his eyes closed like that could shut down his self-castigation. First he hurts her, then he fantasizes about her, and all the while she's trusting him and calling him sweet.

No, strike that. First, he plans ways to get her business away from her, then he hurts her, and all the while, he's abusing her trust.

Her fingers traced his brows and eyelids. He was such an ass that he couldn't even look honestly at her open, seductive face, and she goes and responds with these tender, electric touches that had him involuntarily tightening his grip. He hadn't been aware of shifting them so that her head was cradled in his arm, the one hand holding the ice pack so the other was free to roam up and down her body.

And roaming it was. Even as he realized what a self-serving jerk he was, his palm was memorizing the feel of her hip, the dip of her waist. The outer curve of her breast.

"Greg?"

He opened his eyes. Livia's thumb was idly tracing his cheekbone, her other hand wrapped around his bicep. She was smiling.

"Livia?"

"Are my pupils fixed and responsive?"

Her legs had unfurled down his mattress; his palm on her lower back escorted her pelvis towards his.

"Am I bleeding?"

His mouth was too dry for him to bother answering, but he didn't stop her when she reached back to take the ice pack and pitch it to the floor. Her breasts shifted and strained against her sweater, and she wasn't smacking him for staring, so Greg kept looking until she spoke again.

"Have you noticed any problems with my range of motion?"

And then he was on his back and she was leaning over him, those breasts flush against his pecs while she proved her lack of concussion by dipping to feather kisses over his cheeks and jaw. Stretching to lightly nip the pulse below his ear.

But he was the one who'd thought of biting her first, so Greg evaded when her lips sought his, sliding away so she landed stomach-down on his mattress. Shoving aside the sheets, straddling her, his jean-clad thighs atop her jean-clad ass, thrusting harder than he maybe meant to as he leaned over the curve of her back to growl in her ear, "I'm not done with your exam yet. Hold still."

And she did. Her head cradled on her arms, she looked up at him, half a smile on her kiss-swollen lips. But as his hands gently parted the cool tangle of her hair, she bucked her hips beneath him.

Shit. He'd hurt her again.

But no, his hands were still, and her hips circled again, deliberate. She was grinding her ass up into him, a steady rhythm that destroyed his ability to focus on the lump on her scalp.

Greg's torso covered Livia's completely. She was warm and writhing beneath him, and her half-closed eye and half-heard moan told him all he needed to know about her reaction to the close exam his fingers, then his lips and his tongue, were making of her neck and ear.

His hands were roaming now, following the path out along the tops of her arms, then back to her shoulders, but circling low to her ribcage at the last moment. Livia's pulsing hips stopped so she could lift enough to give his palms access to her breasts. They filled his hands as Greg shifted his pelvis. She was pinned beneath him, ass up and legs wide, so the entire length of his shaft met her body, thrusting in the most exhilarating but most frustrating sexual contact he'd had in months. Maybe years.

He didn't know Livia well enough to just strip off her clothes and plunge into her, no matter how she moved and moaned beneath him. No matter how hot it was, holding her down with his body and hearing her pant his name as he squeezed her breasts and finally bit her shoulder. He'd lost that self-accusatory part of himself, the part that had something to say about guilt and trust and hidden agendas. The only thing left was instinct, desperate to taste every inch of Livia's flesh. More than desperate. Depraved, driven, demanding.

And she propped up on one hand, guiding him under her sweater and shirt, pressing his fingers against her hard nipple. He followed with the other hand, stroking, but she circled his wrist and shoved downwards, into jeans he hadn't been the one to unbutton. So now her core was in his palm, and he rocked the flat of it into her as he thrust against her ass, and she wrapped an arm back around his head, her grip tight in his hair as she pulled his face towards hers.

Livia was throbbing. She was alive, every single molecule of her being alert and hungry. Greg's ocean-breeze scent and rock-formed muscles and hot breath and silk lips and, damn, his energy and his touch and his cock and his fingers and his moan when he touched her. Greg. Gregory with the attitude and the devious smile and the smart ideas and the know-it-all smugness and the hair that was the springy delight she'd imagined and the fucking hot body.

Gregory Forst. Dominant but tender, touching her. Touching, but not enough, not nearly enough. Clothes. Socks. Stupid that they were both wearing socks. Stupider that they were wearing jeans. Jeans were too thick, too restrictive. She could feel the hard length of his erection despite them, but just imagining the jeans being gone was enough to make her wetter, her moans louder.

Greg's fingers plucked one nipple, sure and strong. His other hand pulsed against her clit in time to her moans, his thrusts, the jerking of her hips. Fingers tight against her, blocked only by her underwear, leaving her fervid imaginings of those fingers exploring her depths, executing a carnal promise of more, of longer and harder thrusts.

She moaned again, moving faster, and Greg broke away from her mouth to move down her neck, sucking at the pulse there while he increased his own rhythm. So she covered his hand covering her breast, showed him how much pressure to apply, not that he needed the lesson, but she needed her hand on his strong, sure one. It helped to anchor her above while below, she bucked and writhed. While she ground herself into his hand. He was wild and strong above her, his thighs gripping her hard, and Livia thrashed and Greg bit her shoulder and squeezed her breast and drummed against her clit and ground his cock hard and Livia, crying Greg's name, bucking with unrestrained joy, threw herself headlong into orgasm.

Greg froze.

One hand full of Livia's breast, one hand cupping her core, hips practically mid-thrust, and Greg's whole body just … stopped.

CHAPTER 15

It was not a convenient time for guilty realization to hit Greg upside the head. This was wrong. This was Livia, and this was wrong.

Hot like an inferno, but wrong.

She was subsiding below him, almost melting into the mattress, and despite the urgent signals from his cock, Greg felt himself melting along with her. Gentling his hands from press to caress, lifting his mouth from her neck to bury his nose in the tangled mass of her hair.

Even remembering to avoid the places where he'd already hurt her.

Like she brought out the tender side of him. Like he was building on their neighborly relationship. Like he imagined sharing part of his life with the woman next door.

Like he wasn't a total shit, kissing—no, be truthful; bringing to glorious, uninhibited, sexy beyond belief orgasm—the woman he'd been trying to oust from Aunt Sissy's home since before he met her.

Like he didn't want to do it again.

Greg inhaled, Livia's tangerine scent now heightened by their arousal, and shifted so he was spooning her. He directed his reluctant hands to rest on her abdomen and shoulder, instead of the happier places they'd been.

Not that moving his hands took away from his intense awareness of every curve of Livia's body. They lay, breathing together, while Greg's mind spun.

"What's a frenetic zone?"

He lifted his head. "A what?"

"Frenetic zone," she murmured sleepily.

"Oh, phreatic, yeah." Greg eased gently away from the curve of her body. "The zone of saturation, below the water table."

"Mmmm. Sounds like maybe it's time for me to abseil yours." Her eye half-opened; her fingers reached for his arm.

"No." He tried not to let panic show as he sat up, one hand still on her rounded shoulder. "You really should rest. Why don't you wait here a minute? I'll go get you some more ice."

Before he'd backed to the door, Livia was sitting up and wincing, a hand to her head.

"Greg?"

"You're hurt. I'm—it wasn't—I shouldn't have. I mean, sorry. Your head. Lay down."

"But ..."

"Be right back," he said, and made sure not to slam the door behind him in his hurry to get out of her sight.

His house was too small. The fridge was as far as possible from his room, but he could still hear the bedstead creak as she moved around. Laying back down? Preparing to leave? Getting up to follow him and ask him what the hell was the matter with him? He kept his back to the bedroom door, just in case, and was grateful to the cold air hitting him as he rummaged for something to use as another cold pack. She didn't emerge, so Greg took his time refilling his empty ice trays and straightening the rest of the boxes and bags in his freezer.

Finally, sighing, bag of green beans in hand, Greg turned back towards the bedroom. He didn't go outside to clean up his caving gear. He didn't text Jorge to drop by and provide a distraction from whatever was going to happen next. He just put one foot in front of the other until he stood in front of Livia's prone form.

She was asleep.

Not fast asleep. Not snoring or anything, just sprawled loosely around his spare pillow, eyes closed, breathing steadily. Gorgeous. The yellowish late-January afternoon sun played with her lines, highlighting her dark lashes and pale brow, the barely pink tint of her lips. The reddened scrape on her ear from his helmet.

Only an asshole would take a woman down into the caves and show her the tourism potential—and kiss her—and still expect to buy her out. So, either Greg was an asshole, which might have some merit, or he didn't really expect the buyout to work.

And maybe, asshole or not, he'd picked up on his inner truth that while he still longed for some of her land access, he wasn't the seamless fit for running Chata that Livia was. He wasn't crediting Kent with knowing better; Greg could have figured it out if he'd had the chance he'd told his uncle he wanted.

But when Greg grouched at him, Kent grouched right back about how running Chata on his own, without Sissy, had been like locking him in a cage where he could only watch the wildlife pass by his windows. And Kent was terse and unforgiving, but he knew as well as anyone how much Greg needed to be outside.

Livia stirred, took a deep breath, hummed lightly as she exhaled. Greg watched every moment, feeling like a total creep for staring. For not controlling the baser impulses raging through him, and for getting the two of them to this point to start with.

He should have stayed far away. He'd felt the tug between them from the first second, but instead of considering the warning that meant, he'd gotten closer and closer to her. A wise man would've known that tug would lead him to make decisions counter to his aims, just to stay in her presence. A clever man would've seen that the trips to the diner and the dump and, above all, the treehouse, were all warnings that he wasn't working for himself like he should. A more ruthless man would've used that tug to further, somehow, the goal of getting Livia to sell Chata to him.

At least the fact that he couldn't think along those ruthless lines was a slight comfort about his worthiness. A very slight comfort.

Because he was standing there, cock hardening again with the rise and fall of her chest. Willing himself to move away, but willing more for her to wake up and reach for him again, insistent and eager.

Her hands and mouth and skin on his, and his on hers.

Stripping off sweater and shirt and bra and inhibitions, everything that kept them apart, so he could see her creamy skin, her nipples, shadowed by the approach of his rough hands, determined and strong and unrelenting once those breasts were in his hands. Pinning her hips to his bed as he drove her mad with his mouth, refusing to grant her release until her begging was to his satisfaction, until she writhed and bucked beneath him, discovering within herself deeper wells of pleasure than she'd ever known with any other person, or on her own, or in her wildest dreams.

Orgasms so overwhelming that just the sound of his voice would thereafter have the power to make her wet and willing.

He was lost in the fantasy-haze, breathing quick, ice pack pressed to his balls in a near-futile attempt to wrench his thoughts back to reshaping his carefully laid plans, when Livia opened her eyes.

She was still drowsy, her muscles oddly lax after the unaccustomed demands of the cave and the unexpected release of, well, of release. But she was near-giggling, too, the silly banter and awful puns and intense kisses building a bubbling lightness and the promise of more physical fun that made it hard to suppress her grin.

As her eyes focused, Livia took in Greg's pose. His face was all straight lines again, inscrutable. But one hand was on his hip and the other, oddly, was holding a pack of frozen veggies against his crotch.

Yeah, the grin would not be held back. "Are those green beans in your hand, or are you just happy to see me?"

His eyes closed for a second, then he tossed the bag onto the mattress beside her. "It's for your head."

Livia raised her eyebrows. "For my head? Are you sure? Because maybe my head isn't the one in this room that's throbbing the most." He'd had his hands all over her, which Livia figured gave her more than enough liberty to eye the outline of his erection. She vaguely remembered trying to get ahold of it, too, before zoning off for a blissful catnap. The more wakeful she grew, the more interested she was in how her entire body was waking up in Greg's presence.

He shrugged, though. "You're probably not concussed, but put the ice pack on, anyway. It'll help with the swelling. And you never cleaned the scrapes on your ear. I'll get the antiseptic."

Livia propped herself up. "Don't worry about it. My ear's fine. My head's fine."

He turned, though. Not that Livia ever minded the rear view. She sat up fully so she could watch him rummage in his bathroom drawers. His head tipped down enough that she couldn't gauge his expression.

"Are you okay?"

"I'm fine. I'm not the one with a head wound."

"It's not bad, honest."

He shot her a glance. "Well, I don't want blood on my sheets, so just humor me, okay?"

Unable to match his surly determination while she still fizzed with sensual pleasure, she giggled. "It's okay. I'm not a virgin."

"Jesus." He was opening the disinfecting wipe as he strode back, had her neck stabilized in his palm before she'd stopped smiling. But the alcohol on her abraded ear had her hissing sharply. Without even trying to lighten his mood, Greg pulled antiseptic cream out of his back pocket and set to work slathering up her cuts.

She drew in a deep breath as his fingers played over her earlobe. "Come on, that was funny."

"Yep."

"Because of blood on the sheets."

"I got it."

"Seriously, what's up? Did something happen while I napped?"

He didn't reply, just worked at trying to apply a standard band-aid to the non-standard surface of her ear.

"Are you upset I fell asleep? It wasn't by any means a critique of your performance, you know. If anything, it was a stellar review."

"I'm not upset." Greg crumpled up the band-aid, and bent to blow on her ear.

"Mmmm." Warm breath, shivers up and down her back, and he still smelled like the ocean breeze.

"That wasn't—I mean, the bandage won't work. It's just for the medicine."

"Blowing on the cut is an alternative to band-aids?"

He stepped back from where Livia had set a hand on his cheek, seeming to take a great interest in picking up every scrap of discarded packaging before returning to the bathroom.

"I don't know. My mom always blew on cuts. You should ice your bump."

If it weren't for the spine-shivers, the tenderness of his nursing, and the not-inconsiderable factor of his erection, Livia might start to think Greg was second-guessing the day's intimacies. She, however, wasn't. It wasn't every day a hot guy kissed her in a cave and touched her with passionate perfection. Livia was very fond of the gut instincts that had led to her pre-nap orgasm.

He leaned against the bathroom doorway, finally able to fold his arms across his chest in the 'I'm so superior' pose that meant he was feeling bossy and sure of himself. "Use the ice."

"Not sure I can reach," Livia lied, blinking in exaggerated innocence. "Maybe you could do it for me?"

When Greg didn't move any closer, just held her gaze, she picked up the vegetables. "Or I suppose I can follow your lead and put this on the one spot that aches the most."

To her delight, Greg's eyes tracked her motions as Livia scooted to the edge of the high bed, letting her legs dangle towards the floor as she spread open her thighs. When she'd exposed as much of her jeans-clad mound as possible, she slapped the icy bag against it, instinctively jerking her hips once as the cold permeated and sent more shivers to play up her vertebrae.

"Livia." He sounded irritated, but his breathing had hitched.

"Am I doing it wrong?" Bracing her hands on her upper thighs, Livia used her thumbs to hold the delightfully cold bag to her pulsing core while her fingers traced idle patterns across her legs.

Greg didn't reply, but did prowl forward. Slowly, deliberately, a measured pace at a time.

Livia crossed one hand up her torso, letting just the tips of her fingers land on her thrust-forward breast. "I mean, this is how you were using the vegetables. I just figured it's part of your post-caving routine. Was I wrong?"

One very slow half-smile told her that Greg was tuning in to her energy, as well as watching every movement of Livia's hands on her own body. Another step put him between her legs, and one more pressed her thighs wider to accommodate his hips. It was no effort at all to slide her hand off of her own thigh and onto his, the friction of their jeans raw and exciting.

Greg's irises were a bare two shades lighter than his pupils, and Livia sank into their dark intensity. Her taunting grin broke apart with a gasp when he palmed her ass and yanked her closer to the lip of the bed. Closer to him. The green beans between them rustled loudly in the silent room, and the shivers racing across Livia now were half from the cold, half from the heat, and all welcome.

She opened her mouth, intending to tease some more, unable to think of any jokes. Unable to think of much besides the flex of his ass beneath her hands, the taste of his jaw as she pressed kisses along it, the promising rhythm of the creaking bed as their hips moved in time together.

Letting Greg maintain the connection between them, Livia took charge of lifting his shirt over his back, pulling one hand at a time off her hips until the Henley was on the floor, and Greg was shirtless, and her palms were everywhere across his torso. Oh, and it was just as strong and smooth and sexy as she'd imagined. Gold-toned skin and brown nipples and firm muscles and no hair. Livia never knew she lusted over hairless chests, but there it was: lust, giant shooting flames of lust, and not a chest hair in sight. Learn something new every day. Two new things, if you count 'unusual uses for frozen vegetables,' and it was increasingly clear that Livia wasn't thinking coherently at all.

Greg backed up enough to let the green beans fall to the

floor before pivoting forward and twisting so they were both on the bed, Livia half-straddling his thighs.

"Off," he said, lifting the hem of her sweater. She did him one better, removing the shirt and sweater together, and then he was unhooking her bra while she unzipped his jeans.

It was all fast and fun. Very fun. Until suddenly Greg had one arm stuck through one of her bra straps and the underwire was poking him in the face as Livia tried to ignore their tangled arms in favor of tugging down his jeans.

Oh, lord, never mind the bunched-up socks, there they were, both bare-chested, forearms bound by a fabric strap, and Livia finally had eyes on the hunter-green boxers and the erection Greg was sporting beneath them, and it was just the silliest situation, and Livia burst out laughing.

In a split-second he was crouching over her, jeans hanging loose but still giving him enough play to pin her thighs under his calves. He leveraged their trapped arms to catch her two hands with his one, low on her abdomen and tantalizingly close to his jutting cock. It was all she could see. Right there in front of her, his taut stomach and the faintest line of dark hair and the fabric stretched out, tugging the elastic band away from his waist, and Livia kept trying to look at Greg's stern, hungry face, kept trying to speak, but her eyes kept tracking down and she kept laughing and her shoulders were shaking, making her breasts wobble ridiculously, and his boxers were green, seriously green, it couldn't be more perfect, so no matter how Greg's eyes narrowed and no matter how his hand wrapped securely around her wrists, Livia laughed.

At last, he braced his other arm on the lumpy pillow beside her and stopped her with a fierce kiss. It was the same electric hunger from the cave, but Livia's bubbling merriment kept playing at the surface, even when Greg extracted them both from the bra and flung it aside. Of course, that just meant she was free to press her hands to his pelvis, stroking his cock with her thumbs, which she figured might make it clear to him she wasn't laughing at his dick.

Not that Greg was acting like he was insecure.

His free hand, firm between her shoulder blades, lifted Livia, bringing her into closer contact with him. Her spine arched from ass to skull, neck thrown back, breasts high and tight to his torso, as Greg curled over her, never letting up with his kisses.

She fought to free a leg, eager to wedge his thigh between her own; Greg would not comply. Her hips jumped and wriggled, but no matter what she did, his lower legs pinned hers to the bed. So, fine. She changed tactics, attempting to squeeze a hand beneath his inner thigh and finger her clit herself.

"Nope." He was breathing raggedly, but speaking firmly, low in her ear. "You're not going anywhere until you explain yourself."

Livia grinned, happy to comply, but devilish enough to squeeze the fingers he wouldn't let her use on herself around the base of his cock. At the look he gave her, she started laughing again, never letting go, even as he dropped her back to the bed and captured her nipple between two knuckles.

"Talk, Livia."

He didn't release her, so she didn't release him. Not that either of them seemed to mind the erotic pressure terribly much.

"Okay, okay." She arched into his hold, letting out a little moan of pleasure as he pressed the captured nipple with the pad of his thumb.

"Okay, then."

Oh, this man. He was all fierceness and light, and Livia had already blissed out with him when they were fully clothed. Just imagining him nude had her moaning and then he'd stripped, and the moaning was clearly not going to stop anytime soon.

She bit her lip around her smile before summoning the deepest bass she could as she sang, "Ho, ho, ho."

Those straight brows crinkled into the briefest of vees. "Christmas was last month."

"Not Santa." She stroked up and down his shaft. "Want another guess?"

"I'll tell you what I want."

Livia waggled her eyebrows. "Another guess?"

"Another something." He balanced his weight on his legs, freeing his other hand to palm her other nipple.

Half-laughing, half-gasping, Livia strove for the breath to explain. "Ho, ho, ho! The jolly green giant."

The giant in question jumped in her hand.

"Because of the shorts?" she clarified. "And the green beans?"

Greg glanced at the discarded veggies on the floor, but shook his head.

"You've never seen the ads? There's a jingle," she insisted. "Down in the valley of the jolly green giant?"

"I've never watched much TV."

"Everyone's seen the green giant."

He gave her a pointed look.

"Not *your* green giant. Well, I presume not. He's on the cans. Corn niblets! You have to have seen a green giant guy on a can of corn niblets before."

"He's made out of green beans?"

"No. Well, I guess not. He's a guy, a regular person kind of guy, but he's green and wears some sort of green tunic thing, I think?"

"And he's got a green cock?"

Livia collapsed, giggling. "I can only assume so, yes."

"A giant green cock?" Greg was sitting back now, regarding his green boxers-clad junk.

"Well, I mean, even his hair is green. I have to guess his cock is, too."

"And giant?"

She licked her lips, squirming back enough to lean against his headboard. "I've never really thought about it. But that seems reasonable."

He slid off the bed, bending to pick up the green beans before pulling his jeans the rest of the way off. Livia drank him in. His shoulders and arms were the most muscled parts of his body, but his lean legs seemed plenty strong and more than sexy enough to satisfy her. The boxers rested on his trim waist and molded against his ass, and Livia wanted to be everywhere they were.

He held up the bag to show her. "Generic."

"Well, you'll just have to trust me."

"Don't know about that."

"I can look it up if you want to wait a sec," Livia said, reaching for the side table where she'd put her phone when she'd first rested on Greg's pillow.

"Take your jeans off."

She stopped mid-stretch. Greg was looming over her, one hand cupping his balls, watching the line of her torso as she moved in his bed.

"Excuse me?"

"Jeans. Off. Socks, too."

"Annoying socks," Livia agreed, reaching for them first. "So you don't want to see the jolly green giant?"

"Do you?"

"And the niblets, too," she agreed, unzipping. Greg moved in, dropping the green beans on her stomach and tugging the denim off her legs. Livia squealed, actually squealed, but before she could retaliate, he'd tossed the jeans and veggies both and was warming her navel with his tongue. So that was a quick way to banish any intrusive thoughts about her physique and his appreciation of the bounties of her body. Gone were her thoughts about the plain cotton undies and boring bra, for that matter. The jolly green giant made Greg's feelings about it all clear enough.

"Livia," Greg said, gruff and low. His tongue traced her belly button, and she shivered.

"Gregory." There was no give in his shoulders. It was all muscle, bunching and flexing as he moved over her.

"Is there anything you particularly want me to do before we fuck?"

Well, gracious. How very polite he was. And how very heated Livia was becoming. She rubbed against his side, reveling in the slight release the pressure gave her. "Are you taking requests?"

"Gathering information."

"That tickles."

"This?" He drew his fingers through the damp line his tongue had traced.

"Mmm."

"So you want me to stop?"

"You're the one who wanted info."

"About what you like."

"I thought your liked guessing games." She propped herself up on her elbows. "But I'll give you a hint."

"Yeah? What's that?"

In answer, Livia reached for her breasts, stroking her aching areoles as she met Greg's dark gaze. Her breath was nothing but shallow pants, then gasping as Greg's chin nudged her hand aside and his lips took possession of her nipple. And it was a possession; Livia had certainly never given herself so much pleasure there, so clearly Greg was earning himself some colonizing rights. And he quickly expanded his empire, staking a claim on the other breast as the green giant found a particularly delightful spot between her thighs to plant its flag.

Within moments, Livia was rocking insistently against him, and Greg was the one panting.

"Please tell me you have condoms somewhere in this cabin."

"God, I hope so."

She stopped licking his neck and looked at him. His mouth had lifted into that teasing one-sided smile, and his eyes glinted. "You're kidding? Now?"

"You go on all day about spelunking and blood and niblets but you get outraged when I make a joke?"

She bit her lip. "When you put it like that."

He thrust against her. "Like that?"

Livia groaned. "God, yes. Put it like that again."

"In a minute."

"Now."

And then Livia was looking at Greg's cockiest smirk, as he turned all know-it-all casual and repeated deliberately, "In a minute."

The hunter green boxers hit the floor, and the giant was jolly indeed, if not green. Greg swung a leg over Livia's stomach, straddling her while he dug in the drawer beside his bed.

"Sheath me."

He traced lines inside her arms as she did so, sensual strokes that were far less hurried than the ones she was using to unroll the condom. All she wanted was that thing on and his thing in and, not to be too greedy, another orgasm or two. The first had been great, but the one building as they teased and touched and wrestled with veggies and got tangled up in clothes was, Livia could just tell, capable of blowing her socks off. If she hadn't removed them already.

And they were naked. And the sun highlighted the gleam in Greg's eyes. And he moved to sit on his heels, lifting her legs to bracket his hips. And ... oh.

Oh, oh, oh. Oh.

He didn't leave the bed this time. Didn't even manipulate them so her back was to his front. Just collapsed where they'd ended up, Greg half-under her, with her head on his sweaty, delicious chest.

Livia inhaled, the sea and sex smells settling deep. She bit back a comment about his picking a signature scent that mingled so well with intimate exertions. It might suggest Greg had intended to end up in bed with her. And enthusiastic, and delightful, as he'd been once they got underway, he'd also been following her lead. It was her persistent teasing that took down the wall he'd built with antiseptic and ice packs.

Greg might have been serious about separating them, earlier. What with the sneaking off to the kitchen and the rummaging in the bathroom and the averted eyes.

She yanked one of the lumpy pillows out from where it was wedged under her hip. "Want this?"

He tossed it to the floor. Suddenly pillows and bras and condom wrappers could be on the floor, when before each scrap of the corner of the alcohol wipe was worth tracking down. Yeah, Livia's gut was replaying the afternoon and coming up with a slightly different version of events than the one she'd thought was playing out during the excellently rowdy sex.

"I should go."

The arm around her waist stilled. "It's raining again."

"You can give me a lift back."

"Or we could stay here."

"Or I could go home. Don't worry, Kari and Dante should be gone by now. No one will know."

Greg went from lazy to lightning motion, sitting them both up. "You think I'm worried about Kari?"

Livia shrugged, caught Greg staring at her breasts, snagged the sheet. "It's a small town. I may be new to Honey Wine, but even I've figured out that Kari tells Mason everything, and Mason is down at the feed store every other day talking to Bill and Jackson, and then ten minutes later Ellie will be on your porch asking questions."

"Who gives a damn? They've been gossiping about me all my life. I'm used to it."

"Yeah? That's fine for you." She gave him a light tap on the chest. "But I'm not used to it, and I have to live here, too, you know."

"You don't have to."

She sat with that. Took a breath mercifully free of any ocean breeze. "What's that mean?"

"I just—I mean cause I've got family here. Ties. History. They gossip about me because I'm one of them. Everyone has this narrative, to go along with me skipping a lot of school, and leading friends into trouble, and of dating a lot of people. It's part of the Greg Is Trouble talking points."

"That's not what you said." Livia was the one edging away from Greg this time.

"Sorry, but. What do you mean?"

"You said I don't have to live here, and I said what's that mean, and instead of answering you talked about how you were a player in high school. That's not news, and it has nothing to do with me not having to live here."

"Livia," Greg leaned in, stroked her arm. "No, I mean—I meant—you don't have to get used to gossip, since they won't treat you like they do me."

She eyed him. Frankly, it stunk of a cover story, and she wasn't sure she was buying it. She took some comfort that he didn't mind gossip linking the two of them. But it wasn't the comfort that would come of knowing she hadn't pushed him into going further than he'd intended in the first place.

And no matter how he explained himself, she had his loan contract to put in the balance between them.

Livia really needed to head back to Chata. The sex was unparalleled, but the more her brain worked at it all, the less she liked her gut instincts after all. Fortunately, dressing—no bra, inside-out socks—was faster than undressing had been.

She glanced out the window. "Never mind about the ride; it's clear enough now. I'll walk."

"I can drive you."

"You stay here." She lobbed the green beans towards him where he lay, still lounging, naked, in the bed. "Think up some better uses for those."

"See you soon?"

"Yeah, of course." Livia paused in his doorway. "And thanks for the spelunking lesson."

He lifted the right side of his mouth into that smile that broke up all the serious lines of his face. Livia's stomach did a happy little flip, but she ignored it and set off on the path to home.

CHAPTER 16

Even super-organized Livia wouldn't be able to make a neater variance request packet than the paperwork he'd compiled to the exact specifications in the City Council's brochure. He thought about texting a picture of his work to her, but that felt too much like flirting. They probably needed to talk about the missteps in the previous day's post-cave-and-sex conversation.

Mr. Connor didn't let one scrap of looking impressed cross his face when Greg handed it all over. He hefted himself from behind his desk like crossing the eight feet to the service counter was a Hercules-level task, and spent ninety-five full seconds cleaning and adjusting his glasses before accepting Greg's folder.

"Okay, Mr. Forst. Let's just see."

Mr. Forst. The man had the trick of addressing him with his last name and making it sound like he was barely grown. Too many years married to the vice-principal, Greg supposed.

"I have a flash drive with video and stills from the various activities, but I printed out a few photos as well."

Mr. Connor didn't acknowledge that beyond resting the drive beneath the folder. He finally looked up and nodded once, which felt annoyingly like fireworks of praise. Especially once Mr. Connor pulled out the stamp pad and two different City of Honey Wine stamps and began inking the documents. "City Council meets Thursday."

He nodded, shoving his hands in his pockets to stop from fisting them, or drumming them on the counter, or making any gesture that might be interpreted as rude. "Four p.m., I know. I'll be there."

Since it was between the lunch and dinner rushes, he wandered into the Honey Wine Cafe in search of Ellie. He wanted to talk to just one person who would take his new business seriously. Who would be enthusiastic and proud of him. Uncle Kent's surliness and Mr. Connor's fussiness and Livia's ... well, Livia was okay. Except for how her being enthusiastic about his business reminded him how unenthusiastic he'd been about hers in return.

Ellie was in the front booth, laptop and papers spread across the table. He kissed her cheek and slid in opposite her. She looked up from her work, smiling in that expression that always seemed a little too knowing. She was one of those people who could read him like an open book. "What are you up to today?"

"Been back to City Hall with my variance request. You'll come out on Thursday to support it, won't you?"

Her lips pursed for just a moment before she smiled at him. It was a bit too pat-on-his-head for his liking. "I'll be there."

"What?"

"What what, dear?"

He tightened his core, resisting any of the sullen slouching teen impulses he'd once had. "You don't think I'll get the variance for Cesta Adventures?"

Ellie closed her laptop and regarded him seriously. "Gregory, don't think for a minute I don't admire all you've learned and done since leaving town."

His chest was rubble headed towards a cliff. "But?"

"But all of this, taking people into caves and on the river, it's really what you want?"

He'd shown her his business plan. Why would he have gone to the trouble of creating it if he didn't really want it? "You think it's a terrible idea?"

Her pursed lips relaxed into a sad smile. "I don't. Not really. What I think about is all those treks we'd take, you and me and Zelda, and how it was a joy for her to be the caretaker of the land. It felt ... private, and maybe more special because it was private. It's me being a little stuck in the past, I suppose, that I have trouble imagining all these other people tramping on our pathways."

Greg looked out the window at the same-as-always sights of town. Hardware store, bar, market. The art gallery and the jewelry store. The ice cream shop, which now served bubble tea as well, because, despite appearances, times changed even in Honey Wine. "I don't think my mom would mind so much, me following the pathway I chose for myself. I get what you mean about our memories of her, Ellie, I really do. But it's those same memories that made me want to start Cesta. You know I had to leave Honey Wine after losing Mom. Had to get some space from here. But I missed it. Not just her, not just the land. The town, my friends. You. I missed out on Sissy's last days, and now Dad and Kent plan to just pass through whenever, but that's not for me now. I'm done missing my home."

Ellie reached across to squeeze his arm, and he didn't know if it was pandering or in comfort or because she was admitting she might be wrong. "I'll be at the meeting on Thursday."

She wasn't signing up as head cheerleader, but it would help. The Honey Wine Cafe was one of the longest established businesses in town, and having the owner in his corner, whatever her reasons, held weight. "Thanks. I'm glad I can count on you."

"Of course, Gregory. Just, do remember that this is a small town. We're used to things being as they are, running as they do. The council isn't going to take kindly to someone coming in and changing things."

"I'm not trying to change anything about Honey Wine. This is my land; I'm not dragging anyone else into it." He hadn't told Ellie about his plans for Kent's—now Livia's—property. That didn't matter just now. He shoved out of the booth and began pacing. He hated feeling defensive. "I just want to offer people an alternative reason to come to Honey Wine. More tourism is good for everyone. For you, for Cy, for all the businesses. No one else is bringing in the market segment I can."

He turned back to look at her and saw an expression he'd encountered too often as a teen. She thought he was talking a big game and lacked the skill or drive to back it up. Like Cesta was a sport he was all enthusiasm for until practice took too much of his free time, or a promise to stay put in class that lost the battle to whatever path he set out to wander during lunch. If he'd had Chata already, she'd see—they'd all see—how it worked as an enterprise worth believing in. They already trusted Chata as a reliable business, so his adding Cesta would have been expansion, not risk. Something to ground him. But he didn't, so now Ellie thought he was as fly by night as a free-tailed bat.

He wiped his hand down his face. "Just ... support me on Thursday. I'll do the rest."

She inclined her head, conceding. "I'll support you. You know your mom would come back and hip-check me if I didn't."

Her tone made it clear: it would be an uphill battle, and none of the old-timers in Honey Wine, not even his mom's best friend, had faith in him. Ellie would speak up in his favor, not because she believed he would follow through and be successful, but because she'd feel guilty otherwise.

"Once I get the variance," he said, more confidently than he felt, "Cesta Adventures will take off. People will thank me."

And because having to ask for Ellie's help had drained enough of his pride for one day, he gave her a quick hug and left.

Livia finished up the last of the rooms, putting the final touches on the bedding, arranging the new, not horrifying lampshades, and ensuring the toiletries were in order. She took a step back and surveyed her work. It looked perfect.

She went to her computer and opened up her spreadsheet. Everything was accounted for. She'd sent out the soft opening invitations, and the reservations were coming in. She was actually doing it. She shot a quick video of Persimmon, glowing in the late afternoon sun, to compare to the way it was when she first bought the place. The perfect cap to the time-lapse video of renovations for her to post.

No comparison. Livia deserved every pat she placed on her own back. Thumb fiddling over the contours of her ring, she imagined telling her mom about it. About everything she was accomplishing with the inheritance, and all her own hard work.

In the alternate timeline where she and Mom had found each other again, she'd have been proud of her.

Since that dream-life was impossible, Livia double-checked all the upstairs windows were closed and went down to test out the next batch of breakfast breads. And to text Greg. Because why not get a second opinion? Especially if showing off led to them clearing the air. Even to his staying the night and taste-testing breakfast with her in the morning.

As soon as she pressed send, Livia moved to the porch to pace. They'd left things with a lot unspoken, for all their bad word play and great bed play. Part of it was her own uncertainty about getting into any kind of thing with him. The man next door, the man who met her with designs on her property, but seemed to have exchanged those for designs on her.

Physically, they'd been well-matched. The joking and the touching and the intensity all felt great. She'd thought they were both into exploring their connection, but those 'you don't have to live here' remarks left her on shaky ground. Livia needed his input as they defined what, if anything, would happen with them beyond the one tumble.

She returned to the kitchen table and threw herself into researching reviews for other bed and breakfasts in the area. Her own experience warned her about a lot of potential pitfalls, but understanding more of the customer perspective was always useful.

She got lost in the numbers and the details, blocking out everything else around her until Greg knocked on the back door. Livia forgot all about reservations and spreadsheets. He leaned on her threshold like he was an integral part of the experience. His dark eyes and darker hair and maybe something dark about his intentions, given how much of a smirk he was sending her way. Biting his bottom lip, he eyed every inch of her as she packed away her work and approached him.

"Hi."

"Well, howdy to you, too." He took hold of her hips and yanked her forward.

"Oof." Livia stumbled against him, her body instantly alive with the contact.

"So, I'm sorry I pissed you off, saying all that about the town. It's been a process, reintegrating myself here, and I'm going to keep those issues in their own bucket from here out. Not mix it up with getting to know you better."

It was a good apology. Unprompted, he took responsibility, naming the problem and his solution. She let herself relax into his arms. "Thanks for coming over."

"I missed you." He nuzzled his nose against her hair and inhaled deeply.

"You saw me yesterday." Livia poked him lightly in the stomach, but he only tightened his grip.

"That was too long ago." He finally let her go just long enough to meet her eyes as he began to tug her shirt over her head. When she nodded, his smile went wicked. "Much too long."

Livia melted, almost dizzy with want as he continued to explore her body. He was all hands and lips and teeth, making her gasp and moan in equal measure. "You're making up for lost time. I like it."

"Like it enough to let me past the kitchen door?"

She grinned coyly, like he wasn't having his way with her practically in the open. "Thing about the kitchen is, the frozen veggies are handier this way."

He led with his hips as he walked them past the dining room and towards the stairs. "How about if we do things without the help of the green giant this time?"

"You think you're funny?"

"That's me, the town joke."

She'd have paused at that, if he'd let her. If he wasn't tracing each of her ribs with determined fingers. If he wasn't nuzzling her neck and turning her so his front pressed her shoulder blades, urging them both to ascend towards her room.

But he didn't let her. He kept up his explorations, helping them both shed clothes as they climbed. Soon enough, her B&B would be full of guests, and she wouldn't be able to leave a suggestive trail of shirts and bras through the place.

So. Good. Later, she'd think about cryptic comments and the flash of something urgent in his expression. Like he just needed the oblivion of a long, teasing fuck.

Livia could revel in that, too.

He finally deposited her on her bed, and she sprawled out beneath him, already feeling undone. "God, you're gorgeous."

She widened her legs, happy to be admired. "You say that like you're surprised."

"I am. Every time. Every single time I see you, I'm surprised." He kissed her then, his lips firm and insistent against hers. "Very, very pleasantly surprised."

His hands roved over her bare skin as their kiss deepened. His tongue licked into her mouth, tasting and teasing as he coaxed her to open up wider for him. As he broke away just long enough to go in search of his discarded pants. He returned with a condom, sheathing himself as he approached. Livia couldn't help but admire his efficiency even as she ached for him to hurry up and be inside her again.

"Patience," he murmured, as if reading her mind. "I just now decided to take my time with you."

"Ugh. That's a terrible idea." But she shivered at the promise in his voice and let herself be pulled under again by the intensity of his gaze. He kissed her slowly this time, each press of his lips a separate promise to do some of that deep exploration he was proving to be so good at.

And every time he touched her, every kiss and lick and caress, she felt herself come closer and closer to the edge. She shifted restlessly under him, avid for more. But he continued his slow, lingering assault on her senses, determined to make sure she wouldn't be able to forget this fuck anytime soon.

And that was fine by her. Because if his teasing was any indication, Greg was just as determined to have her gasping in pleasure beneath him again and again in the future. It was the kind of joint operation she could get fully behind.

When he finally entered her, he did it slowly, like he savored every inch. Livia wrapped her legs around him and threw her head back, letting the anticipation drive her higher and higher still. He kept up his steady, deliberate rhythm, and she responded in kind. She dug her nails into his ass and ground her clit against him. It wasn't quite enough, but damn, it was nice. Feeling him full and pulsing inside her, his strength surrounding her, the narrowed intensity of his gaze.

"You need to get there," he said, like he had nothing to do with it. Like his cock wasn't thrusting into her.

She narrowed her eyes right back at him. "Fine." And she flipped them over so she could reach her bedside table. Sank back onto his full length once she had her clit stimulator in hand.

"Mmm?" Greg reached for the toy.

She held it above her head. "Nope. You're in charge of my hips. I'm in charge of this."

"Like that, is it?"

She bucked against him. "You have objections?"

Settling another pillow behind his shoulders, Greg grinned wide at her. "I like you, Livia." With that, he sucked her nipple into the heat of his mouth and started moving fast.

She was almost thrown off balance. Almost at a loss for what to do next. But not entirely. Pressing on the toy, she used her other hand to open up enough space between their pelvises and got it into position. With his moans on her breast and his hand guiding her to ride him hard and, most of all, with his cock sliding in and out of her, she only needed the lowest setting.

"Damn. Yes," he growled against her chest, before sucking in her other nipple.

It sent more electricity reverberating throughout her. She came hard with the toy buzzing between them. She gasped his name, the word almost lost in her orgasm. His hold on her got frantic as his thrusts turned wild, somehow deeper, drawing her pleasure out until he toppled into his own orgasm.

When Livia finally opened her eyes, he was watching her.

His gaze softened, and he reached up to brush the damp hair away from her face.

"Hey." She reached to trace his brow in return. "Come here."

Instead, he slid his hand into her hair and pulled her down for a kiss, soft and sweeter than she expected. When he rolled them to their sides and pulled out, she yelped out a laugh.

"Wow. Everyone's a critic."

His droll tone had her laughing harder. She arched up her torso and grasped at the bedding. Finally coming up with the toy, she silenced its buzz. "Wasn't quite expecting to land on that."

Greg reached for it, and she let him take it this time. "So, this is your answer to the green giant?"

Livia batted her eyelashes. "It's not the size that matters. It's how jolly it can make me."

His smile was slow and a thousand percent wicked. "Yeah? Can I see how jolly you get with just it?"

Her pussy clenched at the mere suggestion. She dropped back down on the bed. "Go for it."

Greg propped himself between her legs and studied the soft silicone for a moment, but quickly found the power button and cycled it through the various settings, head tilted like he was getting to the bottom of a deep mystery. All the while, he toyed lightly with her inner thigh, barely a whisper of a touch here, a few gentle taps there.

Here she was trying to be post-orgasmic boneless, and he was determined to rev her up again. She closed her eyes and stretched her arms above her head, anchoring herself against the headboard.

Greg puffed a small breath of a laugh against her core, and then it was game on. Livia arched to him, open and ready and suddenly out of breath, as he pressed the vibrator to the top of her clit.

His hand glided down her body and came to rest on her hip, holding her steady as she writhed. He kept the pressure light and slow, and the contrast of that against the quick suction of the toy was almost too much.

She shuddered. "Oh, hell."

Greg's hold on her hip tightened as if to steady her.

"Yeah?" He sprinkled a trail of kisses down her body, like he was taming her into a more compliant position, and he shifted his weight to one elbow so he could continue to tease her with the toy, but also to prop up his head. "Too much?"

His tone was teasing, but she could hear the edge of tension. It was almost enough to make her reach for him, but ... "No. More."

He complied, and she gasped. Each soft wake of the toy against her clit sent a zing of pleasure through her. He held the vibrator steady, cranking up the intensity one more notch. She was so wet and aching. For her orgasm, for his fingers, for his cock. Her climax, coiling low and tight, built into an urgent need.

He rolled the toy, and suddenly the buzz was too much. She snapped, exploding around him. She gripped the bedding tight and let out a strangled cry as she came. Tossing the vibrator, he dropped down to eat her out as wave after wave of pleasure washed over her.

"Thanks," she gasped when she could catch her breath.

He laughed. "Livia, believe me, it is entirely my pleasure."

CHAPTER 17

He slid out of her bed at dawn. The advantage of an entire empty B&B was he could go shower in one of the guest rooms and not wake Livia up. Since his hunt for their clothes took him down to the second floor, he ended up in Persimmon.

Even with the new and rearranged furniture, the fresh coats of paint, the high-tech keypad door code he fortunately hadn't needed since the room was unlocked, there was something familiar about stepping into Persimmon's tub to clean up. The decor of the rooms was all Livia now, and she'd done a damn good job updating them while retaining that feeling of a cozy cottage he'd always cherished about Chata. But the bones of the building hadn't changed, and drying himself with her bath sheet, smelling like her honeysuckle shower gel, dovetailed with the familiar experience of dressing while looking over the treetops towards his own home.

It was too early to disturb Livia. He sank into his favorite armchair—into the much more comfortable, new armchair in the place where his favorite armchair used to be—and tried calling Dad.

Tried.

What was the use of being related to the only other man

he knew who rose with the sun, if he wouldn't answer the son who kept reaching out to him?

Greg rose, shoving his phone in his back pocket. Dad would text later, and it would be as innocuous as ever. He'd have nothing to say about Mr. Connors or about Ellie or about Cesta. Nothing more than his usual line about Greg doing what he felt was right, and it was his land now, and yeah, of course he would come check it out. Soon.

He got it. He'd lifted himself out of the pit of memories that twas their cabin for years before Dad faced his need for space. Looking at Persimmon's fresh, inviting vibe, he wondered if he should do more to transform home into something less like the place Mom had raised him. If that would help Dad's comfort when he finally made it back.

He took Livia's pile of clothes back to the top floor suite and peeked into her room. She was still out. He didn't want to wake her, and he didn't want to go. Mittens might finish up the food he'd left and get irked, but that wasn't any kind of incentive for Greg to leave, not when Livia sweet and warm in her bed, curled among all those thousand pillows of hers.

Her suite, now, it felt entirely hers. Maybe because he hadn't spent so much time in Kent and Sissy's rooms, but even with the love seat that had been in Loquat and the bookshelf from the parlor, both her bedroom and her sitting/dining room were wall-to-wall Livia. Her comfortable, organized vibe. Even the boxes she hadn't unpacked yet were neatly labeled and stacked in the correct areas. At least, as far as he could tell from poking into the half-open ones.

She had a two-person dining table beside the kitchenette, and it was totally not snooping to notice the blanket-wrapped stack of stained glass panels atop it. The first panel wasn't even half-covered, so he recognized it as an abstract vase of flowers, even before sliding aside the blanket to inspect it. And lifting it to let the morning light shine through the yellows and greens and oranges meant he dislodged the cardboard separating it from a similar panel, this one showing an abstract pile of books.

He was looking at a third panel, larger than the first two, featuring a large orange cat, when Livia emerged. "Morning."

She raised that single brow at him. "Good morning. What are you up to?"

He set the cat back atop the other panels. "Being quietly nosy? Unless I was loud about it, and that's what woke you up."

"You think being cute will mean I don't mind your being presumptuous?"

"It wasn't a surefire plan, but I came up with it just now and hoped for the best." He leaned against the wall, crossing his arms, cause sometimes that made her walk towards him.

It didn't work. She leaned across from him, mirroring, and it was the most beautiful statement of independence and challenge he'd ever seen.

Enjoying seeing so much heart and strength in her every move was going to end up being a problem for him, if he wanted to keep control of his heart. He strolled towards her and caught her sharp inhale when she must have noticed how he used her bath products.

The glint in her look set his imps dancing. "So, you never let on that you're a cat person. Mittens is going to be so pleased."

She raised her brow. "At what point, since you've adopted him, has Mittens ever shown pleasure?"

He snorted, though the cat had claimed favorite spots in his house, and shown a distinct fondness for catnip toys with feather tails.

She didn't resist his hug. Returned his kiss, and said, "Good morning. Stop deflecting. Why are you going through my mom's stained glass?"

"Those were your mom's?"

She barely stiffened before breaking away. "Thanks for cleaning up the clothes trail."

"Now who's deflecting?"

"I'm being polite, unlike some busybody types I know."

Greg moved to help her stack the artwork back onto the table. "I'm sorry for prying. I glimpsed the top one and liked it a bunch, so I kept looking. Because I'm a busybody. Do you want help hanging them?"

Livia moved to sit on the loveseat, and because he was all about obeying his impulses, he followed her.

"I haven't decided yet if I want to hang them, much less where."

"They'd be pretty in the dining room. You've got those windows so bright and open." It wouldn't be the same as all his aunt's cross stitches, but they could bring in the owner's personality in much the same way. If they looked as good there as he suspected, he'd have to think up something similar, if it ever worked out that he bought Chata from her.

Livia hummed. "She made them. My mom. They were the result of this arts course she took when I was in college. She spent a lot of time learning, planning, and then creating everything. She said she didn't want to be a person who never learned new things."

Greg lifted her right hand from where it rested in her lap. "You're doing the thing again."

The faraway clouds faded from her gaze. "What thing?"

His thumb cruised up and down each finger. "Sometimes when you're talking about your mom, you rub this ring like you want to wrench the stones loose from their settings."

She fisted her hand, but didn't take it from his grasp. "Oh. That thing."

He kissed her knuckles, unsurprised that she was fully aware of the habit.

"It was hers, too." Livia flexed open her hand, let the light catch on the rubies, which were set in three expanding circles around a central stone that was something yellow. They probably meant it to look like a lantana sort of flower, except for how the precision and rigidity of the setting and materials were the opposite of organic. It looked heavy, like it weighed down her entire hand.

"Did she like red?"

Livia shrugged. "Not especially. You saw the stained glass —she was more about orange and blue. This was my great-aunt's, on my dad's side. We both thought it was old-fashioned and, well, not so pretty. My aunt gave it to Mom after my parents divorced, cause Dad took back her engagement ring. They'd used some old family jewelry to make the wedding set, and I guess he didn't want her to sell it or anything. But then Aunt Barbara sent this ring to Mom, and Dad couldn't do much about it."

"You don't usually talk about your dad."

Another shrug. "He hasn't kept in touch. Every once in a while I log into Facebook and look for him in Great-Aunt Barbara's photos, but I decided a long time ago it's not my job to repair a relationship he dropped when I wasn't even old enough for my own cell phone."

"And now your mom is gone, so it wouldn't be fair to her memory if you started getting along with him?"

Livia closed her eyes. "Damn it."

The tightening of her features sent an unpleasant rumble through his chest. "Sorry."

She shook her head. "No, it's fine. I mean, it's not; it's not at all fun to realize something is so obviously true that you picked up on it, when all along I had no idea. But, yeah, that seems like it might be really true. And might be tied up with my whole thing with this ugly ring, too."

He wrapped an arm around her and let loose some tension when she relaxed against him. "How so?"

"I stole it from Mom when I moved out at seventeen. Not stole, maybe—she always called it 'a bit of security for your future' once she had it appraised. But I'd said as much to this horrible guy I moved in with for a while there, and he got pretty insistent about me taking it with me when he was helping me pack up my stuff from her house. So I tucked it in my purse on the way out the door and left Mom's jewelry box open. I guess I wanted to be sure she realized I'd taken it. She never asked about it, not even once I was free of that guy. I'm sure she thought I'd sold it, and if he'd had his way, I would have."

That tension sat tight on his chest again. He rubbed circles on her shoulder. "Yeah?"

Livia huffed a breath. "Yeah. I caught him digging through my bag a couple of times, so finally I decided to just wear the ring to keep it safe. I guess that's when I started doing the rubbing it with my thumb thing, a reassurance I still had it. So, yeah. Now I do it all the time."

Jesus, what a piece of shit she'd dated. He kissed her temple, hugging her tighter. Not that he was any kind of hero, able to make up for the crap she'd gone through in the past. If anything, his ulterior motives regarding Chata from the get-go put him in the villain category.

She knew all about his craving for her land, which meant she likely saw him as just another guy who valued her for something material, instead of for all the wonderful parts of herself she brought to the relationship. Her brains and resilience and style and charm and all the sexiness, too.

"I bet your mom would be in awe of how strong you are."

She was back at the hardware store a couple of days later, picking up S-hooks and chain to use to hang her mom's stained glass. A couple came in, people she hadn't seen before, though Bill's chin-tip was one of long familiarity.

Of course, Bill had that kind of relationship with a lot of

Honey Wine. Livia wondered when she'd be able to say the same. He stopped telling her about the new wood floor cleaner he wanted her to try, and introduced her.

"Livia's running Kent and Sissy's B&B now."

The shorter one, who seemed close to her age, said, "Yeah? Congrats. How're you finding it?"

"Loving it so far. I have an open house coming up soon, so you can check it out. I'm doing it in conjunction with Greg Forst at Cesta Adventures, the new eco adventure place next door to me. We'll be sorting out a date for it soon. Bill, you mind if we put up a flyer when it's all set?"

"Oh, well now, if you're waiting on Greg Forst to be done making plans and get down to the real work …" The first stranger trailed off. The older one, maybe a brother from their resemblance, was laughing.

Livia raised a brow. "What does that mean?"

"No offense to you, of course. I'm sure your side of things is right and tight. But you don't count on Forst to get from eighty to a hundred percent on one of his plans. I'm just saying."

"Unless the plan is to date every unattached gal in school. But just the once," added the laughing one.

"Right. Just the one date. Count on that. Or count on him to fail, that's a safe bet."

"Now, guys," Bill started, but Livia had heard enough.

"So far, I've seen Greg do nothing but come through on his promises. Bill'll tell you how he built a treehouse for Chata, made it far nicer than what I asked him for. He's done all the paperwork to set up Cesta, come up with all the experiences, introduced me to anyone who might make setting up my business easier. I'm not sure why you feel free to laugh about him to someone you just now met, but, no offense to you, that seems like not the nicest attitude."

"Now, Livia," Bill said.

She spun on him. "Now, Bill. You and Jackson like to laugh, too, don't think that's not obvious. But next time you have a joke to make about Greg, can you do me a favor and stop for just long enough to remember what you were like in high school? And then think about if you'd want that to be the only thing people said about you for the next decade or more. I never knew the kid you based all your ideas on, but I know the man who lives next door to me now, and maybe it's worth it to spend a little time taking him for who he is, instead of who you think he was."

She grabbed her purchases and left.

He found Livia on his porch. It gave him a lift, seeing her there. It always did. He liked when she sought him out.

"What's up?"

She grabbed a bag of groceries and followed him in. "Not a lot, but listen. I went down to Bill's to get anchor hooks to hang Mom's stained glass."

"I'd have done that for you."

She stopped petting Mittens and folded one of his emptied grocery totes. "I know, but I was getting restless now that I'm done with all the other projects at Chata. I enjoy having some manual tasks. You were right about them looking great in the dining room, for the record."

"I'm a certified interior decorating genius."

She made a show of examining his living area, which was only slightly less stuck in his parents' era than it had been when he first moved home. He'd let Cy replace his sofa and haul off the old television cabinet, but he was making the changes gradually.

"Just wait. I have a vision."

"I bet." She laughed that quick laugh, but then got serious on him. "So, listen, while I was in town? Not to stress you out, but these guys said something and I thought I should mention it."

"Stress me out? Are you okay?" He mostly respected the people of Honey Wine by common decency standards, but if they were upsetting Livia, he was willing to change his mind, and fast.

"Yeah," Livia said. "With the council meeting coming up, and the way it seems like town goodwill makes a difference to how our businesses are talked about … I mean, first, I want you to know I've been talking you, and Cesta, up."

He put the last of the cold foods in the fridge. "Are you stalling right now?"

She rolled her eyes. "Yeah, some."

"What did whoever this was have to say?"

"Bill told me their names, but I forgot. They looked like brothers, maybe one was Steve? Anyway, yeah. It was more of what you've heard before. Jokes about commitment, and then stuff about you dating a lot of women."

He shrugged. "I did date a lot of women. In high school. Like a lot of high schoolers."

She smirked. "Greg."

"Livia." He sauntered toward her. Backed her against the counter. "Are you bothered by that?"

"About you dating in high school, like a high schooler? No. Why are you so hot?"

He held her closer, tasted the softness of skin on her neck. "I hiked down to the lower bridge before I went to town. Unless you mean, why am I so devastatingly handsome that people can't stop talking about how I dated a bunch in high school?" He cleared his throat, hoping to swallow away the bitter edge in his voice.

Livia kissed his cheek. "I meant the hiking part. But if you want to talk about your devastating good looks, we can do that."

He shook his head. "I don't want to talk about anything."

"Good. We can skip the part about how I yelled at them and at Bill to stop treating you like you're not a full adult with fully adult skills."

He crushed her to him and ground against her. "You defended my honor? Damn, woman. You feel what that does to me?"

Livia bucked right back. He fisted her hair and slanted her head for a deep kiss. Carnal, that was the word.

Her hands were insistent on him. His were reverent on her. They landed on the new couch, Livia on his lap. He cupped her ass, stripped off her shirt, helped her pull his own away.

"Show me those breasts, Livia. I need them."

"Okay," she agreed. "Okay, but take out your dick."

As he yanked down his jeans, she slid to kneel between his legs. For a moment he just sat back and watched her toy with her nipples. He'd never seen a sweeter show. With a long moan, he finally gripped his hard length and nudged it towards her.

The first touch of her tongue to the head of his cock had him hissing through his teeth. Livia took him in her mouth, and he growled low in his throat. His fingers tightened in her hair as she worked the rhythm that made him frantic.

His breath was ragged as she took him deeper. He fought for control, tensing his thighs and his ass and, somehow, his heart, too.

"I need to be inside you," he growled, and pulled her back to him, yanking down her leggings and panties.

She gasped a response, but he was beyond hearing, beyond thinking. She made him feel, and feel, and every feeling left him craving more.

CHAPTER 18

Her first Honey Wine City Council meeting. There was a function room of sorts on the second floor of the municipal building, which had kept most of its 1860s facade but was a warren of fluorescent-lit offices inside. She didn't know whether the two-thirds full room was a normal turnout or not; Ellie seemed unbothered by the crowd, at any rate.

Greg was bothered. He wasn't saying as much, but it radiated off him. She nudged her shoulder into his, and he startled. Then he put an arm around her and dropped his head to rest on hers.

So. That was a public declaration.

Not that she thought the people of Honey Wine, with their robust gossip network, would be surprised that she and Greg were seeing each other. Kari and her husband Mason both knew, from seeing them together around Chata and Cesta, where Mason was learning the literal ropes to work with Greg. Bill would have guessed, from her impassioned defense at the feed and hardware store. Ellie kept commenting about them dating, even though as far as she knew, neither had said as much to her. Or denied it, for that matter.

She reached over and rested a hand just above his knee.

The stones in her mom's ring glinted up at her as she gave his leg a squeeze. He kissed the crown of her head. Most importantly, he relaxed a couple of fractions.

The meeting was procedural. A couple of people who seemed to relish the protocols, a few more who just wanted to get on with things. Some who were energized, some who were bored.

And then it was Greg's time.

He leaned once more into Livia, who whispered good luck to him. Ellie pat his shoulder as he rose.

After the polite exchanges, he looked out over the crowd that had come to see him fight for his dream. Nodding at someone near the back, he said, "Also, I'd like to thank Ms. Svoboda, who gave me such encouragement back in government class, to submit my proposal that Honey Wine institute a heritage initiative for our businesses. I was never much of a student, but this particular project meant the world to me, coming as it did during a time I was grappling with the loss of my mom. It gave me a way to honor all she'd taught me to love about Honey Wine, and our land. I was proud to see that my proposal has finally been adopted, and I'm prouder to say that Cesta Adventures abides by every one of my recommendations."

Ellie's hand closed in a fist over her heart. Livia exchanged a smile with her. It was the kind of smile that said, clearer than words, that Livia was on Team Greg. That she liked him. Maybe more than she'd admitted to herself, even with all the great sex and successful partnership and constant interaction.

It would be wise of her, at some point, to figure out what that meant.

Greg, meanwhile, directed the council to the archeological and environmental reports on his land. Talked them through his map of Cesta Adventures, showed the video he'd put together of the offerings. Stood steady at his podium while he answered questions.

Mr. Connor let loose some grumpiness, and Greg visibly gathered himself to answer.

Before he could, though, Ellie interrupted. "Frank, you don't have a single good reason to block Cesta. Gregory's done everything by the book, and you know it. All y'all need to consider the truth that other kids, like your Paul, got to turn into adults around here. No one still talks about how Paul stole Jackson's tow truck and nearly turned it over in the Clay's goat pasture. So maybe you ought not to dwell so readily on what Greg was like as a teenager, and start considering how smart it is for him to come up with a new way to bring tourists to this town."

The burn of tears at the back of Livia's eyes, entirely because she knew what it meant to Greg for Ellie to speak out for him, suggested she should sort her feelings out pretty damn soon.

Greg leaned back in his chair and took a deep breath. He'd done it. After working all-out to make Cesta a reality, it was happening. With the variance approved, there weren't any more red-tape hurdles to climb over. No one, not Mr. Connor or anyone, could officially hold him back from achieving his dreams. It hadn't been a resounding vote of confidence, but at least the hometown gossips weren't actively working against him anymore.

But there, behind the cafe counter, was the person whose support meant the most. Even if a skeptical part of his mind feared she'd only spoken up because he'd begged it of her. He suspected she still considered Cesta a gamble, no matter how much research he showed her. He could print out every interested comment from his YouTube channel, but she wouldn't believe the demand existed, and that he was well-positioned to capture it, until he had customers booking weeks in advance.

He shook his head and took another sip of coffee. Well, the council meeting was over, and he could finally share his plans with the world. As he reached for his phone to make notes, Livia slid into the booth across from him. Her smile lit every dusty corner of his mind, highlighting just how many places he was trying to hide his lingering worries.

"You did it. Congrats."

"I did," Greg said, clinging on to the relief.

"I knew you would." She reached out and put her hand on his arm.

Greg mustered a smile. She was so full of faith in him. "Do you believe in me?" he asked, trying to make a joke.

"I do," Livia said. "I don't know why Mr. Connor was such a pill about it all. He was nothing but kind to me when I went to him about my permits."

Greg sighed and turned to look out over Honey Wine's darkening Main Street. Across the square, February's cold air wasn't putting any kind of dent in the line of customers at the ice cream shop. A van parked outside Bob's Bar suggested there'd be live music later on.

It wasn't just the tourists who could have fun with what he was building at Cesta, but other than Lee and Jorge, he wasn't counting on much local business. Not with the way people still elaborated on every scrap of their memories about him, building him into some sort of demon child with a vendetta against the town.

He glanced towards Ellie. "Well, he's been put in his place. For now." It might not last, but while it did, he'd take it.

Anything to get people to stop labeling his hard work as some kind of flash in the pan. And to stop making out like a few rowdy teenage moments had long-term implications about his life.

As if sensing his more sour thoughts, Livia leaned forward again. "What's next on your plan?"

He smiled, feeling the possibilities unfurl in his heart like tendrils of fresh growth. "I'm already editing together my footage from the zip lines and ATV trails. Once I post that with that fancy branding of yours, I'm going to look into those merchandising ideas."

He knew it would take time for everyone to see how much potential there was in Cesta. But if he could make a splash with the right people, they would spread the word and he could transform this dusty little town into a bustling center of sustainable adventure tourism. He'd make sure Ellie and the other town businesses had their own chances to shine, and before long, people would stop thinking of Honey Wine as just a pretty place for swimming holes and antique shops. It would be a year-round destination for a new demographic.

And if Livia and he could work out the rights … He looked back out the window. Every time he thought about losing that last zip line anchored at her property, or how he'd had to move the raft's landing stage, his heart was pierced by some mixed up shard of guilt and longing and anger and despair.

He needed to get Cesta opened as-is, if nothing else to prove to Honey Wine he didn't need to hook on to Livia's success to make his own. But if he launched well, and kept such … cordial relations with his beguiling neighbor. Well, it was an idea to keep in his back pocket.

"You know what we should do next, though?"

She seemed to buy the false cheer in his voice. "What's that?"

"We should go over to Bob's and find out if whoever they've got playing tonight is any good to dance to. Text Amalia and whoever, and I'll message my guys. I feel like celebrating."

Amalia and Patti were already at Bob's, which was part of that small-town thing Livia was still getting used to. Everyone turning up at the same place, because that place was one of the few places around for everyone. Including Lynne, who was Kari's youngest, and Livia took a sec to think back on Kari's talk about her kids to reassure herself the woman was of drinking age.

"Am I turning into a crone?" she asked Patti.

"Because you think that one looks no more than fourteen?"

She faked wiping sweat from her brow. "Okay, I'm not the only one."

"Nope. But feel free to help me remind Susanna that Lynne's totally legal."

She followed Patti's gesture to where Greg was talking with a few people she hadn't yet met. "Susanna the vet?"

Patti lifted her soda in acknowledgment. "And former prom date of your guy there, yep."

She was all class, and trained at public-facing situations, so she didn't snort her beer out her nose.

"Is it the prom thing or the possessive that got you?" Amalia asked.

"Weren't they a few years behind you two in school? Why do you know about Susanna's prom?"

Amalia leveled a don't-even-try-to-be-slick look on her. "Setting aside how chronicling the feats of the supposed bad seeds is a town preoccupation—which reminds me, someone please text Dante that he needs to be better at keeping his little primo's antics under the radar."

"Because you can't text him yourself?" Livia pressed her lips together to hold in her snickers.

"Because I've already told him, but he thinks he's got everything under control, as always, and I am in no mood.

And I told you, we are setting that aside. Everyone knows about Greg taking Susanna to prom because they left early and he took her on some trail hike, rented tux and strappy sandals, the works, and that was the first thing he made public on his YouTube channel."

"It wasn't like she wanted to dance with me," Greg said, slipping a hand low on her back and dropping a kiss to her neck as the group shuffled to make room for more people. Livia's nerves were suddenly all creepy-crawly in a way she'd call fun if they were alone. Somehow knowing the old-timers were gossiping was a different feeling from open affection in front of their peers.

Susanna laughingly introduced herself, and so did Jorge and the other newcomers, but by then Livia was covered with imaginary fire ants and she needed to shake them off. "Well, come on then, let's go find out why you're such a bad bet on the dance floor."

They wound through the crowd, and soon enough, she discovered that Greg knew how to move. Well, rediscovered, because she knew from all those times of his intent, intimate focus on her, that he had the right rhythm.

The prickly feelings fell away as they danced, sometimes swaying together and sometimes getting more deliberately hither-and-yon about it all. But as she reconnected with her body, things deep within her chest and her brain fizzed around. And she blurted out mid-song, "I like you."

It wasn't any kind of surprising declaration, not between people who'd been working side-by-side for so long and spending many nights lately in the same bed.

So Livia was startled by how giddy she was, saying it.

And close to shocked by the way Greg, once he heard her, shut his whole self down for a long moment.

It wasn't a grand declaration. Wasn't demanding more of him than he'd put out there on his own. So his reaction? Kinda pissed her off.

What if she'd been asking for his heart? Was that so beyond the realm of what they had going on, that he had to escape her trap? She wasn't that person; hadn't ever been that person. She knew what it was to be trapped, and she wasn't signing up for that. For either of them. So it was good that, after all, their relationship was only practical and physical. She would make a point of not straying from that one defined path.

One minute Livia was all soft spice and sweet swells up against him, not even laughing at his faux-suave moves, and the next she—well, she was all the same goodness as before, but with a new intent behind it. Not just sex-based intent, either. Emotion intent.

And he hadn't teamed up with her to get entrapped by emotions.

Not by hers, and for damn sure not by his.

He pressed harder into her, feeling her words melt away in favor of motion. Of looks and licked lips and lust. Lust, he was on board with. It suited this odd brief window of their working together. His grip on her tightened reflexively, and he slanted his head, a cocky invitation to move off the dance floor.

Livia was a wildfire, and he was just trying to feed the flames between them without getting himself burned. Her smart eyes and her bright face and her laughing way of mimicking the goofy dance moves that always seemed to rack up the hits on his channel when he broke them out.

The song shifted, and they tripped together, pressed in close. It was too hot in Bob's. The air was thicker than was warranted by the size of the crowd, and someone must have spilled beer nearby, because the hoppy tang and sticky floor weren't adding a damn thing to the atmosphere.

But Livia's body up against his. Her flushed cheeks and chest, glowing in the low light. She was caught up in whatever this was, this thing he wouldn't name. The sickly sweet taste of adrenaline and a tang of uncertainty melting together into something else entirely.

It took a few more songs, a few more rounds with friends, for them to make their way out onto the street. Livia leaning into him, her grip tight on his shirt as they waved off the others. Her head pressed into his shoulder.

The fresh air did little to clear his head. When she looked up at him, eyes dark and pupils blown wide, he was ready to tell her whatever heart-truths she wanted.

"You'll drive me back?" she whispered, and it was half request, half plea.

He didn't need to be asked twice. Bring on the fire.

Backing her against his vehicle, fitting her length along his chest and hips and thighs. Their smiles matching in wicked intent. One of her hands wove into his hair, and he let out a low noise in the back of his throat before capturing her lips with his own.

The kiss was electric. An ignition to all the tinder they'd built between them. She tasted of smiles and sass and sin. Her body met his, pulsing and pressing, hard to soft and rough to gentle, like they were made out of a perfect fit.

He wasn't thinking about it. Textures, urges, the drive to get Livia into his bed as immediately as he could navigate them there: Greg filled his brain with all of that, and left the danger of emotion to dissolve into the dust of Bob's cracked-up parking lot.

CHAPTER 19

For once, she was the first one awake in the morning and not laid flat by a night of drinking and dancing the way she would have expected. Of course, it was Honey Wine, not Dallas, so they'd been home and in bed by eleven. Her spine and calves weren't complaining of the high heels she'd have worn clubbing in the city, and she sank deeper into the mattress, relishing the relaxation of her entire self. Funny how when she'd moved to a small town, she'd figured nights like the one before were as out of reach as coffee shops on every corner and superstores on the interstate.

Not that coffee shops were entirely a thing of her past, though she'd have to trek into town and post up with the nosy regulars to access them. And that would generally be after she'd provided a cup or three to Honey Wine visitors, even if she was out of sorts from a late night. What pleased her was that things like late nights were still accessible in her new life. She hadn't left behind everything she'd once relied on to fill her time.

It was just the scale that had changed. Bob's Bar had all the parts of a night out vibe that she'd always liked best: friends and motion and touching. The buzz of drinks and music and laughter. All of that had followed her to Honey Wine, and she basked in still having immediate access to it.

If she wanted higher octane live music, and smoky neon rooms, and dancing well past midnight, San Antonio and Austin weren't that far away. But a little contented ember burned away in her at the realization she hadn't entirely left her nightlife behind when she fled Dallas.

And now, she also had Greg sprawled out flat beside her. His broad chest rising and falling softly as she gazed at him. She bit her lip, remembering all the descriptions she'd read of people looking at their lovers fast asleep, and thinking about how young and innocent they looked.

That was not Greg. Somehow, he looked more devious in his sleep. Like he was dreaming up all kinds of evil plans and machinations she should watch out for.

His brows slanted, like they were quirking up with malicious intent, and it made her ache to thumb them smooth. Even if that meant waking him up. But it was so unlike him to sleep in, and he'd cleared such a big hurdle for his business the day before. She wanted him to enjoy the restorative rest. Maybe wake him in a bit with fresh pastries. Though he rightly rhapsodized about every one of her baked goods and breakfast treats, so providing them wouldn't mark this morning as special. And she wanted, with the kind of urgency that was setting her heart on triple time, to convey something new to Greg.

Something about being proud of him, and glad for their friendship. He didn't want more; she'd gotten that message clear on the dance floor. She wasn't hurtling all-out towards romance, herself. Not after his obvious worry about having to confront her affection.

So she was resetting them: friends, business co-conspirators, neighborly dating. Enough of a claim on each other to be gossiped about, not enough to fret about the dark wounds on his soul.

As her friend, he deserved thanks for the way he'd helped make Honey Wine her home. For all the generosity of his insider knowledge. For helping her realize that, although she'd set off on this path sure of herself, sure she was honoring her mother, she'd begun more and more to hold Chata as a dream that was just hers.

It wasn't until she recognized how much she loved what she was building at Chata, for herself, that she understood how much her buying it sight unseen and moving her whole life to Honey Wine had been a referendum on what she'd been trying to prove to the mother she'd barely spoken to in so many years.

Not that Greg was magic.

She wasn't giving him the credit for her revelations, or supposing that she wouldn't have reached it without his eagerness to team up with her as they prepared to launch their businesses. She hadn't forgotten that nonsense about his first right of refusal, though they'd neither one mentioned it in a good long while. She'd set up an auto-payment on the loan; maybe that was enough to set his mind at ease that she was good for it.

Setting aside their contract, Livia wasn't denying that these days, and especially these nights, with Greg had been a key as she began to truly think of Honey Wine as her comfortable home.

His chest expanded deep, and she looked up to find his eyes on her.

"Morning."

"Isn't it though?" she asked, drawing down the blankets and straddling him. Because, introspection aside, she wanted to celebrate his success, and her comfort, and their chemistry.

His eyes darkened impossibly as she leaned into the way his hands trailed up her stomach. "Gonna be a good morning, I think."

She pressed her ass into his hips. "If this is what you think is only good …"

He caught her waist and held her tight against him. "Great. Did I say good? I meant great."

She executed a little swivel that had him groaning.

"Fantastic. Exemplary. Beyond compare."

"That is more like it," she laughed.

"Sorry to have been inadequately enthusiastic."

"I'll let it slide this once." She captured his mouth with hers.

"You are beyond generous."

"Damn straight."

"Also, did I mention? Really sexy."

"Pretty cute, your own self," she said, just to make him growl.

"Listen here, temptress, I'm not cute." He flipped and pressed over her, weight in his grip and in his gaze. It was that gaze that really held her in place, glowing with the wicked delights that his sleeping face had hinted he was dreaming up. His expression promised carnal pleasure and a deep satisfaction she'd learned, going back to their first encounter, he could—and would—make a reality.

Never mind the breakfast pastries or the wonderful coffee. Livia had carnal ideas of her own to share with him. To make it clear to them both that what was between them mattered to her in, and, importantly, out of, her bed.

He'd woken a little hungover and a little groggy and not in his own bed.

It wasn't more than a blink before he placed it as Uncle Kent and Aunt Sissy's room.

Livia's room.

Livia was the warmth radiating at his side. Livia was the

enticing smell of sex and morning time. Livia was the gentle drift of breath on the air.

Livia under him and welcoming him and encouraging his body with her own. Driving away other thoughts with the urgency of kisses and responsiveness of passion. He was all action and reaction and urges that felt more important than anything.

More important to coax her body to not-quite its peak. To trace her curves and taste her skin and tease her senses. To force her to whine in frustration when he pulled back too fast, to grin at her glower, both of them knowing he wouldn't leave her teetering too long. Tightening his grip on her wrists as his other hand feathered light taps on her folds, his body demanding she open further to him and her body demanding his supplication in return.

And he gave it to her, readily. He lavished attention on her core and her breasts, kept them both moving in sync as he coaxed them both to deeper need. Released her hands so she could dig fingers into his ass while he sheathed himself and found the tight, wet welcome his cock craved. A hand to cradle her head, a thumb to press her clit, and every muscle he possessed dedicated to joining her in joyful, greedy, delicious release.

After, he collapsed on Livia. Lay there too long, relishing the closeness of her body, and trying to stave off his guilt. He couldn't bring himself to move. Moving meant admitting things his heart and mind hadn't agreed on. Facing the day meant facing how he'd let himself slip, all too easily, into a relationship.

They weren't just hooking up when they were free. They weren't mere neighbors with conveniently similar sex drives.

They were making time for each other. Going out with friends together. And all of that unity on top of working their new businesses in this complimentary way that, to Livia, was all about mutual success.

And to him, had started as a ruse to be the one nearby when she failed. She looked to be brilliant at her job, and he was enough of a mess that the had to remind himself to be only impressed with and glad for her.

Livia finally stretched and ran a tickling hand up his spine. "You staying for breakfast?"

He edged off her and fixed on a smile. "Please."

She had that morning glow she got, coupled with a languor that seemed to spread, diffuse, all across the bed. Greg marveled at it, remembering how other mornings she'd gathered up her energy all in a rush and was fully alert and ready to accomplish more from her clever to-do lists as soon as she rose.

Good trait in a B&B owner, that. His Aunt Sissy had been a morning person, and it'd always served her and Kent well. Greg's mind kicked into gear easily enough in the mornings, but he wasn't someone who relished interaction until he'd had plenty of time to move through the world in silence first.

It ... made it even more sensible of Kent to have sold to Livia. He'd still deserved fair notice, but getting to see her in action made clearer by the day that she was really built for this B&B business.

He owed his uncle a somewhat conciliatory call.

He sat up. "I'll go put the coffee on."

Was he hiding from her? Was he pushing off, again, the need to be honest with himself about balancing this relationship and his business?

Yes. And yes.

And Livia was letting him get away with it. Seemed almost delighted with him, despite his twisted-wrong insides. "Thanks. I'll be down after I shower. There's a cranberry coffee cake in the freezer if you want to slice some for toasting."

"Sure thing."

He pulled on his clothes and headed down, mind a mess

but body savoring the familiar feeling of his feet against the floorboards. All his life going up and down these stairs, but they were Livia's now. Her food in the kitchen, not Aunt Sissy's pitcher of lemonade and omnipresent chocolate cookies. Her up-to-the-second online reservation system, not Uncle Kent's big date book. The same sturdy walls and glorious views, but now each windowsill was painted in the colors Livia chose, and her mom's glass art tinted the morning light filling the dining room.

It was all something he could get used to. Maybe it wasn't a curtailment of all his dreams. Maybe expending his dreams wasn't as important as supporting hers.

After all, not everyone got to achieve all their dreams. There was compensation in sitting with Livia as the morning sun laid colorful, wavy lines across the table he'd grown up at, and which now held space for all her own plans.

Later, inhaling deeply as he crossed the bridge, he could feel his heart giving up a heavy grudge. As if by putting one foot in front of another on this particular morning's walk home, everything would magically be okay. Deep down, he knew it wasn't magic that was going to make things right. It was hard work and honesty, imagination and passion. But most importantly, it was knowing that no matter how starting Cesta affected his life—whether it went smooth or rough—he was forced to work the land he had now. To let go of all of those grander dreams.

Never mind if letting them go struck a blow to his soul. He could resign himself to living a smaller life, to dreams that almost came true. It wasn't the worst fate his heart ever had to accept.

CHAPTER 20

In her wildest dreams, she never dared expect Chata to launch so seamlessly. Her junket guests were posting with her hashtags from the first evening they arrived, and the attention was already generating new business. She had Kent's records as a baseline, and already her bookings for the next few months met or exceeded his five-year averages.

Everything was coming up Chata, and within a couple of weeks, she'd settled into the routine she'd longed for. Everything she imagined her mom would have hoped for, and most of what she'd dreamed up for this step in her career.

She woke one Friday to an alert and followed the link to a glowing write-up one of her junket journalists placed in a state-wide tourism mag. She was excited to get over to Greg and show him as soon as she had time.

That shift, to not working, and playing, so tightly in step with Greg as they got their businesses ready to run, was the only downside to everything else going so well.

Livia just about trusted her new Wi-Fi enabled door lock system to allow contactless check-ins, and didn't mind spending chunks of time over at his place. Especially once she'd hired Kari's daughter Lynne to come in on Fridays and

Saturdays afternoons to staff the common areas and host the guest happy hour.

So it worked for her to see most of her guests settled in before retreating to Greg's for the night, counting on her cell's alerts, and Greg's habit of rising between five-thirty and six, to rouse her and send her back across to Chata in time to prep breakfast. Then she and Kari would spend a few hours cleaning and turning over rooms before new customers arrived.

They'd worked out some glitches and learning curves, and it all energized Livia. Left her happy in a way that let her ignore a half-acidic suspicion about why Greg was reluctant to visit Chata since she opened.

So that afternoon, after updating Lynne about the last guests they expected for the night, she slipped across the bridge and let herself into Greg's cabin. Her greeting faltered when she found his brow furrowed as he hunched over his laptop.

"Hey?"

He sat back and rubbed his face. "Hey." A deep breath later, he smiled. "Hi. How are you?"

"Better than you, maybe? Something up?"

Greg shook his head. "Well, I'm kinda hoping this booking software is extremely messed up and was a waste of money."

Now her brow was the furrowed one. "You … hope that?"

"Yeah. Because if it's perfect and you were right to recommend it, I'm maybe in trouble."

She came up behind him as he clicked to the report graphs. Assuming her setup was as like hers as they thought, she saw the problem. Not a one of his experiences was more than a quarter booked, not even on opening weekend.

Livia hoped the noise she made was kind, instead of distressing or pitying. "Sorry, hon. You'll get there."

"I know. I've got to build this starting from scratch, and it's not even to the scale I'd envisioned promoting. Nobody knows my work here yet. I'm inventing a new niche market that takes time for discovery."

He rattled off all the comforting platitudes that might have occurred to her, so she kept her solace to herself. And didn't mention the splinter he'd lodged, mentioning his lingering irritation about not buying Chata from Kent.

"Well, it's possible this will help." She pulled up the review, scrolling to the part where it mentioned Cesta. "It's only been live since this morning, so I'm not expecting much of an uptick just yet myself. But it has to be a boost for us both."

Instead of reading from her screen, Greg open the article on his computer and read the whole thing, scrolling through every picture and even glancing at the few article comments before he navigated back to the 'what else to do in Honey Wine' inset and clicked on the link to Cesta.

His smile was tight. "Well, it works, anyway, so all that website curation you helped me do is paying off."

Greg slapped closed the laptop lid and turned to her. "But you." Capturing her hand, he brought it to his mouth and laid a tender kiss on her palm. "That review is excellent stuff. Congratulations."

She didn't even try to shrug it off his praise. She'd earned it every bit and more. She pulled him up to spin them both into a dance. "I know, right? Witness my excellence."

"Don't threaten me with a good time. Are we celebrating?"

"Lynne's at Chata until six."

"Works for me." He towed her to the bedroom. "Move it, Mittens."

Mittens delivered his best glower.

Livia grinned. "The furry giant never did decide to fear the green giant, did he?"

"You know better than calling me that."

"Why? What happens if I do?"

He crowded her to the mattress, and she slipped into the narrow space between him and the cat. Mittens huffed at being jostled, but set his head back down, so she didn't worry about him.

"What happens ..." Greg kissed his way down her neck and across her collarbone. "Is I put some of that chicken casserole in the oven and set us a timer so we can do other things while it bakes."

Livia nestled against the pillow, made a face, and reached for the decent pillow she'd informed Greg was a requirement if she was going to spend nights in his bed. She tucked it under her shoulders.

"I was thinking we could go into town and eat. I'm confident about the doors now, and the guests for Mulberry are supposed to get in before Lynne leaves, anyway."

"My chicken and stuffing won't cut it?"

"I have complete faith in your ability to feed me. I'm just excited. I mean, having this kind of buzz for Chata at this point? It's not even spring break yet."

Greg made a face, and she held back a wince. She kept her voice matter-of-fact. "Spring break is a perfect soft opening time for you. By then you're going to have so many testimonials and people on your waiting list, you won't have time to assemble casseroles in advance, never mind the energy to go dancing."

His chin tip suggested he believed her, but the quiet way he retreated to the kitchen without innuendo or joke suggested he wasn't so sanguine about the success of Cesta Adventures. And because they were friends, and partners in getting their businesses underway, she would do what she could to push his plans uphill.

He was being a brat, and he knew it. His mom had been gone almost half his life now, but he could still hear her reprimands; he ought to know better than to let his gut reactions of jealousy and pettiness stand when he was in the place most redolent with her spirit.

Gregory Jacquin Forst, you are a good looking, charming rascal of a young man, and I will not sit back and watch you grow up to be one of these boys who feels entitled to success, or any kind of anything, when you face some little setback. You have too many wheels greased in your favor in this life, and you can darn well refute this idea that anything going someone else's way is a mark against your path. Even if that someone else has no more friction in their way than you, you better learn to admire what you think comes easy to others, instead of getting pouty that it didn't come easy to you.

Predictable as sunset, the demons on his shoulder laughed and laughed about the ghost of his mom giving him a dressing down.

Greg breathed deep to recenter himself in the present, not willing to give any of the nonsense in his head the satisfaction of admitting he was in the wrong. He'd promised Livia dinner and a good time, and that's what he would deliver.

"You never sleep at mine anymore."

He turned from the freezer to find her, still shirtless, stepping deeper into the kitchen. Mittens was draped across her torso, glowering narrow-eyed at him, but it was Livia's carefully neutral expression that stung him.

He straightened, setting the casserole dish on the stovetop. "Sorry?"

"It's not that I mind coming over here to you, but before I opened, most weeks we'd spend a night or two here, and a night or two at mine. These days I'm over here just as often, but you're never at mine."

"You've been—"

"Yeah, I've been busy, of course. I know my opening has

cut into our time together. What I don't understand is why—" She cut herself off, shook her head.

Mittens chose that moment to chirp-growl and leap heavily to the floor, complaining as he wove his way between Greg's stone-still legs and the kitchen counter. Since that didn't conjure up any food for him, he took himself off to catch the last low beams of sun streaming through the windows.

Livia was unfazed by the loss of her shield beast. "Why haven't you uploaded the video from when you took me caving?"

"I ... What do you mean?"

"Back in January, that first day we kissed."

"No, obviously I remember that. But?"

She plucked her phone from her back pocket, waving it like it was proof of something. "You made that video of Jorge and Lee on the ATV trails. You have Kari's whole extended family on zip lines. I just checked, and those are all on Cesta's website." She jabbed the blank screen. "On your channel you've got extended cuts of all those things, plus you hiking around your land, and even caving over in the state park."

He nodded. "Right."

She nodded right back, and when she poked the screen this time he could tell her browser was on his site. "But there's none of your video from the day we went caving."

He shook his head. "It isn't—"

"I know you have it. You showed some of it at the city council meeting."

He nodded. "Right, yeah." Mittens returned to headbutt his shin. He un-froze to grab the cat food canister from his cabinet. Once the beast had sustenance, he stepped closer to Livia, whose crossed arms did very little to hide the impact of how she was confronting him.

Bare shoulders, and bra, and breaths a little too rapid for his liking, not when he wasn't causing her chest to heave for mutually pleasurable reasons. He wanted to take her hand, but didn't know if he should. "I have the video mostly edited. It's on my list."

"And so, what's the holdup?" Her shoulders hunched in, and he didn't know if she was cold, or curling tighter into her shell. "Is it the same reason you don't want to go into town with me to celebrate my article? The same reason you don't want to sleep at my place?"

"No, it's nothing like that. I mean, those aren't things with reasons behind them." He had edited the video. He had several versions of it cut together, not just the rapid fire shots of all of Cesta Adventures's offerings he'd used for the City Council presentation. So why was he still dithering over them instead of clicking upload?

"Is it because you're not all in?"

He scrubbed at the nape of his neck. "Of course I'm all in. I didn't come back to Honey Wine and give up my job and spend all my time and money and put up with the Mr. Connors of the town without being all in."

At that, she turned and went back to the bedroom.

He followed. Of course he followed. He knew without the help of any ghosts or demons that he'd been deflecting. He knew he answered wrong. "You didn't mean about Cesta."

Her snort was plenty of confirmation. She tugged on her shirt and spun to face him, her eyes narrowed with ire.

He stepped back and pressed his weight up against the solidity of the doorframe.

"There's never been a question about you being all in on Cesta. Even when it meant you having to negotiate with me in hopes I would fail, so you could take Chata away. You've been a hundred percent focused on building your business, which I admire and respect. And I think you'll be a success. That's why it's so odd you haven't put up a caving video."

He could almost feel the grain of the doorframe through his T-shirt, so much of his weight was pressed into its support. "Livia, I'm not connecting dots the same way you are. If you'd rather go eat in town, we can."

"No." She slumped to sit on the bed, as if all the live wires keeping her animated lost all their juice at once. Mittens jumped up to curl at her side. His rumble of a purr might have drowned out her words if he hadn't grown so attuned to her voice over the past months.

"Maybe I'm picking up three or four different pieces and trying to make them fit one puzzle, and ending up with entirely the wrong picture." She drew that big soft pillow of hers into her lap, leaving his smaller one to float alone across the expanse of his bed. "Maybe I'm staring too hard at the gap between what is happening and what I kinda wish was happening. Between reality and what I wish was reality. And lashing out because of how it comes up short."

He would move towards her if he could get his muscles to cooperate. "What do you wish was reality?"

Her eyes shuttered completely. The pillow dropped to the floor as she stood. It seemed like her muscles could work just fine through this morass. Her smile was sharp, the shake of her head sharper. "You've made it clear from the outset: first right of refusal, your uncle was wrong. You're waiting for me to fail. All of that. Don't worry that I've forgotten." She tapped her temple. "It's all up here, no matter what."

Her hand moved to her heart as she passed him. She held it there, the last of the many protections she'd used since Mittens first let her hold him to her chest, and said nothing more.

She slipped on her shoes and walked out the door, leaving him with a defrosting casserole and a gut filled with ice.

CHAPTER 21

Had she overreacted? Livia called Mags as soon as she had free time the next day, and went through the whole thing.

"Okay, so what do you need?" It was the softest tone she'd ever heard from her usually blunt bestie. "Affirmation? A curse upon his name? Tickets to that Scorch Madigan show that's coming through Austin?"

She laughed. "Yes, obviously we need to catch that concert. Text me the dates. But I guess, for now, can you tell me if I was wrong?"

Maggie snorted.

"I know, I know, it's ridiculous. I feel like—well, you know how I am."

"Do not say over-sensitive. Banish that word from your vocabulary."

She couldn't help but smile. Maggie had no patience for Livia's claim that she'd gone from enduring Terry's many transgressions at twenty to being a thirty-year-old intent on throwing any other person under the microscope at the slightest provocation.

"That relationship, every relationship you have: with your mom, with Terry, with what's his name, and now with

Greg? Even with me. Every one of them is a chance to learn more. About yourself and about others," Mags said, not for the first time. "We're all works in progress, and if your instinct put together all those pieces and came up with him holding you at a reserve, I don't see why you shouldn't believe that."

"Okay, but ..."

Maggie busted into the silence she'd left hanging. "You're gonna say something about 'that was never the deal' or 'I never meant to fall in love' or whatever, right?"

"Never said I was in love."

"Your failure to deny it spoke for itself."

Livia gusted out a breath.

"Yo, watch the eardrums."

"Sorry. I'm just irritated."

"At how I'm naming the fact you're in love? Yeah, I got that."

"Love you so much. Even when you're the worst."

She could hear the smile in Mag's reply. "Don't even try. You know I'm the best."

"Whatever."

"Whatever your own self. So, are you going to do something about it, or just keep it tucked in the back of your mind and refuse to take any action?"

"Ouch."

"Sorry for the reality check, babe. I'm just wondering: I know you laid all this out because you're not happy about it. So what's the next step?"

She held in another sigh, but she was so deeply without answers. "I don't know. I don't even know how my unhappiness makes any difference, if he's not willing to move forward with me."

She didn't love the way neither of them had an answer to her question, but as Maggie said, it wasn't the kind of problem that got solved with brute force determination.

Or without working with Greg to achieve whatever the solution would be. If there was an attainable solution.

"So lay out your own options," Maggie said. "Your ideal outcomes, what you're willing to accept instead, all of that. And then go talk to the man. Meanwhile, I'll check my calendar and let you know when I can meet you in Austin for the concert."

She sniffled, which was the first sign that she was, annoyingly, about to cry. "You are my best friend."

Maggie's growl was so like Mittens' she nearly lost all her tears to laughter.

For six and a half days, every text Livia sent, every email—so many emails—was about their damn open house event. Not that he'd responded with anything but polite logistics and follow up. He didn't know if he could, or should. Every one of her professionally crafted messages reminded him that their relationship, first and foremost, was a business one.

One of the imps in his head fell over laughing about that. About how he'd known damn good and well from the beginning that getting involved with Livia was going to complicate his life, and result in a messy situation. Well, congratulations to all the wise demons in his past, because now he'd gone and fucked everything up. Turned his life into something that stung sharper with each of Livia's increasingly professional and impersonal messages.

So. Yeah.

Now he was in the position of having no choice but to address the situation, to explore the meaning behind her accusations of his holding back. To think about what she meant, and about what he felt.

About if he wanted to un-mess their situation and convince her of ... something meaningful to them both. Or to leave personal things in a void and only discuss business. As if the thing Greg felt least capable of doing wasn't establishing a professional footing with the woman he couldn't stop dreaming about.

Until he could figure it out—if he could figure it out—he just answered each question. Kept the conversation going, didn't delve deeper. Either because he was a chickenshit, or because the imps and demons were right to agree with the bulk of Honey Wine's inhabitants that he wasn't a string-of-successes kind of guy. They likely suspected him of hitching himself to Livia's star in order to drag her down with him.

Anyone in town could see on his site how many open slots he had for every day of his new venture. Anyone in the world could, but it was Honey Wine where the opinions mattered. Where Bill and Jackson and Ellie and even Cy still saw him as the reckless boy who'd tried to make himself famous on the internet, and ended up right back at home. Returned to Honey Wine with every one of his hopes tied up in one half of his family lands, because even his uncle didn't think he was worth giving the chance to establish his grand new ideas.

Meanwhile, every old timer in town had embraced Livia like a long-lost granddaughter. Once they learned just how badly he'd fucked up things with her, it would reinforce their already low opinion of him. He did not need to give them any more ammunition, so he answered Livia's texts and emails with respectful and professional replies. Read her suggestions, made a few of his own, kicked up no fuss. Locked down his emotions as if the only things that mattered to either of them were Cesta and Chata.

After a final survey of everything in the outbuilding serving as his office and equipment shed, and a glance to check the signage in his parking lot, he headed across their private bridge to Chata. Their joint open house began with a tour of the B&B's renovations, and a sampling of Livia's breakfast breads, in case anyone needed convincing they should recommend the place to visitors. Hell, her coffee station alone was enough to get people buzzing about the idea of coming in for breakfast, even if they weren't staying with her.

Like every other marketing plan of hers, this one seemed to be a stroke of genius. Ellie, Jackson, and Bill were holed up in the same spots at the big dining table where they'd always sat to gossip with Kent and Sissy and his folks. They looked content and proud.

Cy kept dragging people off for tours of the redecorated rooms as if he'd been the one to hand-turn each bedpost and could personally guarantee Livia's success. Not about to be outdone, Jackson was going on and on about the termite-ridden sewing machine table he'd talked Livia into refinishing to hold the guest book in the foyer. Ellie took credit for hooking Livia up with suppliers of local produce. Even Dante was leaning back against the bannister, slow talking about the benefits of tankless hot water heaters between totally inappropriate moans at each bite of Livia's jalapeño jelly cornbread muffins and raspberry white chocolate bundt cake.

Every damn person in town acted like they had a stake in Chata's success. He caught sight of three different people posting about it on TikTok, like that was the best platform to lure people to an antique filled B&B a beautiful-for-lounging tree house. Which had been his own damn work to start with, not that anybody seemed to know anything about his building that part of her dream. He wasn't the kind of asshole to go around taking credit for all the time, money, and labor Livia had invested in her business.

Instead, apparently, he was the asshole incapable of figuring out how to apologize, but still capable of standing hip to hip with her on her staircase as she called for the crowd's attention. More people than he'd imagined could fit in the rooms pressed forward to listen, including several listening from the open porch windows.

He might resent how eager they all were to claim her, but some vise tightening his shoulders fell away as he stood above them all. Seeing so clearly their sweet admiration of what she'd built.

Livia deserved that.

Maybe he didn't deserve to feel the warmth radiating off her, not anymore, but he was glad the rest of the town was clear about her value.

"I see so many familiar faces here who were instrumental in getting Chata back up and running. Cy, Dante, Jackson. Amalia and Ellie. Know I can't thank you enough for all you've done to help my dream become a reality. Same goes for Kent, who wanted to be here today—but was tempted away by a poker tournament, and apparently our little shindig wasn't as appealing as that."

Everybody laughed, so Greg laughed with them. It would have been odd if he hadn't. If he'd given the crowd the completely correct impression that he'd not known she'd even been talking to Uncle Kent, never mind that he'd turned down a trip to their open houses.

Should he have invited his uncle himself? He'd thought about it, but his own dad left his invite on read for two days. And then ignored it to text about some TV show his campsite neighbor recommended for a binge watch.

After that, he'd confined his invite list to a strictly local one. He didn't even post it on his channel. It was all part of his generally chickenshit situation, wherein he decided that if the open house was a success—by which he meant that many of his currently open slots would get booked—he'd share footage of it.

Let the world judge then, whether his hometown had welcomed him back with at least a modicum of pleasure.

Greg stood on the stair beside her, making a show like there was nothing wrong. Like: message received, no further explanation necessary. So her only conclusion was that she'd been right about his lack of intentions, and what could she do about that? Her own feelings didn't make a bit of difference, not if he had none of his own.

Livia aimed her best 'over to you' smile at his ridiculous, once-touchable cheekbones. Not at his eyes. She couldn't quite manage that. It would be enough to fool the crowd, but not her. Or Greg.

He lifted his chin towards the crowd, projecting a confident stance she could tell was a lie by the way his Adam's apple bobbed in his throat. He'd be nervous about Cesta Adventures, of course. She knew how desperately he wanted it to launch well. So, sure. He was bound to be nervous about that.

Not about the inadvertent touches as their bodies took up space on these too-close stairs. Not about how to keep up a polite facade for the rest of the open house event. Not about standing beside her, and revealing to the entire community, via the agonizing discomfort of stilted body language, how she'd misjudged something as basic—as essential—as the relationship between the two of them.

"Livia—" he cleared his throat and hid behind a brief smile. "Livia is so right that today wouldn't be possible without the help and support of so many of you. And even if you aren't supportive—I'm looking at you, Paul—you're still part of what we've built here at Chata and over at Cesta. Because you're all Honey Wine, the place that defined adventure for me. Back when I was clambering all around with Lee and Jorge, and even Paul, with so many of you, I learned to value and to love the land. To stand in awe of the thousands of years of inhabitants shaping and caretaking the ecosystem. To appreciate the sheer beauty of a red-tailed hawk circling on an updraft or stream water tumbling along towards the aquifer.

"That love brought me back to Honey Wine. I'm so thrilled to be able to guide more people up Cesta's trails, into its caves, along its waterway, and over its ravines. The adrenaline is one thing, but every person who comes to Cesta Adventures will also come away with knowledge about the land, and about our community, and about everything Honey Wine offers. Including the pleasures you're all discovering today at Chata."

Livia aimed another smile at Greg, because that's what the script called for. He'd fallen into his role, and garnered the crowd's interest. She stood listening to him talk about passion and love, her expression fixed like she heard that kind of spirited enthusiasm from him all the time.

Like his passion was still a part of her life.

She noticed Ellie, standing rapt in the dining room doorway. The woman had her hand over her heart, face soft and eyes tender. Jackson's arm rested over her shoulders, and he was giving her arm a squeeze. Livia hoped Greg's sweeping gaze over his audience took them in. Hoped he saw how hard Ellie was rooting for him, and balanced that against his fears that his collection of elders didn't expect him to succeed. Hoped he came to know how much they saw the man he was, and not the boy they underestimated.

Livia wanted that for him, too. The success, the acclaim of the town. For him to finally shed the label of young miscreant like it was an outgrown rattler skin.

Even though it meant potentially years upon years of next-door businesses interaction. Even though it meant running into each other in town, hanging in mutual friend groups, handing over mis-delivered mail.

Standing in crowds like this, polite polite polite. Agreeing that he makes a fine speech. Joking about her initial fear going into the caves. Bragging on his skillful construction of the treehouse.

Listening to him praise her entire repertoire of breakfast breads and not—*not*—picking apart his tone to see if he was telling Dante something more than just his carb preferences as he detailed the things she'd made that weren't set out for the crowd.

Every day would get easier. It had to. Most days wouldn't include Greg at all, and she wouldn't have to debate if it was better for him to be across the room, or right up in talking range, or walking, as he was now, out of her place and down the porch steps like he'd never once barged his way up them in the first place a few weighty months ago.

Jorge was handling the ATV tours while Lee guided groups across the zip line course. Kari's husband Mason, on his first official day of desk duty, embraced the chance to direct crowds from one spot to the next. Greg watched his crew long enough to feel it was all under control before taking the first set of adventurers into the caves.

It was all going just about as fine as he could have hoped. Even if, every time he scanned the crowds, or skimmed over Mason's signup sheets, or flipped through the pile of liability and photo release forms, he was only looking for signs that Livia had arrived.

Even if there was no reason why would she would.

The plan had always been for him to show up at Chata for speeches before escorting a crowd back to Cesta. It was sensible she'd still be busy there, not only chatting with the more sedentary people but also, as they cleared out, resetting the rooms for her afternoon check-ins. Anyone in town would think the same, so he wasn't braced at all when Ellie passed her safety harness off to Lee and approached with her arms open for a hug.

Instead, he fully basked in her praise for the beauty of his set-up, and the excitement of flying over the ravines, and the burrows she'd spotted on an outcrop. Her adrenaline high delighted him, and settled a blanket of warm comfort over nerves he knew were frayed from more than just his anxiety over how his business would do.

"Your dad told me you'd aim high like a firework and light up this place."

Greg laughed. "He did? When did you talk to him?" Because getting his dad to answer the phone wasn't one of his strong suits.

"Oh, this was a couple of weeks back. He wanted to be sure I'd be out here today. He told me you'd been all over this place in your videos and made it look real spiffy. Professional."

"He keeps up with my videos?"

Ellie rapped a knuckle on his forehead. "Of course he does, Gregory. He texted Jackson the link to that one about you trying at domesticating Mittens about four times."

Huh.

Okay, so his dad was doing the thing where he told other people what he thought about Greg, instead of telling Greg directly. Somehow, although it must have been over two decades since he'd first been told that was how Dad operated, he'd forgotten. He kept trying to gauge Dad's feelings about their relationship based on their actual interactions. It seemed, to him, like the fair way to do it. And it left him wrong-footed every time somebody reported on all the ways Dad was not just keeping tabs on him, but also expressing pride and admiration. Bursting with words of love he never actually said to his son.

Ellie gave him a piercing look before turning to gaze

across the land. Chata wasn't visible through the trees, but she knew as well as he did exactly how far away Livia was.

She shook her head at him. "Sometimes I get to despairing about how little influence me and your mom and Sissy had on you. Not that I don't love him to bits, but I don't think even your dad would have hoped you'd end up being quite such a chip off the old block."

Instead of giving him even one second to process what she might mean, Ellie patted his shoulder and walked off, calling to Jackson, "Stop futzing around with Gregory's brand new equipment, and take these old bones of mine home."

CHAPTER 22

It was getting busy enough that she went in and scheduled closed days every fourth Wednesday through May, just to be sure she had time for maintenance and a bit of a break before high season. Her staff was working out great, but a consequence of living on property was, even when she was scheduled off, she was on. And she didn't want to head off property every time she needed to be sure neither she nor her employees were breaking the boundaries.

Meeting Maggie in Austin for a concert was a treat, but her in-town nights with Amalia and Patti had a disquieting conspicuous quality she was in no rush to experience too often.

These things always got better with time. She didn't need to avoid her adopted hometown forever. But Honey Wine was too small for people not to have noticed that they never saw her and Greg together anymore. Even if they didn't ask, she was all too aware that nights out without him meant people would speculate.

And sure, she could make what passed for an official statement around Honey Wine by mentioning the break up to Ellie or Jackson and letting the efficient grapevine get to work. The only problem was, she wasn't the one who'd known Ellie all her life.

It was obvious Greg had said nothing, and Livia couldn't figure out what that meant. For all her confusion and irritation, she still respected the journey Greg was on with his hometown. It wouldn't serve him for her to add in distracting gossip. Not to mention, the open house had made her feel, more viscerally than ever, like part of the community.

It was something Greg had claimed, back when they were prone to lying around in bed chatting about their businesses together. "Right now, Dante is working with you, and Cy's interested in what you're doing here, and Ellie has offered up a few supplier names, and Mr. Connor thinks you're a paperwork queen. But that's each of them acting as individuals. Once you get them all up here, so they can see that you're relying on so many people in town to rebuild Chata, they're going to look at everything you're doing as part of their community."

When he'd said it, she'd flinched at his suggestion of her relying on anyone, much less an entire town. They were just vendors on a list. Tasks to be completed. Not some sort of net that was drawing closer around her, acting like she couldn't do her job without them.

She could.

She didn't have to use a local co-op for her eggs and veggies, or shop Bill Moll's place for her painting supplies, or get Amalia to fashion her new logo into a sign. She could have sourced all of that stuff from bigger towns, or ordered online. But ever since Greg first took her to the dump and talked her into the tree house plan, he'd dragged her from place to place, introducing her. Acting as her own personal hyper-local hype man. Making his own way back into the heart of the community, by showing her all the different ways the locals could meet her needs.

Yes, he'd been combatting the ways people had him

pegged. But he'd done it while all along, promising that there'd be this payoff of her being taken under the town's wing. As they'd stood there making their open house speeches, as she acknowledged all the different people who'd helped during the renovation, she had caught the way they'd looked around at each other—and at Chata—with increasing approbation.

It was exactly as Greg predicted, and she hadn't told him so.

But he'd not told Ellie, or anyone, what was going on with them. And Livia wasn't sure that her newfound sense of belonging would hold if they knew, or if it would turn out that part of her ease with everyone was the fondness they all had for their returned reprobate.

Because deny it as much as he liked, the town was Gregory Forst's number one fan. She saw it in how quickly his bookings filled up after the open house. Heard about it from her guests who gathered around at her evening reception after a day of tubing or antiquing, mentioning all the adventure opportunities they'd heard about from the town's shop owners. Caught their excitement every morning as she served breakfast and the guests who'd already experienced Cesta enthused to the newer ones about zip lining and caves and nature walks.

Livia kept a tablet in the dining room for guests to browse local activities. The link for Cesta was second only to the icon for the Chata site. She told herself it was just logic to order the options based on their geographical distance. It was the same system she used for the QR code sheet she'd printed for each guest room. And even if she sometimes found herself scrolling through his availability, and admiring the way he was integrating customer feedback in his offerings, she could chalk it up to her excellent customer service. It was only smart, knowing how to talk up his offerings, so her guests had a more delightful experience in Honey Wine.

She didn't waste time wondering how Greg felt about not booking many customers for his caving experiences, or what exact thought processes had led him to add nature sound bath walks to his offerings. At least five of her customers had raved about them, so she had confidence in her recommendation as a businessperson. That was as deep as it needed to be.

Even if she couldn't scroll his site without misplaced pangs of pride at all he'd accomplished. It wasn't her hard work that had got him to this point. He'd returned to Honey Wine with a vision—with, in fact, a fully formed plan. And even though her own plans had thrown his awry, he'd still executed them with great success.

It was all to his credit. Constantly adding to his view count wasn't doing a thing to help him, or to soothe her thrown-awry heart.

He was used to getting calls from the B&B by now. The first couple of times it happened—maybe the first dozen times—his heart would race when he saw the caller ID pop up with Chata's number. His reaction was all adrenaline, followed by the realization that it was just a potential customer. Someone calling with a question he'd already addressed in his session description or the FAQ of the site they clearly had open in front of them.

"Cesta Adventures, how can I help?" He was proud of himself for answering with a friendly customer service voice, rather than with the humiliating, "Livia? Hi?" desperation he'd used in the past.

It was an unwelcome déjà vu for his heart when it was Livia's voice answering. "Greg, good, thank God you're there. Listen, I know you've got that ATV tour about to start, but can you get down here as soon as possible?"

"Of course, what's up?"

"Mittens is here. I think I've got him contained, but you know how he is."

He started towards his house to check, but pulled himself up short. Livia knew Mittens. If she said the cat was there, he was there. "I'm sorry. Damn. I'm on my way."

"But your tour?"

"It's fine. I have a new guy who can take over."

"Are you sure?"

"Course. I'm almost there." He doubled back. "Shit. I've gotta put this phone back, and then I'm almost there."

She let out a bit of a laugh. There went his damn heart again, but there was no time to think about that.

"Okay, I'm hanging up," he said, before thrusting the phone at Mason and telling him to give the first tour over to Manuel.

Mason didn't even pretend confusion. He and Kari were obviously texting each other about this entire situation from his and Livia's respective businesses. He'd spend more than enough time over the last month hearing about his personal life from both of them, as if they'd never been through their own fraught situations. Never asked for a break from the gossip about their relationship. Although, fair enough, they kept most of their pointed comments under wraps if they noticed Greg making whatever face he seemed to put on when he'd spent all day dwelling on whatever was going on with him and Livia.

He wasn't out of breath when he reached Chata's porch, but he took a beat to scrub his sleeve over his forehead and smooth his hair into some kind of shape before letting himself in. Livia and a handful of guests clustered at the head of the table. She kept herself in neutral, but the guest faces were a mixture of concern, irritation, and amusement as Mittens launched into what was clearly not the first chorus of his "I am disgruntled" yowl-song.

The noise emanated from beneath the china hutch. A

couple of chairs were on their sides near the foot of the table, and as he approached he saw their backs were blocking Mittens in. He channeled that customer service voice. "Sorry about this, folks." And, finally meeting her beautiful eyes, "Livia."

He started to pull straight the mess of her tablecloth and spilled food, but it was a losing battle. "It seems like my cat and I are interrupting breakfast."

Livia shot him a glare.

"Did you make those cornbread jalapeño muffins again?" Her eyes narrowed, but he turned to the guests. "They're Mittens's favorite food in the world. I swear I keep him securely locked up at home, but I might need to ask Livia for an alert every time she puts them in the oven, cause he can smell them from a mile away. And my place isn't near that far off."

A couple of the customers chuckled, and Livia rolled her eyes a little. "Yeah, but at least he avoided the peppers this time," she said.

Greg nodded. "It's true. My cat can't handle it when Livia gets spicy."

But he wasn't going to keep testing her patience, so he righted a chair and plopped down beside Mittens's hiding place. "Okay, pal, come out here." He twiddled his fingers and made that smoochy noise he normally wouldn't have let anyone but Livia hear. Mittens growled at him.

And he caught Livia's pursed lips, and his heart lurched, and he laughed. "I hear you, buddy. You don't have to tell me her baking is better than mine. But you can't just be inviting yourself over. Those muffins are for the paying guests, not the likes of you and me."

Mittens let loose with another complaint about that, but there wasn't much either of them could do about how throughly he'd been cut off from Livia's food supply. He was surprised it'd taken this long for Mittens to get up in arms about it, honestly. Livia maybe didn't know how often he'd smuggled bits of baked goods home to his cat, back when he'd had access to them. The other day he'd gone so far as to follow the instructions on a pack of cornbread mix himself, topping it with shredded cheddar like Livia always did.

Mittens had seen him at work, but hadn't even wandered in from the bedroom once Greg had the muffins cooling on the counter, in case he needed confirmation they were going to end up dry and bland and not even a shade as tasty as what Livia made.

And now he was sitting on his ass in her dining room, being berated by an angry cat while more guests wandered in to observe how useless he was at pet ownership. If all this got back to Susanna, everyone would tease him for a year.

Finally, Livia approached and handed him half a muffin that looked to have slid off from someone's plate. Presumably when Mittens had catapulted himself into the middle of their peaceful meal. "Not to reward his destructive behavior, but …"

He took it, hoping she would interpret his gratitude as related to her help, rather than to his joy at having any kind of excuse to be near her.

The traitor hurtled into his lap as soon as he proffered it, forcing him to raise his arm in a damned game of keep away. He didn't need the bark of laughter from one of the guests to realize how ridiculous he must look. One thing he'd noticed, running Cesta, was that he got to send people on their way after a few minutes. Maybe a few hours, if he was leading an excursion. Not all day and all night and in his home space at all times.

He was trying to figure out how he could hold on to Mittens, rise even half gracefully, and not reduce the cornbread to a collection of crumbs scattered across Livia's floor. Once he let the cat take a bite of the muffin, he positioned him a little more securely against his chest. And then his entire arm was on high alert, because Livia took him under the elbow, giving him a bit of leverage. He hoped how urgently he wanted to be close to her didn't show.

What mattered wasn't his yearning, but how Livia was clearly—and correctly—still frantic-mad about Mittens disrupting her breakfast service. About the guests she needed to feed, about the spills she needed to clean, about the potential for negative reviews. He got his feet under him, nodded thanks, and said, "I'm sorry, Livia. Sorry, everybody. I hope no one's allergic."

Thankfully, they all claimed not to be, so that was one problem sorted out. He turned on the charm. He stepped to the mess of a table to wrap the rest of the muffin in a discarded napkin before tucking it into one of his pockets. "Hi, everyone. You've met Mittens here. I'm Greg Forst, and I run Cesta Adventures just up there," he nodded his chin towards the tree line out the dining room window. "This is not the kind of adventure I normally try to provide for anyone, but like I said, Mittens is seriously devoted to Livia's cooking. I know you can sympathize with that, even if you only got down a bite or two before my cat disrupted your morning."

One of the guests approached like she would stroke Mittens, so he covered his paws with his free hand, just in case. "He's mostly Maine Coon, part of a family of them that's wandered wild out here for a bit. I've been working on domesticating him, semi-successfully, since the first of the year. Part of my mission over at Cesta is wildlife management. We aim to manage the land so that our native species can thrive, which is easier if semi-feral cats aren't running around hunting their food sources. Or yours, for that matter."

Another quick glance of Livia, and, wow. He needed to wrap it up. One guy in the back had started filming him and panning around the currently destroyed dining room. "Anyhow, if you want to know more, I'm happy to get into it all.

Maybe once you've gotten a chance to finish your breakfast, and fuel up with some of Livia's excellent coffee. She's gonna pass along all your names so I can set you up with either forty bucks off one of my adventures, or a meal down at Ellie's cafe in town. Today's special is her fried catfish for dinner, and if you're there for lunch, I gotta recommend the roast beef sandwich."

Mittens wriggled against his chest, so he wrapped it up. "Livia, you let me know who wants what, and I'll get everybody sorted."

He backed his way out the door, Mittens's tail slapping irritably against his thigh, and waited until he was out of hearing range before informing his cat just exactly how uncool his little stunt had been.

CHAPTER 23

She toyed with the ends of her newly colored hair. She'd used the home kit again. It wasn't like she lacked the time now to go into town and let a professional handle highlights and layering and everything else she'd once deemed necessary to maintain while working in a high end boutique hotel in Dallas. But it'd been a couple of months, and her roots were showing, and ... Greg had confessed to getting a little starry-eyed about how her hair smelled all fresh and herbal and vibrant, the last time she'd colored it herself. And that had been the day they'd met at the treehouse for Patti's photo shoot.

Patti had posed them close together, fingers interlocked in front of glasses of wine, a simulacrum of romance that had eventually become their reality. It was the first time they'd deliberately touched since shaking on their business-building agreement, and they'd later kissed while confirming the sparks that had flashed between them that day.

This time, she was the one asking him to meet at the treehouse. If there was a chance they could find their way back to those sparks, back to the something more they'd shared, she was doing what she could to nudge them that direction. Stashing a bottle of wine on the deck he'd built. Turning on the fairy lights and positioning the chairs like Patti had for the photos. Dying her hair in hopes the scent nudged him towards those memories.

It couldn't hurt, all this scene-setting. Not compared to the hurt she'd been living with since walking out of his cabin all those weeks ago. So she brushed out her newly vibrant hair, and sent a text asking him to meet her at the treehouse she was, undoubtedly, getting way too symbolic about.

He agreed, and her nerves got silly, and she headed up the path. Maybe this would be stilted, and maybe it would push them irrevocably apart. But she'd rather take the risk than go on not knowing, so she put some faith in the magic of treehouse sparks to help them be together again.

He needed to hang a mirror in the office. He'd seen several customers using their phone cameras to check their appearance once they'd been kitted out with safety gear. The knowledge grew in him, like a shoot rising from the leaf mold of a wooded path, that Livia would have one, if it were her customers. If he had her knack for attentive service.

Plus, if there was a mirror he could glance at in passing, he'd be spared Mason's sardonic expression when he paused on the porch to check his reflection in the window. His giggling demons assured him he was giving his every hope and dream away. But Mason would gossip whether or not Greg gave him fodder, so he may as well be open about fussing with his shirt and ruffling up his hair, mere moments after texting Livia he was on his way.

Talk about giving everything away. Her request to meet him at the place they'd created together had set all of him on fire. The magnitude of hope that barreled at him, tempting him with the idea she was open to hearing him out, might end up being a brutal weapon he wielded against himself. But he had to handle it.

Halfway to her, his dad called. He was damn close to sending it to voicemail, but they'd spent too long in the cycle of just missing each other. And he missed the man. "Hey. What's going on?"

"Something has to be going on for you to call me?"

"You called me."

"Oh, relax, Gregory. I'm making a funny joke."

Dad's laugh relaxed him. The man might be a bit impossible, but he never hid his happenings behind false cheer. "Ha, ha."

"If you're going to be that way about it, maybe I won't come after all."

Greg stopped fast, eyes tracking the tumble of water past the bridge. This section of Forst Creek wouldn't cover much over his head now he was grown, but when they were kids, he and the guys had felt like courageous explorers daring to plumb the depths as they plunged straight down from the bridge railing. "You're driving in?"

"If you still got room on your driveway for my camper, I am."

"Yeah, always. You know that. I don't need advance warning." He'd as soon park the camper at the cabin forever, but Greg had figured out he hadn't gotten all of his adventurous spirit from his mom. Dad needed to wander, so Greg would be the haven when he needed it.

"I guess I do know. I just didn't want you worrying I'll be trespassing on your love life. Obviously, I'll sleep in my camper."

Greg ran a hand down his face and kept walking, crossing to Livia's land and heading up the deer path along the bluffs to the treehouse. "Honestly, I'm not sure I'm gonna have a love life for you to trespass on. But whether or not I do, you don't need to sleep in the camper when your own house is right here."

"It's your house now. You signed the papers."

"Dad. It's always gonna be your house."

"Your Uncle Kent says, from what he heard, you're moving in that hotel woman any day now. I don't want you all awkward about it. It's a good house for a young couple. Me and your mom—"

"Dad, stop. I'll happily make my own memories there if I get a chance, but I think I'll make them better if I don't have any of yours stuck in my brain."

"Ha. You're too easy, son."

"Well, that's sure as hell not what Livia thinks, but I'm on my way now to try and do something about that. When you coming?"

"I expect it'll be a week from Thursday."

He swallowed thickly, staring up at a stand of crown-shy mountain laurel, letting the magnanimity of the news settle down to his core. No more checking in on him via proxy; Dad was coming to see for himself all he'd built. "Outstanding. Looking forward to it."

"Me, too, Greg. Love you."

There was something about the smile he wore as he approached the treehouse that set her jangling nerves into a more sedate kind of motion. Something more like the wind that riffled through the woods before a cleansing spring rain, rather than the frantic whip-around of trees in the approach of a tropical storm.

She took a deeper breath than she had all day, inhaling the sweet scents of cedar, leaf mold, hair dye, and vanilla from the diffuser she kept in the treehouse. It was calming, but what she missed most was being close enough to catch Greg's ocean waves smell. There were plenty of reasons to keep her distance until they'd talked, but avoiding being tantalized by all the Greg-ness of him was pretty high on the list.

Her heart had its own opinions about the situation, and it was because of those opinions that she'd wrestled with the factors, and talked it through with Maggie, and come up with the treehouse plan.

Maggie claimed that the traditional thing was to leave it up to him to make a grand gesture of apology, showing he understood the error of his ways. Demonstrate the actions he'd take to not screw up again. Beg forgiveness, and so on.

"Mags, since when do you even pay attention to any kind of traditional narrative? And, more than that, since when is that your go-to advice for anyone? I thought you'd tell me to be attentive to my part of the dynamic and remind me that communication is a shared task in any relationship."

"Stop being a brat," Maggie'd grumbled back, which was a highly suspicious answer.

Still, Livia still couldn't stop thinking about what an apology would mean from him. And what actions from either of them would show a commitment to moving forward, together.

If her treehouse plan worked—and Greg's smile as he approached beamed promises she was eager to explore further—she might end up in a situation that satisfied even the most trepidatious of hearts.

She just … fit, there in front of the tree house. The shades of her—hair and eyes and clothes—all resonated with the colors of the treehouse. The festive lights beckoned him near.

Also a beacon? The way she looked at him, like she wasn't the only one who belonged. This, on top of Dad saying he looked forward to seeing what he'd done with Cesta. That news had unlocked a layer of contentment in him, but seeing the open pleasure on Livia's face? Especially as she stood there, so completely and perfectly a part of how they were both managing his grandparents' land. Opening it up to invite others to experience the beauty of nature while still protecting the environment.

He shoved his hands in his pockets to stop himself from tucking her flyaway strands behind her ear. Rooted his feet so he wouldn't plant himself right up against her. Focused on filling his lungs so he wouldn't spill out a jumble of words, before giving her a chance to say why she'd invited him over.

Spilled an eager greeting anyway. "Hi. I'm so glad to see you."

She smiled, and his cheeks felt inadequate to the task of containing his happiness.

"Good to see you, too."

"And, thanks for the message I've been hoping—planning—to see you soon." He was stammering with politeness and it was excruciating. He blew out a breath. "Livia, I've got so much I want to say. But you're the one who reached out, so I should contain my apologies and explanations. And I will. But I need you to know that those things are on the table. Only if you want to hear them, I mean. It's your call."

He was studying every facet of her expression. The slight flare of her nostrils when he thanked her. How she blinked fast and glanced away when he mentioned hoping to see her. Her quickening breath and briefly bitten lips when he explained he would hold his apologies until she was ready.

He didn't know what reaction he'd been expecting, but her body language seemed to indicate she was okay with this level of interpersonal talk. Like she asked him over for more than business. Like she wasn't there to convey that they were done for good.

All he'd had to go on, in that regard, was that no one in town seemed to suspect anything. Except maybe Ellie, and she wasn't spreading her suspicions, according to what his dad had said about Honey Wine gossip. Maybe Mason and Kari ruminated about them, but no one knew for sure how much Greg was wrestling, alone, with Livia's accusations. And his failure, so far, to address them.

With the way her eyes met his, as she tilted her head to the treehouse deck and suggested they sit, he was willing to let those dancing demons of his stir up each and every kind of hope that Livia was inviting him into a shared life.

CHAPTER 24

Closing her eyes to compose herself, Livia focused on the rustling of the trees and the cacophony of grackles on the other side of the bluff. All that talk of wanting to explore, and explain, and apologize. It was everything at the top of her wish list, and Greg was setting it before her without her having to ask.

She poured herself some wine, then gestured with the bottle in offer to him. He glanced at his watch, sardonic, but nodded.

"Thank you. Is there a specific occasion?"

After passing him the wine, she lifted her own glass in a toast. "I'm celebrating a milestone, and wanted to do it here. With you."

His crow's feet flashed as he clinked her glass. "Yeah?"

She nodded. "Yeah."

"Well, congratulations on whatever it is. Something to do with Chata? I saw that review in the Austin paper. Noticed how few vacancies you're having."

So she wasn't the only one peeking at the other's site. "Thanks, yeah. I booked a couple of wedding groups for early summer, and it's put me in the black sooner than I expected."

"That's brilliant. You deserve all this success you've worked for."

His smile was that one that delved into her and made her heart skip a beat. It smashed through another of the tight bands around her chest, allowing her to release her uncertainty, along with an answering smile. "Thanks. And I meant all I said at the open house, about how important you were in helping get me here. Here, as in me finding my place in Honey Wine, but also here, specifically, in how you agreed to build this magic treehouse for me."

He searched her face, his own expression flattening a little. She wasn't explaining right. Wasn't following her own script. "I'm not suggesting that's all you were good for. But it feels, to me, like if we're going to be open with each other. . . If we're wanting to trust and understand each other … That it's a good idea to make sure this cornerstone of our relationship is squared up and set in place. If that makes sense?"

She handed him a printout.

"What's this?" he asked, unfolding the paper.

"I was going to write you an actual check, but that seems silly since we've already got electronic payments set up. So this is just a new amortization schedule, taking into account the extra principal I've paid back."

As he read, his straight brows slanted down into a vee. "So when you asked to meet me here, it was because of the loan?"

"Right. I'm not making hot tub money, not yet, but everything's going well. And I thought, this way, it's kind of a signal. You know?"

Still intent on the paper, Greg shook his head. "A signal for what, exactly?"

"That we can get the problem of the loan out from between us. You don't have to wonder anymore if I'm going to meet my obligations. You'll know I'm not squandering the money, and I know you're not holding that right of refusal over my head."

"... The hell?"

Greg was normally easygoing. She hadn't realized she'd never actually seen him angry. There was no mistaking it. His tone, his flushed face, the way he moved as far away from her as possible without leaving the Adirondack chair.

Any of his stated intentions flew out of the air between them, as if those hurricane winds were back in play. Livia fell silent, at a loss. She'd imagined any number of scenarios to go with her treehouse plan, but not Greg visibly reining in his anger.

He settled against the back of the chair, covering his face with both palms. His voice was tattered, slow. Deliberate. "Okay, wait. We're at cross purposes. I know that was a harsh reaction."

She could only nod, once.

Even as his voice smoothed, he shot her a weary smile that did nothing to sweeten the atmosphere. "Sorry, Livia. Can you wait here for one sec? I'm not going far."

She nodded again.

He took off.

It was not what she'd expected. Not by a long shot. He paced away from the treehouse, returning long seconds later from the far side. Shoving the amortization schedule into his back pocket, he stepped onto the deck. Quietly, focused on her like he was forcing himself, he said, "Feels like I'm making a lot of apologies these days. It's the kind of thing that can make a guy feel a bit like a jerk, you know? However much you deserve the words."

"You're not a jerk."

"Thanks. But I'm not my own favorite person just now."

"I'm not my own, either, these days. But we have to fix our expectations. To understand that whatever we are to each other, neither of us is perfect. Not even in the 'perfect for me' sense, no matter how much about being together was good. All we can be is imperfect, but willing to accept that about each other. And about ourselves."

They sat, letting the words sink in as the sounds of the woods fill the surrounding space. This high above the creek, only the occasional splash drifted up for the water to make itself heard above the calls of birds and chittering of squirrels and rustling of leaves. All her months at Chata, and she couldn't tell one avian cry from another, and was at a loss to identify any but the most populous trees.

Greg knew it all. Not only from his lifetime exploring the environment around his home, but also because he'd set out to study the ecology, history, and management of this land. He wasn't a know-it-all about it, but from the moment they walked past their own front doors, his experience, and love, showed in the way he spoke to her about their surroundings.

She would learn. Given half a chance, she would come to understand the ways the woods and earth and rainfall and animals and humans interacted. Not like he did, but in her own way. Before coming to Honey Wine, she could tell an oak from a pine, but now she could differentiate red and Chinquapin oaks, pinyons and the rare loblolly. Not to mention her new friends the cypress and the mulberry and the Mexican plum, whose white blooms had harbingered an early spring.

And if she had the capacity to learn all that, couldn't she also hope that, if they worked together, they could learn the wisest ways to be in a relationship?

The heat between them dissipated as the silence crept in.

He studied Livia for signs of resignation or impatience. But he found her quiet and open—perhaps even interested in—what he had to say. He knew he didn't deserve her attention, her grace, but was also selfish enough to take everything she gave him, including the hopeful fact of accepting their imperfections.

And prideful enough to think he could give her, in return, some understanding of herself, of the way he saw her. Speaking from his heart, sharing what he'd learned when he'd viewed the world from her perspective. Hoping the words would guide them to a path forward they could take together.

He owed it to her, after the ways being with her, listening to her advice, had taught him how to be easier within himself. Made him aware of all those learned habits Ellie mentioned, of backing away and going to ground when he needed to step up to his emotions.

At his little snort of laughter, she gave him a quizzical look. "What?"

He winced a little. "I am officially better at making suggestive comments about caves than at expressing my feelings."

Briefly—way too briefly—she rested her fingertips on his forearm. "Give yourself a chance. You may surprise yourself once you get started."

How was he lucky enough to know this person who could set him on fire with a fingertip and crumble his defenses with a blink? She was too much, and he couldn't get enough.

His voice roughened as he spoke. "Sorry about the outburst, first of all. On top of everything else, it was just rude. You don't deserve that. Earlier I … never mind, that doesn't matter. Or excuse my reaction. I have something I want to say about the loan, too, but can I tell you my other thoughts first?"

She relaxed as she nodded. "Tell me whatever. Even after this past break, I still want to know what's going on with you. And about your other thoughts, too. But what happened? Is everything okay?"

"Yes, fine, it's only that Dad called while I was walking over here. He's finally coming to visit. But I think it threw me around an extra loop, on top of how upside down I've been since that day at my place. I've known forever, since well before the open house, how much it matters to me that we have a chance of being together. I should have gotten my ass over here to you long ago, instead of getting run down with the work of opening Cesta and all. It wasn't fair to you, and it wasn't even fair to me."

His chest hitched at that last statement, which was a signal that he'd hit on something unresolved in his own heart. A glowing arrow pointing towards how much his self-sabotage had contributed to his recent pain. It wasn't the right time for him to process the ways he'd been beating down on himself, but the realization clarified his thinking. Allowed, at last, for a dulling of those lingering sharp bites of resentment towards Livia, for how she'd pushed the issue in the first place.

He was through letting his imps revel in laying the blame elsewhere. "Also, it's not fair of me to hold the work, or anything, responsible for my not coming to you."

"I've been busy, too. We're both on a steep learning curve." The tenderness in her voice nearly set him to tears.

"We are, and that's not to mention my learning curve about serious relationships. You're the first person I've dated who made me think real, long-term thoughts, but I knew that months ago. So long ago, we were barely out of the cave, so I went and told all those feelings to back off. That it was too early to think that way. But then I never let them resurface."

"How many comparisons to my phreatic zone are in this speech?"

He sunk his head into his hands, laughing. "Oh, shit. Livia. I'm doing the video narration voice, too, aren't I?"

He looked up, saw her raised eyebrows, and collapsed again.

"Sorry. I'm sorry. Every bit of my apology is sincere, I

swear, but I'm so damn happy to see you again. And you're so perfect at busting me. So perfectly imperfect for me in so many ways, like you said. Even though I don't think I can be right for you if I'm grinning through every second of my speech."

Her answering smile was such a relief. She ran fingers up his arm, and he stretched it towards her. Offering a hand to hold.

Offering himself.

She took it, and their interlaced fingers wiped the smile right off his face. So did her words. "I'm not holding your happiness against you, Greg. Or the way you obviously practiced this speech of yours. In fact, those things answer a lot of questions I've been nervous about asking. They tell me you've been thinking about us. That you've missed us."

His hand tightened on hers. "I've missed us so damn much, Livia."

"And I have, too." She retreated, tucking her hands under her knees. Her tone went from its usual strong and light flight down into a rocky gravity. "So I'm glad you want to talk about it all. About us. About these past weeks, and what's going on today. I want to talk about the future. But, Greg, we fought. Or maybe what I mean is, we failed to fight, about the way we jumped from signing a contract to sleeping together, and never sorted out what that meant. For you, for me, for Chata and Cesta. It's like we zip lined from one kind of interaction to another, but never really examined the pitfalls of all that terrain below us."

Greg's arm dropped to his side, and she swallowed hard, wishing her breath didn't feel constricted along the path from her throat to her heart.

He was nodding, but not in a way that seemed entirely

connected to whatever he was thinking. But she'd had to say what she'd said. As much as everything in his semi-prepared speech had moved and soothed her, it made little sense to go back to where they were. They had to deal with the realities that had caused the problem in the first place.

She ached for all that would be possible, moving into the future, if they did some work about the past, and their present. It seemed so much to hope for, to go back over the parts they'd skipped and ensure their relationship was strong.

So it was almost a surprise, when she looked back to him, to see his expression so clear and so sure as he nodded. "You're right."

A little effervescence twirled up her limbs, growing bubblier the longer he studied her. It was so like Greg, for him to tune in to her feelings. That same careful attention he used to observe the world around him, he was focusing on her.

"I can't keep wanting what I want with you," he held his hand out again, "with us. And there's a lot I want with us, Livia. Without wanting us also to build it on a sound foundation."

The calluses on his fingers were so familiar, as they brushed across her knuckles. The way her palm tucked neatly into his larger one.

"What it comes down to is, that day, you asked me why I wasn't all in. And I didn't give you the right answer."

She squeezed his hand. "To be fair, I didn't give you a chance to say much one way or another."

Something about the afternoon light caught in Greg's waves, burnishing them with a bit of gold. "You don't need to temper my failures with your forgiveness, not before I'm even done telling you how wrong I am. You've got to be a little more hard-hearted than that, Livia."

How did he have her giggling when they still had heavy topics on the table? Damn, but she'd missed his silliness.

Being around Greg, even as uncertain as she felt, meant the world was a little lighter and easier to navigate.

She had complete faith in her ability to manage owning and operating the business she'd dreamed of, without him to talk things over with. To take her out of her sometimes-fretful mind, whether it was because they were exploring the woods, or because they were having great sex. But knowing she could succeed wasn't the same as enjoying the problem-solving.

It wasn't all she'd missed about Greg since their fight / breakup / whatever that might have been. Whatever it was now. But it was thrilling to feel that lightness settling in, now that they were side by side in the treehouse they'd built together.

"The thing is, when you asked about me being all in, I didn't give you the right answer. Because the right answer wasn't what I'd imagined it was going to be. Not after all that time of telling myself that all we had was a casual business arrangement with benefits."

She laughed. "A what?"

"I know. I'm not saying I made sense. Matter of fact, I know I didn't make sense. But it turns out you can tell yourself all kinds of illogical nonsense, right up until the minute someone you care about questions it."

He made the most self-deprecating face, and the chambers of her heart turned into butterfly wings.

"There I was, Livia, caring about you so much. And needing you so much. And wanting you so much to be a permanent part of my life, when I hadn't even admitted anything like that to myself. I kept thinking about how it was so great for right now. Like, today is great, tonight is going to be spectacular, so never mind how much tomorrow and tomorrow matters to me. And then you asked what I thought about tomorrow, and I had this urge to, like, rip out my own imperfect heart and set it at your doorstep. But I froze, and didn't give you even one drop of myself, so you did the logical thing and walked away."

His open vulnerability scraped away maybe the last of her lingering resentment. Her eyes stung. "I gotta admit, it didn't feel very logical at the time. Or since, for that matter."

"Well, it struck me as a smart move. Better than letting me keep lying to myself, and to you, too. Even if it took me this long to come to you about it."

"You know what? I just made a decision about us." She pointed at him, then at herself. "You and me, from now on? We're going to accept that the past few weeks have been intense for us both, and that we've both been doing some thinking about our relationship, and that it does not matter how long it's been since we talked, or how we ended up here today. What matters is that we are here, together, and talking."

"God, I love you." His eyes gleamed, and the words burst out of him, and she caught her breath in a moment of utter stillness.

He licked his lips.

She couldn't stop staring.

Throat bobbing, Greg nodded. "Okay. So, yeah. I said that. I … meant it. Mean it. Not that I'm trying to bypass the conversations we should have, or expecting you to trust me with your own feelings. Or even for you trust me about my own, not out of nowhere like that. But you astound me, and I got overwhelmed just now with your grace and your strength and your big heart, and you're so completely beautiful and, okay, I've been so full of tension, holding that back. So. Now you know. That I love you. Yeah."

It was part of his rock-solid character, the way he tipped his chin like he refused to look away from her, ready to accept her reaction, whatever it was.

His chest hitched once, and he smiled softly, when she blinked loose her tears. "Yeah?"

"So much yeah."

Biting back her smile was impossible. "Okay, then. Good."

Greg slumped so dramatically, he practically slid out of the chair. "Livia," he groaned.

"Gregory."

"I can't believe you're being so cruel to me."

"You've got something against giving a gal a moment to process?"

"A gal with your lighting-fast brain? You're all decisiveness and action and lists and plans and execution until this moment? Nope. I know you better than that."

She stood. "Fine. You want decisiveness? Come with me."

He grabbed her hand, leaping up before she could haul him. Their coming together was like having him fall into her arms in the best possible way. A recapturing of all those things she'd missed about his physical presence—his solidity and his chest snug against hers and that elusive ocean smell, all right up against her aching, grateful heart.

She floated up the stairs with his hand in hers, his solid footsteps echoing her lighter tread as they crossed under the threshold he'd painted a welcoming deep red-orange.

As soon as they were near a wall, he pinned her against it. All muscle and deep breaths and smiles. "Livia DeLacroix, do you have something to say to me?"

She tipped her head back, letting the cedar plank walls support her weight as she finally let loose with her own truth. "Just the one thing."

He nudged impossibly closer. "Yeah? Which one thing is that?"

She let her fingers sink into the curls at his nape. Let her smile reinforce the truth of her words. Word. "Same."

His grin was huge, his growl tender. "Livia."

Her heart swooped. "I love you, too, Greg."

And then, even though they both kept laughing, they kissed for an impossibly long time.

CHAPTER 25

She wasn't aware of anything, but she could feel everything from her center on out.

It was the giddiness of sharing her declaration that pushed her lips to meet his, so ferocious and firm in his intent.

It was the relief releasing the tension in her gut that propelled her body against his, every place they rubbed together, rekindling the memories of their most intimate moments.

It was the ecstatic leap of her soul towards his that jump-started her every nerve ending, as she ran her hands up his pecs, over his shoulders, shaping all the flexing muscles of his back before groping his beloved backside.

Apparently, his senses were on high alert, at least enough that the crinkle of paper in his back pocket seemed to trigger him to slow down. To pull away. To cup her cheeks while brushing slow kisses down the bridge of her nose, and gently guiding them to one last, soft kiss.

She wasn't done holding him tight. Wasn't ready to break away and begin the process of moving forward. Not when the present was everything she'd been craving.

But he pressed their foreheads together and slid his palms

along her arms until they interlaced their fingers. He rested their joined hands in the space between their hearts. "I can't tell you how happy I am."

His words broke her free from the ways she'd been grounded within herself, and dropped her into a hard-world reality.

Her face must have conveyed something of her disgruntled, horny thoughts, because Greg squeezed her fingers and said, "You've got no arguments from me on that score."

"And yet, we're not moving to the extremely convenient lounger right there."

He raised his brows. "Hopefully soon, though."

"You're telling me. Did I ever tell you about the ideas I had about it and you and me when we were moving it up here?"

Greg's face blanked for a delicious moment, and somehow, that was the last evidence she needed that they'd emerge stronger once they'd talked. So she slid away from him and took one of the chairs by the window.

"Okay, happy as I am, too, let's hear it. Why did you freak out when I gave you the amortization statement?"

Instead of taking the adjoining seat, he flopped onto the chaise lounge.

"Wow. Rude."

His grin was a touch wicked, and she was glad to be sitting down. "Gotta maintain my distance or I'll get derailed."

She shook her head, but he had a point. They were both too handsy to get through the conversation if they didn't impose some discipline. At least his tender and understanding expression allowed her the full release of a blown-out breath.

Greg nodded. "So, you weren't wrong to call it a freak out. These past few days, while I've been thinking about our breakup …"

"So you have been thinking of it as a breakup?" She knew she blurted the words, but wow. He was putting names to things when she'd been careful not to. Maybe too careful.

"I never thought of it as permanent. I knew I couldn't let you go like that, not without trying and trying again—as much as necessary—to explain myself. One thing I discovered about myself, and I'd never have known this if I hadn't fucked things up with you and been forced to grapple with how I did it, is that I'm more like my dad than I ever knew. I don't want to be that guy who disappears when it's time to examine his emotions. Or even just to name them. When I have a feeling, I need to claim it. Like I claim my love for you."

Her nod felt a little jerky, but her pulse was settling down. "Okay, yeah, that's ... important. Naming. I'm glad you thought through all that."

"I am, too. Very glad. And like I said, to my way of thinking, our treehouse contract is just business. Not relevant to all the feelings between us. I admit, when I came back to Honey Wine, fired up by Kent selling without telling me—all I was thinking about was how I'd grown up freely roaming both sides of the creek. How my dad and Aunt Sissy grew up the same way, and there's all this ... shared memory, I guess, in what the land means to me. My dreams for Cesta were always built based off those memories. So, yeah, I came here hoping to get my hands on your property."

His eyes were pools, and she was happy to sink. "You were hoping I'd be incompetent and run away, flailing like a Kermit meme."

"Kermit is always excited in those memes. I was thinking more along the lines of you melting like the Wicked Witch of the West."

She snorted. "Thanks."

"And instead, it turns out there's no place like home, because my home is with you."

"Insert eye rolling GIF here."

He bit his lip, but then released the entirety of his smile. It somehow pushed her own mouth into a grin, and that somehow banished her remaining resistance to hearing him out.

Greg's voice dropped, turning almost grim with intent. "My point, and granted, I should have said it sooner, is that I knew from way back before your soft open that you were here to stay. I knew you weren't going to leave, and I was for sure prickly about it, but I changed my plans for Cesta accordingly. Not in any kind of half measure while I waited you out, but because I knew both our businesses would thrive. I knew I could love building Cesta on the land I own, and God, Livia, with the strength and brilliance and dedication you bring to the table, you could make anything thrive. I never had a second's doubt that you'd pay back the loan and get that hot tub and everything else you dreamed up for Chata."

She crossed her arms. "And so I will. I appreciate how you've adapted, and how you see good things for us both. But why are you sounding like it's a bad thing that I've exceeded my goals? I'm proud that I can handle my finances so well. And why can't it be smart for our relationship if we take the money out of the equation? If I don't owe you, it puts us on an equal footing."

He slid off the lounger and onto the chair beside hers. "But Livia, that's the thing. We are on an equal footing. We always have been. The contract does exactly that. It creates a structure for the loan with terms and conditions. Same with our agreement to help each other out with launching the businesses. We talked about everything, wrote it all up, and abided by it. What is that if not equality? Or that's the way I've always seen it. But when you gave me that paper, it was like you were suddenly turning me into your dead mom."

Shit. Her face had gone stark, and he wanted to chop out his own tongue. "That's not when I meant."

Her mouth worked a little, and she swallowed, looking at him for the briefest moment. "Okay."

Restraining his impulse for agitated motion, he scooted right to the edge of the seat, so his knees could bracket hers. "Livia, I'm sorry. Listen, that sounded so much worse than I meant it."

She blinked. "I hope so."

He wanted to touch her, but was wary about reaching out. "Okay, so, listen. Remember you told me about your gut feelings about Chata, and why you bought it sight unseen? And maybe this is just my perspective being different from yours. Because of course we're different people, and come at things from different ways, but … it feels like you have a kind of scorecard about your inheritance. Like you feel that with enough checks in the pro column, you'll prove to your mom, to her memory, that you deserved it. That you're worthy of what she gave you."

"Well, but …" She trailed off and looked away, but he saw her tears before she wiped them.

"Livia, you don't owe her anything. Not when it comes to the money. From what you've told me about her, it's clear she loved you. And that what she would care about is things like you being close to your friends, and kind to your community, and open with your heart. Those are all the things that she instilled in you, and that's always who you've been."

Livia's shoulders quaked, and Greg couldn't stand it anymore. He gathered her in and guided them to the lounger, where he could hold her close and give her space to process his words. He buried his nose in the fresh herbal smell of her hair, glad he'd changed after his morning expedition, so the clean cotton of his shirt could absorb her tears.

He stroked her shoulder and back. "Do you think what I said about your mom could be right?"

She sniffed and nodded. "That kind to my community thing ... I don't think I've ever thought about it that way, but it's exactly who she was."

"I could tell from the way you talked about her, from the stories about working at food banks and canvassing for your local libraries."

Her laugh was watery, but it thrilled him. "All those times I had to talk my friends into block walking with me during election season."

"Yep, and that's the person your mom knew you to be, Livia. And that's what mattered most to her, it seems like."

"But then I moved in with Terry."

He'd never heard that kernel of self-disgust in her voice before, and decided the best way to live his life was to never cause her to feel anything like it again. "Oh, love. I know I never got to know her, so I can only guess. But she sounds like she was pretty smart, so she likely understood that as people hit adulthood, they need to break away from their parents, to some extent. To establish themselves in their own right. I'd bet your mom had faith that you two would come back together if only fate hadn't intervened so suddenly."

She'd gone quiet against him, the stillness of deep listening. He hoped his words, and his heart, were both ringing truths into her. "You don't have to prove anything, Livia. Your inheritance was a gift with no ties to it. It didn't come with qualifiers, because your mom's love for you didn't come with qualifiers. You couldn't be any more worthy of it, no matter what you do, because the money is not a test of your mother's love. It's just money. And it's horrible that your mother died, but you're not doing wrong by her. Not if it turned out buying Chata was a horrible mistake, or if you run it into the ground, or when you turn it into an international chain of rustic B&Bs. Then you can be grateful for the generational wealth that helped you start your empire, but none of the outcomes ever alters your mom's love."

She sat up a little and wiped at her eyes. "So when you said I was treating you like my dead mom, that was even harsher than I first thought?"

His breath caught. He forced himself to not resettle her against his chest. "I'm sorry, love, Probably so. I felt like you were holding yourself back from our relationship, because you've felt like the money had a bad emotional component. And paying it off early was leveling the ground. I understand everybody has their own hangups and issues around money. It's not an easy topic, and if you need to pay it off early for us to move forward, I'm not gonna fight you on it. I want you to feel you can trust in our love, and maybe the contract has stopped you from feeling that."

She shifted in his arms. "I didn't think I was the one holding back."

He ducked his head. "You were definitely not the only one. And at least you let me mention your issues without shutting down."

"I don't want either of us to shut down. I don't want us to have a scorecard. But I can see it now." She bit her lip. "I know Mags has said the same thing to me. I guess I was never ready to hear it before, the thing about how I feel like I owe it to Mom to make Chata a success. Even, a little, that I was trying to prove myself worthy."

She squeezed his torso like she needed all the air he was holding in. She could have it, along with his heart.

"And I never thought I was doing anything like that with you. I felt …" She arched her brows at him. "Do not throw this back in my face."

He snugged her against him. "Oh, there is literally nothing you can say to push me away, Livia. I am so done with my flight or fight nonsense when it comes to you."

She shifted in his lap, and let out a surprised huff of

laughter when she encountered his erection. "I guess you're channeling all of your energy into a third F response."

He groaned. "Well, it's not freeze, not unless you've stashed another bag of green beans up here. Ignore my dick and tell me what you were going to say."

Somehow, she melted her body even closer into his. "Just that you're right about the money. When I calculated up the new amortization schedule, I felt like it was a way of clearing the decks. That it would force your hand about discussing our relationship, and, ugh. This is so petty. That it would prove I was, maybe, the bigger person."

He kissed her crown, and her forehead, and her cheek. "I have no problem ceding all the higher ground to you. Including the literal higher ground of these bluffs. I meant all those compliments I paid you, because you're amazing to me. Not perfect—I understand what you meant there. Neither of us is perfect, but, Livia? I am so willing to do the work to make this relationship as perfect as it can be for us both."

The next time she shifted, she seemed deliberate about undulating against his cock. "You are, are you?"

This stunning woman. Their treehouse, and the companies they built, and the feel and sound and smell and taste of her in his arms. The way she teased and joked and told him her truths and listened to his in return. And every sexy, luxurious curve and dip and dimple of her body. He was unbelievably lucky in love. "I am, and it would be my absolute pleasure to prove it to you."

EPILOGUE

"Okay, that's it." Greg lowered the camera and clicked swiftly through the footage with his usual practiced ease. "I think we're good."

She moved in to peer over his shoulder, but it was more an excuse to snuggle than anything to do with concerns that the video was good enough. It had taken maybe three seconds for her to take up his offer to do all the filming for their social media and websites. She'd gotten better than the year before, with what Maggie had called the Blair Witch Tour of her first impressions of Chata, but every one of his videos made her rooms look intimate and inviting and comfortable and compelling. Which they were, because she'd made a point of making them so, but her camerawork didn't prove it.

And as for the photographic evidence of their relationship, somehow she never lost her shaky hands. So many blurry selfies and shots centered on their chins. But Greg captured them in the golden light filtering through the trees, or in black and white heading out of the caves, or with a few strategic lights and shadows among the pillows of their couch.

Their couch.

She'd moved into his cabin in the fall. Not long, actually,

after installing the hot tub off Chata's back porch. Mittens turned out to be a lot more agreeable about domestication once Livia devised a treat recipe that catered to all his faves—cheese and bread and bacon—and he spent most of the time Livia was home trying to hold her down under his bulk.

The cat's favoritism was Greg's only gripe about their new arrangement. It became a joint complaint when Uncle Kent came to Honey Wine for Thanksgiving, Mittens, fickle beast that he was, followed Kent around like he'd invented the concept of head scritches. Even Livia's cornbread stuffing didn't entice the cat back to her side. Kent just hid his smile in his beard and said it was a good thing they'd put him up at Chata so the cat couldn't stow away in his luggage.

Once Kent headed out, she and Greg found themselves super-settled into all the couple things: date nights, negotiating who did which chores, making dinner for friends, redecorating the cabin in a way that merged their individual styles.

Lots and lots of invigorating sex.

She made it over to Chata most days, but once she and Greg had the staff they needed, they spent most Tuesdays and Wednesdays not working. And now the holiday season was behind them, they had ample free time for her to enact her plan. She'd had him meet her on the bridge connecting Chata and Cesta, telling him it was to capture some footage for the socials.

He tucked away his equipment. "I'll upload that later. After you tell me what this is really about."

Livia laughed. "You are rotten at letting a surprise be a surprise."

His arms circled her, and she pressed up against his comfortable chest. His kiss was full of nips and laughs. "Maybe you're rotten at surprises, ever think of that?"

"Maybe you're a sneak."

"Cause I saw you slip something out of your bag and into

your pocket this morning when you were standing nine feet from me? Yep, it was incredibly devious of me."

Since she and Greg fell in love, everything in her world was *more*—more sunlight, more deep moments, more fun. More complete.

She handed over the printout she'd nearly fumbled that morning while transferring it into her jeans. "Okay, fine. But just so you know, this isn't going to be like the last time I asked you to meet up so I could hand you paperwork."

His eyes crinkled. "No?"

"No. There's hardly any numbers on this at all."

He shifted, so they both leaned against the bridge rail. "What is it?"

Instead of answering, she nudged her shoulder into his, focusing on his expression as he read.

"This … is my original plan for Cesta?"

"Not quite. I got Mason to show me where you'd planned the trails and such. And I decided no matter how quiet those electric ATVs are, it wouldn't work to have them around the south and west sides of Chata. But if you reinforce that log bridge up past the bluffs, you can extend those experiences by a few miles. And you may as well move the sound baths and orienteering to the gulch up here, since it seems like half my guests want to do those."

"Okay, but, Livia, what are you thinking, exactly? Because it looks like you want me to move some of my operations onto your land."

"I'm thinking January and February will be slower months for you, so it's a good time to expand."

His face. She had to bite her cheek a sec before going on.

"Also, since your dad is coming through again in a few weeks, I'm thinking that's a good time for us to get married."

He lost his grip on the printout. "Married?"

She caught the paper and tucked it into his back pocket. "Yep. See, if we marry, Chata and Cesta become community property. Makes the paperwork side of things so much easier than if we have to set it up like you're leasing part of my acreage, all those liability issues and such. I'm not conflating money with emotions, so don't worry about that. I'll run my business and you'll run yours. You'll just run yours with an extra mile of zip lines. It's a perk of loving me, the same way my extra profits now that I'm putting guests in the Chata owner's suite is my perk of loving you."

"If we weren't in public right now, I'd show you some perks." His growl only encouraged her to squeeze him tight.

"I'll remind you of that later. After you get around to accepting my proposal."

Greg hauled her up into a wild spin across the bridge deck. "Livia DeLacroix, you're the best thing to come to Honey Wine in at least a century. Of course, I want to marry you. And not for the zip lines."

Their mouths met in a fierce kiss, all lips and moans. Even once he set her down, she was flying with happiness, and grounded in the certainty that their partnership was the perfect basis for whatever came their way.

Thank you for reading COMMON GROUND. I'm delighted you've taken the time to get to know Livia, Greg, and Honey Wine.

As you know, honest feedback helps other readers find new books. Please take a moment to review COMMON GROUND at some of the top retailers / review sites. 🤍

Amazon / Goodreads / BookBub / Other Retailers

ACKNOWLEDGMENTS

The world of Honey Wine has lived in my head almost as long as I've been a romance writer. Chata grew from fond memories of visits to Wimberley, Texas, and other small Hill Country towns, including the one where my parents retired. I've bounced bits of this narrative off, I expect, everyone I know—from my sweet first critique partners: Brandi and Michelle and Temple; to my excellent, insightful editor Jen Prokop; and my mom, Karen, who cheerleads and copyedits with equal enthusiasm and skill.

And my sweet sons. It delights me that I can ramble about imaginary people and places and you'll take me, and my craft, seriously. Of course, so does your father, in yet another way that he's an unmatched example to us all.

I'm grateful to everyone who's helped me bring Honey Wine to the page at last, and to the readers who take a chance on Common Ground. I hope you love Livia and Greg, and are eager to find out what Amalia and Dante get up to in book 2!

ABOUT THE AUTHOR

Melanie Greene lives in a tiny woodland cottage in a big skyscraper city, with her husband and kids and pets and plants and all the people inhabiting her imagination.

For more info, visit her at www.melaniegreene.com, where you can sign up for her newsletter to access new releases and bonus content.

facebook.com/MelGreeneBooks
instagram.com/melaniegreeneauthor

www.ingramcontent.com/pod-product-compliance
Lightning Source LLC
Chambersburg PA
CBHW061526250926
52052CB00010B/2821
9781941967515